CYCLE OF FIRE

THE CLOUD WARRIOR SAGA

D.K. HOLMBERG

ASH PUBLISHING

CONTENTS

1. A Draasin Hunts   1
2. Return to Xsa   11
3. Maelen's Ask   24
4. Child of the Mother   35
5. Understanding the Cycle   47
6. Disciples Attack   58
7. The Athan Returns   72
8. A Place of Convergence   85
9. Return to Norilan   96
10. A Shapers Garden   106
11. The Sacred Pool   118
12. Filled With the Mother   128
13. Blessed by the Mother   142
14. A Daughter Speaks   150
15. Return to the Mountains   160
16. The Voice of the Mother   173
17. After the Attack   184
18. Questioning the Disciple   191
19. The Mistress's Plan   200
20. A Daughter, Lost   210
21. Return to the Pool   213
22. Understanding the Seals   224
23. Restoring the Seals   228
24. Tenebeth   233
25. Maelen's Call   237
26. Shapers of Spirit   246
27. Shaper of Bonds   254
28. Fire Reborn   264
29. Cycle of Light and Dark   270
    Epilogue   281

Soldier Son sneak peak   287

About the Author   315

Also by D.K. Holmberg   317

A DRAASIN HUNTS

The clouds appeared thick, touched with a hint of darkness, like something solid, almost as if Tannen Minden could truly walk across the clouds like one of the Cloud Warriors of old. He sat atop the draasin with his daughter Alanna as together the three soared, diving from high in the sky where the sun beat on him but didn't give any warmth, piercing through the clouds, feeling a mist swirling around him, before they were free and diving toward the ground once more. Alanna giggled as the draasin's wings brushed the ocean waves, sending even more spray toward them before she climbed once more, reaching into the sky and gliding just beneath the clouds.

Tan wrapped his arms around his daughter and she turned toward him, her face glowing with a wide smile that carried a hint of mischief to it. The draasin obeyed her more than him, though Tan could hear their conversations within the fire bond.

Barely more than two, Alanna spoke to the elementals with maturity. More surprising, they listened.

Wasina dove once more, and Tan recognized that there was nothing in the bond that steered her this time. This was entirely about what she saw below her. Wasina caught a current of air and plummeted, her graceful fall more controlled than most of the draasin. Flying with her was a thing of beauty.

What is it? Tan asked, connecting to the draasin.

The hunt, Maelen. Nothing more than the hunt.

Alanna giggled and threw her hands into the air. She was precocious, and he suspected that were Amia with them, she would be displeased that he allowed their daughter to be in danger like this. Then again, both knew how she could be, how she had been from the first days. Between her earliest demonstrations of an ability to shape to her bonding, there was much about Alanna that was accelerated.

She is a Child of Light, Maelen.

She is my child. Is that what you mean?

The draasin turned and peered at him with a bright, golden-eyed stare. Steam drifted from her nostrils, and he imagined the corners of her mouth curling in a smile, though he wasn't certain how much of that was truly imagined and how much of it was real.

You are the Shaper of Light. Your daughter is a Child of Light.

Like Amia?

The Daughter is different.

The Daughter. It was the elemental term for Amia, though he had never learned why they referred to her that way. He'd assumed that it had to do with her connection to spirit, but given what he'd seen, and now the way that they referred to *his* daughter differently, he no longer knew whether that was the case.

Help me understand. She's different. I can see that myself. But there's more to it, isn't there?

I don't know that the elementals will be able to provide answers to you, Maelen. You are the Shaper of Light, and you are connected to the elements in ways that we have not seen from man before, but the Child is a different connection altogether. Be patient and know that the Mother has a plan for you.

The draasin had grown philosophical. Did seeing the power of the darkness do that?

They hadn't seen any evidence of the darkness in quite some time. It had been over a year since it had been freed, more than a year since he'd faced Marin and she had managed to escape, and more than a year for him to have searched, looking for evidence that the seal had failed. So far, he had found nothing to indicate that it had. The bonds remained, holding strong on the island of Norilan, preventing the escape of the greater darkness. He studied, searching for answers, but there were none. Even the archivists had not found any. Neither had Elanne. There seemed to be something they were missing, though he couldn't tell what it might be. The one person—or elemental—who *might* be able to help had been so devastated by the last attack that he had retreated, becoming something different than he had been before. Lessened, in many ways.

You blame yourself, Wasina said.

They were bound tightly within the fire bond, perhaps too tightly, and she could reach his thoughts. He didn't mind her knowing, but she shouldn't be able to reach him so easily. *I don't blame myself. I reached him as soon as I could.*

3

Even then, it had almost not been enough. Honl had been trapped, captured by some of the ancient warriors who had remained faithful—or seemingly remained faithful—to the old ways and preventing the escape of the darkness. Even they had been corrupted. It had proven that anyone could be corrupted by the darkness, that anyone could lose themselves to it, even those dedicated to protecting the rest of the world from it.

You search.

The plunged into the ocean, diving briefly below the surface, long enough that Tan gripped Alanna more tightly, preventing her from slipping from the draasin's back. He didn't think she'd really fall from Wasina—Alanna had proven herself a skilled draasin rider—but he wouldn't take that risk. She *was* only two.

I search. We need answers, Wasina. If he returns, then we all will suffer.

You will be able to stop him, Maelen. You are the Shaper of Light.

He wished he shared the draasin's confidence. It wasn't that he didn't think himself capable. Far from it. He knew that he was better equipped than almost anyone else to withstand an attack like they'd faced. Between his natural shaping ability and his ability to speak to the elementals—and now to the element bonds themselves—he might be the only one who *could* face the darkness. That didn't make it any easier for him, not when the power that they encountered was so much *more* than anything they had ever faced. And he had thought the Par-shon a formidable foe, but at least the Utu Tonah had been single person. A man, if only bonded to all the elementals and dangerous for that connection. To stop this darkness, Tan would have to overcome something greater than the elementals themselves, something that might rival the Mother. How could he rival that which created everything?

They soared, Wasina thankfully not interrupting his thoughts again. She listened through the bond but no longer spoke to him. He wasn't sure that she would have anything that she could say.

He leaned against the spikes on Wasina's back, feeling the heat surging through them. His connection to fire—and the fire bond—kept him safe, much like it kept Alanna safe. Others would need for him to shape a protection, or to have their own resistance to fire. Not his daughter. He wondered what the full extent of her abilities would be when she fully developed them. More than him, possibly, especially with the connections she already possessed. Would she one day surpass him? Would *she* be the one the elementals called on to keep them safe?

It would only be fitting. Someone needed to maintain that connection. The elementals had gone for so long without having anyone able to speak to them, or at least able to speak on their behalf. Even those who had bonded to the elementals didn't fully understand. His mother recognized what the elementals could do for her, but she didn't have the same ties to all of them and didn't seem to fully grasp the need to take those ties into consideration as she viewed the world around her. It was her failing, and one born of the world she'd lived in, the world that had existed before Tan had changed it.

Alanna giggled, gripping the spikes of the draasin with her bare hands.

How could he think he'd done anything but change it for the better? This world, the one where his daughter would grow up —and the students within Par and now the university, for that matter—would not know a time with a barrier between the kingdoms and Incendin, a time when Par-shon existed, even a time when there were no draasin. She would know only that the draasin existed and were not to be feared. That barriers between countries only prevented them from understanding each other, and that the elementals should be considered, not suppressed and used.

It was a better world. That didn't make it less dangerous.

No, in some ways, this world was more dangerous. With the darkness now managing to get free, even if only a little bit, there was much more danger to the world than only that which Incendin posed, or even what Par-shon had once posed for the people. This darkness could unmake everything that the Mother had created, and could undo all that the elementals were.

You worry for that which you should not.

I've seen the way it uses the elementals, Wasina.

You have protected us, Maelen. You have added spirit to the bonds. There is nothing that Voidan can do to us any longer.

Tan wasn't certain that was true. The darkness could still influence things in ways that would create problems, even if it wasn't able to damage the elementals. It could possess shapers, much like it had with Marin, and the way that Jorma had been corrupted. If that happened to others, it might be able to impact the elementals, especially if it corrupted those who were bound to them.

We should return, Wasina. There is nothing for us here.

She snuffed, and steam and smoke breathed out from her nostrils, creating a fine mist in the air where they touched. Arching her head back, she looked at him, catching him with one eye. She fixed him with it, concern flashing across it. He didn't need the fire bond to know that she worried about him.

I am not the only one who worries for you, Maelen. The others see the way this consumes you. You will find answers when he comes again, or he will not come again.

The bond is not fully secure.

You have created enough of a bond. It will hold, Maelen. The others have added to it.

He knew that they did. The archivists in particular, led by Amia, had continued adding to the binding that he'd placed. Norilan was different now than it had been when he first encountered it, a place that now had colors and life, things that were not artificial and shaped but that allowed the land itself to return, much like what had happened in Incendin.

They did create a bond, but it was entirely possible that the bond would fail. In fact, it was what Tan expected, what he feared. It was why he searched for answers, why he continued to push himself. He needed to understand how he could suppress the darkness and use the binding that had been created centuries ago.

But... there *had* been no further attack. As much as he searched, there had been no sign of the darkness. Nothing. It was as if Tan truly *had* suppressed it, even though he didn't think that he had.

Which was why he continued to search. If they could find something, a sign of some sort, a way for him to understand what the darkness might do next, he needed to be ready. There was only one way to do that, and he might be the only one who *could* do it.

He sensed Wasina's disappointment but she didn't say anything more.

Through the fire bond, he detected a growing sense of another presence.

Tan twisted in his seat, looking back into the sky, and saw the massive form of Asgar streaking toward them. On either side of him were two of the newest hatchlings, both now almost half his size, large enough that they could carry someone with them, though they did not. Neither did Asgar.

Why are you here, Asgar?

You must come with me, Maelen.

Tan motioned to Alanna. *I have her with me. I can't leave. Let me bring her back to the city and then I can come with you.*

There is no time.

What did you find?

What we've searched for.

Tan's heart started racing. *You found the darkness?*

A part of it. We have found her.

Marin. They found her.

After a year, they had finally found her.

The draasin?

Not the draasin. Ara discovered evidence of her. We should go or she might begin to leave and obscure herself from us again.

Where?

An image formed in his mind, one of a series of islands with an enormous central island.

Tan had seen it before, and had even been to one of the outer islands before.

Xsa? How could she be in Xsa? Wouldn't we have seen her by now?

8

Xsa was too close to Par for them to overlook. They had looked—at least, Elanne and several of the other bond wardens had looked. They wouldn't have missed Marin.

Unless those of Xsa hid her from them.

It seemed unlikely, especially since they had made it clear what Marin had done. But Tan didn't know enough about Xsa. They were an island of people he had only seen a few times, even when he had been in the kingdoms. Others knew them better and had more experience with them.

Come, Maelen.

Tan turned his attention to Wasina. *Can you take her back to her mother?*

Of course, Maelen. She will be safe.

No more diving.

Are you certain? The Child seems to enjoy the dives. She is much like you in that way.

Tan laughed. *I do enjoy the hunt, but not when it places her in danger.*

She will be safe. You know that the elementals will keep her from harm. She is the Child of Light.

He patted Wasina's side. *Thank you.*

Tan squeezed his daughter and she turned to look at him. For a moment, she had a knowing look in her eyes, one that almost made him think that she understood what he had to do. Then it faded, disappearing with a giggle, and she squeezed onto Wasina's spikes. Through the bond, he sensed Wasina's approval.

Tan jumped, carrying himself off Wasina's back and onto Asgar's with a shaping of wind and fire. When he landed, the draasin turned to the side, streaking away. Tan looked down to see his daughter giggling, holding onto Wasina, as the other draasin rode the current of air, drifting with it, a beautiful sight.

With a sigh, he pulled his eyes away. Much as he did every time he left her, he hoped he would return to her safely. With what he faced, it was a sacrifice he was willing to make. He hoped that if it came to it, she would one day understand.

RETURN TO XSA

The flight carried them over the ocean, with massive white-capped swells rising below. The clouds grew thicker, as if a coming rain made its way toward them. The air smelled of hot sulfur—that of the draasin—and the damp hint of the rain. Tan leaned forward, gripping the draasin's spikes, holding on more tightly than was necessary.

You can relax, Maelen.

When? I've sent Alanna with Wasina. A two year old, alone atop a draasin.

You know the elementals will keep her safe.

Tan shook his head. He knew that they would, but it didn't make it any easier that he had left his daughter. *Human children aren't the same as draasin. She is unsafe at that age. She cannot even hunt.*

She has no need to hunt. Wasina will keep her fed if you fear for her.

Tan almost smiled. The comment amused him, though he knew it shouldn't. He *should* be filled with worry, and a part of him *was*, but there was the other part that knew the draasin would never harm his daughter, and that they would do everything that they could to keep her safe. He hoped Amia understood. She'd had a hard enough time with him bringing Alanna with him in the first place.

You're mistaken, Maelen. She wanted you to bring the Child. You have been too focused lately.

I don't think I can be too focused. Not with what we face.

Even with what we face, you must live.

Tan wanted to counter him, but there was nothing he could say that would convince even himself.

The islands came into view. In the distance, Tan could see where they'd been attacked by the stone creatures and he'd been forced to use a binding on them in order to escape. He'd barely managed to get away, and had he not known how to use the binding, he doubted that he would have managed. That was when he'd learned that he couldn't destroy. Even with all his abilities, he couldn't destroy. He could kill—he'd taken the Utu Tonah's life—but what he needed to do with the darkness was something else entirely.

You cannot counter the Mother. If you think like that, you risk becoming what you would oppose.

He's not only destruction, he wants to end everything that we are, Asgar.

I know.

Tan sighed. Asgar had been tainted by the darkness, if only briefly. Long enough for him to fear it happening again. If the draasin could be tainted, what prevented others from being tainted, other than his binding to spirit?

It was one more thing that he had changed. The bond—something that he had not even really known about until a year ago—had changed because of him. The elements connecting to the bond didn't *seem* like they'd been changed, but could he be certain?

That was something else he'd watched for. He owed it to the elementals to observe and see if there was anything that changed because of what he'd done, and so far he couldn't tell. The draasin and the hounds had always been visible, but now he was beginning to think that the wind elementals were becoming visible as well. Tan didn't know if that were true, or whether it was his imagination or fear. No others seemed able to see them, so maybe it really *was* only his connection to the bonds.

Where is she?

Tan sent the connection to wyln. The wind elemental was more common in Xsa, stronger in much the way saa was stronger in Par. He asked the question through the wind bond, not bothering to send it on the wind as he once would have. Spending a year practicing had made his connection to the bond much easier than it had been. Now he remained connected most of the time. There had to be a danger to doing so, but so far he had only experienced fatigue, and even that began to fade.

Maelen.

It came like a breath, nothing more than a whisper, but with a distinct voice. Not ara—that was cold and strong—and not ashi—that was hot and breathy. Wyln had always been weaker, quiet and hard for him to fully understand, except here.

I search for the Mistress of Darkness.

That was how the elementals referred to Marin, and Tan figured it made the most sense. She was no longer the Mistress of Souls, not as she had been in Par-shon. Mistress of Darkness gave her a more ominous feel, but it was well deserved.

She is here.

Can you hold her?

It is dangerous, Maelen. She can control the darkness. If we intervene, she destroys.

Spirit should protect them, but why wouldn't the elementals believe that they would be safe? *I have connected wind to spirit. She can't corrupt you the way that she did before.*

She can still destroy.

That was the first that he'd heard of that.

Asgar?

The elemental seemed to ignore his call.

What does it mean that she could destroy?

Asgar snorted, steam spewing from his nostrils. *There is the possibility that she can use the connection to the darkness to destroy. The Mother cannot, but Voidan can use its power to undo what the Mother created.*

That was something he hadn't considered, but the elementals must have. Was that what they were keeping from him? If so, then the threat of not only Marin, but of all of this darkness, was much greater than he'd realized.

I think you've been holding back on me.

Only because we know what you will do if you know the truth.

Which is? She needs to be stopped. The darkness needs to be confined. Knowing how dangerous it is only makes me more motivated to see that it cannot harm any others.

That is my fear, Maelen.

They circled an island that was set aside from some of the others. On one end of the island, Tan noted a pile of rubble, debris that he suspected had once been a building of some sort. The air here had a stink to it. Not the foul odor of rot or of decay, but a slimy sort of odor, one that he couldn't quite put his finger on why it bothered him so much.

What is it? he asked Asgar.

That is the scent of Undoing.

The way he said it made it sound like something more than a simple description. *What do you mean by Undoing?*

It is why you must be careful, Maelen. She has grown more tightly connected to Voidan. If she has discovered the secret to Undoing, then all that the Mother created is in danger.

How can I stop her?

You are chosen by the Mother. You are the Shaper of Light. You are the only one who can.

He sensed there was something more than what Asgar was telling him. *You cannot come closer, can you?*

The Undoing.

That was no answer, at least, not one that made any sort of sense to him, but Asgar said it in such an emphatic way that Tan knew he couldn't ask the draasin to risk himself and get too close to the island.

And he understood why wyln didn't want to help him.

There *was* something the draasin could do.

If she escaped, do what you can to confine her. You can form a binding—

The elementals cannot do such a thing.

Tan had had this argument with them before. He suspected

that were he able to get the elementals themselves to help form the binding, they would be more powerful than even what the shapers were able to create. The elementals had helped stave off the attack from the darkness, but using them in the actual creation of the binding seemed like something else, something that would be far more effective.

Asgar. You have to try. If she escapes me, we will be in real danger. If we know where she is, you and the other hatchlings—Tan looked over at them, flying alongside him and mostly silent during the flight—*need to confine her. The other elementals need to participate in the binding. They know the pattern.*

You know what you ask?

Tan swallowed. He suspected the price it would require of the elementals. As with so many bonds, it would likely confine them and hold them in place. It would be the end of those elementals. For Asgar, it meant a loss of freedom. It meant he would be lost. The other hatchlings. Whatever wind, earth, and water elementals were involved. But it would hold Marin. Tan prayed that it would.

I know.

Then we will do this for you, Maelen.

He jumped from Asgar, pulling on the wind and shaping his way toward the island.

As he traveled, he felt the pull of the wind against his hair, the salt spray of the sea, and even the tug of earth on his senses. Tan ignored all of it, focused on the absence of spirit—of *every-thing*—on the island. That would be Marin.

She was there. He felt her, and shaped himself to her.

Wind whipped around him, brutal in some ways. Tan didn't add spirit to his shaping as he would when traveling by lightning, jumping from the clouds the way the warriors of old once had. Doing so gave him less of a sense of movement and less control over where he appeared. This way, he was able to use his connection to the elements—and even to the bond—and sense where to find Marin.

The landscape felt as awful as it smelled. There was a foulness to it, one that he'd detected before when facing the darkness in Norilan. This was a sort of blackness, something that came across as simply *wrong*. There was no other way to describe it.

Bleak black rock piled around him. Once there had been trees, but now there were only the husks of the trunks, nothing more than towering black twisted fingers, rising from the ground as if a taunt to the Mother. Even the grass that once must have grown here had been changed, less grass and more a dark gray, as if life itself had been sucked from here.

How long had Marin been here?

If this was the Undoing, then Tan needed to intervene, but was there anything that he *could* do? Pulling on the energy of the bonds, reaching for each of the elements, and through them reaching for spirit as well to bind them, he sent a shaping through the ground, through a clump of grass. Where his shaping struck, life bloomed again, the grass taking on color and brightness. Some of the foul, slippery evil faded.

And then it was gone.

When he'd released his shaping, everything else had gone out with it. The Undoing pushed back, removing what he'd done, taking on something of a life of its own.

Would it spread?

What would happen if the Undoing reached the sea? Would

it spread across the water, reaching toward the next isle, and the next? Would it be able to reach Par and then the kingdoms?

Tan probed through his connection to water and discovered the sea itself contained the Undoing. Water, an element of healing, did what it could to prevent the spread of the Undoing. Tan couldn't tell how long it would last and whether it would remain indefinitely, but for now it held.

There was something else he could try.

Reaching for the shaping, he created the binding, layering it in the air above the dried grasses, twisting it together, forging it in such a way that the binding itself gained strength. When the twisting shape formed, Tan began to settle it upon the grass, pressing it into the ground, and forcing the binding deeper. As he did, the shaping pushed back the darkness, doing what his other shaping had been unable to do.

Life returned.

Green began to spread out from the binding. Tan waited, wondering how far his shaping would affect, and was disappointed to see that it spread in a circle only a hundred feet or so around him. To really help this land, he would have to layer the binding over and over, pressing back the Undoing. At least there was something that he *could* do.

Where was Marin?

He'd allowed himself to be taken by the intrigue of trying to discover a way to thwart the Undoing, enough that he ignored the very reason that he'd come in the first place.

The Undoing itself was like a void upon his ability to sense, but through it, he searched for a flicker of anything that would indicate life. The elementals had detected her here, and Tan could sense her, but wasn't certain quite where.

Now that he was here, he was impressed that the elementals had been willing to search. With the Undoing, he didn't know what effect it would have on the wind as it blew through. If the unnatural stillness around him was any indication, the impact was not good. Would it destroy even the wind?

Before leaving this place, he would need to create as much of a buffer as he could. He would need to layer protections around the outer edge of the island, use them to prevent the Undoing from damaging the water elementals, and from risking harm to the wind. He would need to take the time to restore what Marin had done, heal the land from her touch. If he could—

There came a flicker.

That was all the notice Tan was given.

He looked up. Had he not, the finger of darkness streaking toward him would have struck him and caught him unaware. As strong as he might be with the elements, he doubted his ability to withstand a direct attack, especially with the Undoing that surrounded him.

Tan pressed back with a shaping that called on each of the elements. He'd fought Marin before, and in the time since they had last encountered each other, his strength had grown.

So had hers.

She no longer looked the way she had when he'd first met her. Black hair fell limp around her head. Her eyes were sunken pools of a starless night. A heavy black cloak hung motionless from her. Even the smile on her face bore menace and no warmth, no life.

The finger of blackness streaking toward him had more force, and more control, than she'd possessed when they had last faced each other. Maybe it was this place, the fact that he couldn't draw upon life and the elementals to aid his shaping, but she pressed him back, meeting his shaping with an equal strength.

"Maelen," she said, her voice barely more than a whisper. It hung on the air, a taunt that she would use the term the elementals had for him.

"It ends now, Marin."

Tan twisted the shaping and began cutting her off from the blackness, using the element bonds to form the binding that he knew would contain even the darkness. As he did, he twisted it, settling it toward her.

She shot a streamer of blackness from her palm and obliterated his shaping.

Tan was thrown back by the force of it.

"You will see that I have learned a few things in my time away."

"Is that what you've been doing?"

She smiled and wagged a finger at him. Even the skin of her hands had taken on a blackish hue. Darkness seemed to ooze from her skin and poured out of her mouth when she opened it to speak.

"You can't begin to understand what I've been doing, Maelen."

Tan surveyed the darkened landscape around him. "I think I understand enough."

"Is this all that you think I've done?"

"The elementals call it the Undoing. You realized the harm you're causing?"

"I realize more than you can understand."

She sent a lancing bolt of darkness at him. Tan deflected it, but found that it was more difficult than the last time. He had to focus on the element bonds, but the more that he was here, the more that they remained in this place of Undoing, the harder it became for him to reach the bonds as he should be able to.

Was that what this was about?

Did she think to separate him from the bonds? Without them, he would have no way of defeating the darkness. Tan could use the elementals, and he could shape, but pushing that back required a strength that only came from reaching the source, from tapping into that which made him a Shaper of Light.

Marin seemed to recognize the dilemma playing out in his mind. She smiled, a dark flash of teeth, and stepped toward him.

It was more than stepping toward him, it was as if she oozed forward. With it came the effect of the power she could shape, the dark power of the creature the elementals called Voidan, that which those who preceded him called Nightfall or Tenebeth. She was powered by a dark god, and she was stronger than Tan.

Tan summoned all the strength that he could.

As he reached into the bonds, as he pulled on the elements, he could barely detect the elementals. Even his connection to shaping was weakened, taken from him. It was there, but faint and faded. The only connection that remained strong was his ability to reach the bonds… and even that was starting to fade.

She was Undoing him.

He didn't know how she did, and didn't know if there was anything short of leaving that he could do to resist.

There had to be something that he could try.

It would require a level of desperation, but he felt desperate now.

With a deep breath, he sent the shaping down and all around

him. At the same time, he forced it up, creating a barrier of sorts, a wall that kept the rest of the Undoing away from him. The ground turned green once more, the shaping that he used bringing back life that he hadn't realized had been missing.

The connections returned to him. Power of the bonds flooded into him, strength coming with it. The elementals spoke through the bonds, their voices a steady murmuring within his mind. Even his sense of shaping began to return.

Tan sighed, breathing it in.

The barrier that he'd created exploded away from him.

Marin had destroyed it, the darkness overcoming his ability to shape.

But he'd been given enough of a reprieve that he could reach the bonds once more. The connections had returned, and strength still filled him.

Tan knew what he had to do.

It wasn't that he had to destroy Marin. That would come. It *had* to come, though the elementals didn't believe that he could or should. But he needed to restore. That would be what kept him stronger here.

Power pulsed from him, a shaping that he sent deep within the ground.

It called to the elementals.

The murmuring in his mind increased and became something of a steady roar. The voices understood what he asked.

Power surged into the island, pounding into it. There was no real binding, not like what Tan suspected he would need to do in order to suppress the Undoing for long, but it was something different. It was life, in a place where it had been removed.

Marin jerked her head around.

Tan slammed a shaping into her, power of each of the bonds, adding what he could draw of spirit into it.

She screamed.

And then disappeared in a flash.

Tan sighed and sank to the ground, fatigue overwhelming him.

3

MAELEN'S ASK

Tan awoke to wetness and heat. Asgar rested nearby, his tail wrapped completely around Tan, his nose pressed close to his head so that the steam coming from his snout filtered around Tan, leaving him damp and hot. It was not entirely unpleasant, only an odd sensation.

Lifting his head, Tan saw that the island had changed in the time that he'd been asleep. Grass once again had life. Flowers bloomed somewhere, though he wasn't able to detect quite where. The trees, still twisted husks of what they had once been, now had color to their bark and a sort of pride to them.

What happened? he asked Asgar.

You sent the Mistress of Darkness away.

He remembered that, but didn't like the fact that he had fallen after doing it. What would have happened had there not been a draasin to watch over him? What would have happened had Marin returned with others able to pull on the dark, those the archivists had taken to calling the Disciples of the Dark? Tan had destroyed most of the disciples during the attack on Nori-lan, but given Marin's connection to spirit and the way that she could use it to force others to do her bidding, it wouldn't take her long to develop new disciples.

She was nearly too much for me. She has learned much in her time hidden.

Tan dusted himself off as he stood, drawing on power around him for strength. He no longer knew whether that power came from the element bonds or from the elementals. There had been a time when that distinction mattered, but it no longer did, not in the same way that it once had. Connected to the bonds, he could tell that the power was essentially the same. Shapers reached the bonds the same way the elementals did. Reaching the power of the bonds directly only bypassed the help of the element bonds but gave Tan a direct access to the source of power.

Was that what Marin did with the darkness?

It might explain why she had been so able to nearly over-come him. Tan hadn't effectively managed to reach the spirit bond the same way. It was there, and he knew that he had tapped into it in the past, but touching upon spirit might be the only way for him to finally stop Marin and the darkness.

How? The only times he had really reached that kind of power had been when he'd stepped in the pool of spirit, held the artifact and dared use it, and defeated the Utu Tonah, drawing upon the power of everyone around him. Otherwise, he had pulled on spirit, but not with the same strength, nor the same depth to that power, that he had otherwise. To defeat the darkness, he would need something like that.

Was *that* why the artifact had been created?

Tan paced, letting the awareness of the island fill him. The Undoing wasn't gone from this place, not completely, and he sent a quick request to the wind elementals to summon Elanne. He would need his Bond Wardens now.

The artifact had been held in a place of incredible power. A place of convergence, where each of the elementals would congregate, where power bubbled to the surface. Tan had thought the shapers of that time had abused their relationship to the elementals and forced them to serve, to create the protections that went into the making of the artifact, but that hadn't been entirely true. The nymid had been there voluntarily. Golud and ara as well. At a time when he had thought that those were the only great elementals, Tan hadn't known why they would have remained bonded there, held in the place of convergence.

What if it had to do with binding the darkness?

Even if it didn't, it was possible that they protected an item that could be used against the darkness. Those ancient shapers *did* know more than he did about shaping. They might not have been as tightly bound to the elementals, and they might not have been able to reach the bonds, but they could shape, and many could speak to the elementals.

They must have known.

And a device like that… it *was* powerful enough to counter the darkness.

If he could create something like that, it wouldn't have to be only him facing the darkness. The others could help, much more directly than they were able to help now. As much as they wanted to assist him, they were not able to, not fully, and not when facing the full might of Marin and those she had trained to reach the darkness.

Maelen?

Tan looked over and saw Asgar watching him.

Your thoughts are moving too quickly to follow, but I catch flickers. Within them, I see the Elder, and see him bound. Is this something you would recreate?

Trapping the draasin had been terrible. They had been forced into service, and Tan suspected—especially knowing the draasin —that they would have served willingly had they been asked, especially if they knew what they were asked to do. Defeating the darkness was something that all of the elementals understood.

There is something from a long time ago, Tan began, sending images of the artifact to Asgar. *This was what had confined Asboel. At least the reason that he was confined. This device contained power and allowed those with the ability to shape to reach into the source of the Mother.*

You would allow others to reach that source? If the Elder were confined to protect it, then those who came before you saw the danger in possessing it.

There was danger, Tan agreed. Enough danger that many had died trying to reach it. The archivists and Althem had wanted nothing more than to reach that power, and had been willing to sacrifice many—and doing much more horrible things—all in the sake of possessing that power. *I don't know how we can defeat her without having some way of reaching the Mother. I can reach her, but the others cannot.*

There is another.

Who?

The Child.

Tan blinked. Alanna could reach the Mother? That shouldn't surprise him, but it did. His daughter was only two. Even if she were able to reach the Mother, the source of creation, she shouldn't—and couldn't—be called on to face someone as deadly as Marin. This was not her fight.

I can't let her face Voidan. She's not old enough to be able to fight.

Perhaps not in your years, but the elementals know that she is powerful. She continues to grow. You must feel it as well.

I know that she has strength. She would not have bonded already if there wasn't strength there, but what you're suggesting is letting a child, one who can barely even walk, face something that fully grown adults cannot face.

You think of age, rather than in connection to the Mother.

Tan frowned, turning to the draasin. Could Asgar really be telling him that he should allow his *daughter* to face Marin and the disciples?

I think of understanding. The draasin do not have full understanding when they are born.

Are you certain? Many are fire returned to a body.

Tan hesitated. *What do you mean?*

Fire does not end, Maelen. It returns to the bond but then it returns. Fire is life. You have said so yourself.

All elements were life, but getting one of the elementals, especially the draasin, to see that was not something that Tan had ever managed. Now wasn't the time to attempt to convince Asgar. Other questions came to him from what Asgar had said.

Does that mean the Elder—

Could Asboel be returned?

All return eventually, Maelen. If the Elder returned, he would not be the same as you knew. He would be changed. The memories that he possessed would be gone, nothing more than a reflection, like flickers in the flame.

Tan had not considered the possibility that Asboel could ever return, even in a different form. He had felt lucky to have been able to speak to him through the Fire bond, but would that ability disappear if Asboel returned?

There were plenty of draasin eggs remaining… but Tan had a sense that those already were life, that they had begun the moment the eggs were lain. Which meant that it was possible that Asboel, if he were to return, was not an egg.

They were thoughts for another time. Now he had to focus on what Asgar told him about the knowledge of those born of fire. *How many of the new hatchlings possess memories of their times before?*

Asgar snorted. *As I said, it is faded. There are memories, but they are flickers, and nothing more. Fire burns, and what was is changed.*

Tan detected the struggle that Asgar had in describing it, and realized that he had gone through something similar. *What's it like?*

Asgar huffed out. *There are hints of what I had been, but that is all. Things I see… there are certain things that trouble me because I know that I have experienced them in some way before. You describing this device. I have seen this sometime, though I cannot tell you when. It troubles me.*

But we could use that power to stop the darkness.

At what cost, Maelen? If the wrong person controls it—if the Mistress of Darkness comes into possession of it—what will happen to the Mother? Will she be able to harm the Mother?

It shouldn't be able to be used to destroy.

The Mistress has proven that she can twist power. If she does it to a device like you describe, the danger is great.

Tan felt a stirring on the wind and looked up. Elanne appeared on a shaping of wind, carried by the elementals and her own shaped power. Two other bond wardens came with her, both men Tan had met before and tested with spirit. He had taken to testing everyone with a hint of spirit, needing to know if they could be trusted. The work that they did now depended on it.

We will continue this conversation later, friend, he said to Asgar.

"Maelen. The wind tells me that you requested my presence."

Tan sighed. "Thanks for coming. Do you know this place?"

Elanne looked around, a frown on her lips as she did. When she turned back to him, she nodded. "This is one of the Xsa Isles, Maelen. There should be a temple here, but I do not see it and the wind tells me that it has been destroyed."

That must have been the pile of debris that Tan had seen before. What kind of temple would there have been here, and why would it have been destroyed? He knew little about the people of Xsa, not enough to know whether they had a god they worshipped, or whether they were tied to the elements and the belief in the Great Mother.

"What happened here? There is… something not quite right here."

"The Mistress of Darkness was here," Tan said. "She used something the elementals called Undoing to change the land. That's why I need your help."

All of the bond wardens tipped their heads, as if to listen. Tan suspected they waited for the elementals to share with them their understanding of the Undoing. All were bonded to elementals, and each of them were powerful shapers. That was another reason that Tan trusted them. He would know from the elementals if there was something off about them, and if they had become tainted by the darkness.

One by one, their faces turned ashen.

"You understand what happened here?" Tan asked.

Rogan, a man with an easy smile and thin frame, nodded. He was a fire shaper, and bound to saa. Unlike with other fire shapers, those like Ciara, heat didn't radiate from him. He didn't have the same temper that other fire shapers often possessed, men like Seanan. Instead, he seemed to radiate his warmth in a different way, almost a friendly way.

"Saa tells me there could be nothing here. They are impressed that you have managed to return what you have."

"I will return all of this island," Tan said. "That's why I need you here. We need to place bonds throughout the island until everything is fully restored."

"That will take…" Elanne started and saw Tan's face before nodding. "Of course, Maelen. We will do this. You do not need to remain. I suspect you have other things that must be done."

Asgar nudged him with his nose, and Tan sighed. There were other things that he *could* be doing, but this was important. Besides, in doing this, he would discover how difficult it might be to stop Marin if she attempted this again, and he had little doubt that she would.

"I will help. The work will go faster."

Rogan and the other man, Teln, both nodded. Elanne watched Tan with an expression of worry, one that pinched her brow into a wrinkled line.

They started away and stopped at the edge of Tan's binding, starting to create another without waiting.

Elanne watched him and then approached. "Maelen—"

"I know you're worried about me," he said to her.

She nodded. "It's more than that."

"What is it, Elanne? I've been trying to do what I can to protect us. That means finding out what Marin intends." And he still didn't know. The Undoing gave him a hint, especially if there was as much destruction tied to it as he had seen. If they were able to prevent him from using his connection to the elements, and to the elementals, then the Undoing might be the most dangerous plan they had come up with.

All around him, he felt the surge of bindings as they took hold. Teln and Rogan made their way around the island, slowly circling out, placing the bindings into ground they had already recovered and widening the preserved land. As they did, Tan could detect the return of life, the surge of the elementals back into the ground.

"You have changed, Maelen. That is what this is about."

"We've all changed."

"But you no longer teach the children. You no longer spend time in Par. You come, you visit with Amia and your daughter, and you depart again. Even the elementals worry about you."

Tan kept his attention away from Asgar but could feel the draasin as he fixed his gaze on him. Had the elementals instructed Elanne to tell him this? He wouldn't put it past them to work together to see that he did what they needed of him.

"The masters lead Par. I've seen to it that there are leaders."

Elanne smiled and shook her head. "Do you know that when

the Utu Tonah came, he forced himself on the people of Par? He forced the people to serve him, and then began forcing the bonds. The longer that he was there, the more he forced. Over time, there were those who sought more power, who wanted nothing more than to reach power, and they began to serve him."

"I know this, Elanne. That is why I forced him out."

"You know this, but you don't know how much the council rebelled against his presence. I wasn't always the bond master. There were others before me."

The others had all been killed by Tan during his cleansing of the Utu Tonah's attack. It was because of Tan that she had come into her role. "Do you wish you would never have been given your title?"

"You miss the point, Maelen. The council wanted no other. They did not want the Utu Tonah to lead, and then when you came, they did not want you to lead."

"And now I've given them a chance to take on leadership. I've stepped away, letting those who want to guide the people of Par to do so."

"They only thought they wanted to lead. Now that you've been gone, they feel that loss more than they realized." Elanne stepped toward him. Tan felt bindings continue to flash all around him. "I know you think the elementals need you and there are other responsibilities you have placed upon yourself, but the people of Par need you, Maelen."

She waited and then nodded, hurrying off on a shaping of wind to join the others in creating the bindings.

Tan stood there a moment before leaping to the air on wind and fire. Asgar leaped into the sky on his massive wings and circled around him but didn't reach through the fire bond to him.

He placed a few more bindings, but it became clear that the bond wardens didn't need his help as much as he thought. They were skilled, trained by Elanne, who had been partially trained by him—and by the Utu Tonah—and didn't require him to help.

We can return, he sent to Asgar.

As you wish, Maelen.

Tan shaped himself to Asgar's back, watched the cleansing of the island a moment longer, and then rode with the draasin as they made their way back toward Par.

4

CHILD OF THE MOTHER

The inside of the estate glowed with a soft warmth. Seasons had changed, and the usual heat of Par had begun to clear, leaving a cool bite to the air that drifted with the heavy northern wind. Tan imagined the wind coming from Norilan and from the ice that he'd once seen surrounding the island, though now that he'd been there, he knew the ice little more than a mirage. He shifted the heavy wool cloak on his shoulders as he strode through the estate. The sense of both Amia and Alanna pulled him with an urgency. Amia, at least, needed to know what he had faced.

A tall man with a thin face and a serious expression joined him as they made their way through the hall. Maclin was now the Master of Souls, a title Tan had essentially bestowed on him, and one that made him a leader within Par. He had provided a type of guidance from the first moment that Tan had come to Par, and Tan normally valued his opinion. Today, he only hoped the man wouldn't make a point of telling him the same things that Elanne and the elementals had.

"You appear well, Maelen," Maclin noted.

"The elementals don't tell you when I'm well?" Tan had discovered Maclin had a connection to earth, to the elemental ghosh that was not native to Par. The bond had formed sometime after Tan had freed Par-shon and after he had released all of the bonds.

"They tell me were I to ask."

"If you don't ask, then you must be the only one who doesn't," Tan said. "It seems the elementals *and* your council worries about my commitment."

"It's not your commitment that has people—and elementals —talking. I would say there are those who fear your passion. They have seen it before."

Tan hesitated. The door into his quarters was just down the hall, close enough now that he could hear Alanna laughing inside, the sound tugging on his heart. "I am nothing like him, Maclin. You of all people should know that."

Maclin nodded. "I know, as much as I also know how you share the passion he possessed. His was directed at collecting elementals, and through them, reaching for power. Yours is a more singular passion, but carries with it the same risk of overwhelming the ability to see others around you."

Tan squeezed his eyes shut. He tried not to let the responsibilities he now possessed weigh on him, but there were times when they were almost impossible to ignore. Most of the time, he kept his focus on the elementals and serving the Mother. That had been the one constant through everything, and the reason he thought he'd managed to succeed so far. Were he to allow himself to think about personal gain, he wondered if he would have managed the same success.

"I hear what you're saying, Maclin."

"Do you, Maelen? All I ask is that you consider the others who would share in your burden. If the Mistress of Darkness succeeds, we all will fall. You do not have to be the only one responsible for stopping her."

Tan started forward again. "Ask ghosh about the Undoing, Maclin, and then tell me if there are others who can help."

He continued on, leaving Maclin alone in the hall, his head tipped to the side as he seemed to listen to the elemental. Tan could almost hear part of the conversation through the earth bond, but he ignored it. It was not meant for him. Were he to want to, he suspected he could listen to all the conversations between elementals, but that was a violation of the gift that he'd been given, and one he didn't feel was at all appropriate.

Pushing the door open, he hurried inside. Alanna met him at the door, as if waiting for him. Likely she had been. He sensed her connection to spirit, one that was at least as deep as his and likely as connected as her mother's. Tan lifted her, spinning her around as he hugged her tightly. She giggled and power surged against him.

"You sent her back with the draasin?" Amia asked. "She hasn't said her first words yet, and you let her travel alone?"

It had troubled them that Alanna hadn't spoken, though there was nothing for them to do about it but wait.

She stood with her arm resting on the back of a chair, her long, golden hair flowing around her shoulders. A band of silver around her neck marked her as the First Mother of the Aeta, a title that she reluctantly still possessed. Eventually, he knew, she wanted to pass that on to someone else, but among other things, he doubted there had been time to find the right person. She barely spent any time in the kingdoms anymore, and that even with the draasin willing to fly her there anytime that Tan wouldn't be available.

"We found Marin."

"We? I thought the elementals found her."

Tan nodded. Since he'd bridged the connection between the element bonds and spirit, using spirit to protect the bonds, and in effect, protect the elementals, she had been able to hear much of the same conversations as he had. Even without that, she had her bond to him, one that connected them in such a way that she could listen to him.

"Wind found her. She was creating something they called an Undoing." Alanna stopped wiggling in his arms and studied his face. Her fingers traced his cheeks as she frowned. Tan detected a soft buildup of pressure from a shaping, but couldn't be certain that it came from her. Could she already be that subtle with shaping that he couldn't even detect it anymore? "It's a terrible thing, one where everything the Mother had created was destroyed, pressed away from the land."

"And you couldn't return our daughter to Par before taking this on? You couldn't bring other shapers with you? If you were willing to take others who could use spirit—"

He shook his head. She had tried getting him to work with the archivists, but he still struggled with them. Amia trusted them, which *should* be enough, but for some reason it was not. "The draasin didn't think we had the time."

Amia glanced over his shoulder and he turned, noting Maclin standing there. The man had an unreadable expression on his face. "Is there anything we can help you with, Maclin?" Amia asked.

"Now that the Maelen has returned, there are a few who would speak with him. I can give you a few minutes, but they would really appreciate a few moments of your time."

Tan expected Maclin to tell him who waited, but he didn't. A hint of a smile tugged at Amia's mouth, and she nodded.

The door closed behind him, leaving them alone. Amia took Alanna from his arms and set her onto the ground. She walked to the fire and pulled on a brick, lowering the stairs that were recessed into it, revealing a hidden passage that ultimately led to the massive tower.

"When did she discover that?" Tan asked.

"I think she's always known."

A small shape slithered out, something like a snake, only thicker. It had the snout and eyes of the draasin, and stubby legs the creature didn't use. There were no wings on it. Since hatching, Tan hadn't known what to make of the creature, but it clearly had bonded to his daughter. The creature climbed around her legs and wound up and around her torso, settling in. Alanna giggled, and the creature's skin glowed a soft orange.

None had known what to make of it. Even more than Light —and where was the lizard, now that he thought about her?— no one really knew what to make of this elemental. She had been nearly broken, healed only because of what Tan had done and how she had been shifted, but that had changed something about her, much as he seemed to often change things about the elementals.

Alanna took a seat near the fire and her mouth moved, as if speaking to the snake. The creature's head bobbed and its mouth opened and closed, a long tongue sliding out as it responded.

It wasn't quite like kaas. That elemental was both fire and earth. This one was more a combination of many elementals, though Tan couldn't quite determine what that meant. He could *hear* the creature within the bonds, but had not ever managed to get it to respond to him. So far, it only spoke to Alanna. It would trouble him if he didn't know what he did about the elementals.

He pulled his attention away from Alanna. "She was as safe as the draasin could make her. You know they would never do anything to put her into danger."

"Are you certain?"

He nodded, but a growing sense of doubt rose within him. He hadn't thought that the elementals would lead his daughter into harm, but with the comment that Asgar had made, a suggestion that Alanna be used in the fight against Marin, he wasn't certain. Would they press her to fight, thinking that she was more like them than like a human child?

"Wasina brought her back safely," he said.

Amia nodded. "She did, but that doesn't change the fact that she shouldn't have been out there with you in the first place. She's too young to be riding on the draasin. What would happen were she to fall? What would you do then?"

"I would shape myself to her." He worried less about that happening than about the possibility of the draasin getting ambushed by Marin or her disciples.

Amia turned away, fixing her attention on Alanna. Through the bond between them, he could tell the mixture of annoyance and relief she felt at having Alanna back. She didn't really think that anything would have happened to her, just as she didn't think that Tan would have left her where any harm could come to her.

He went and took her hand in his, squeezing. "We've been through so much together. We shouldn't let the stress of this drive a wedge between us."

Amia took a deep breath. "You're right. I know that you are, but that doesn't change the fact that all I think of when she leaves with you is what other danger she might face. With you, it's bad enough. I know you can defend yourself and even if you can't, the elementals will fight on your behalf. With Alanna... she's helpless."

It was the same thing his mother had tried to do with him. She'd wanted to protect him from the Incendin threat for as long as she could, preventing him from even realizing that she had been one of the more powerful shapers who had been helping protect the wall until she was forced to reveal herself.

With the thought, a smile crossed his face.

"What are you grinning at?"

Tan shook his head. "Just... just thinking of Zephra and how she attempted to protect me." He squeezed her hand again and smiled. "What was it like for you? Did the Mother try to keep you out of anything that might be dangerous?"

Amia stiffened for a moment. "She thought to keep me from harm. It was part of the reason we wandered. Keeping moving prevented anyone from discovering our connection with spirit."

"Incendin discovered."

"They did. Others suspected, but we had always been so careful with who could shape."

"To the point that the men who could shape were sent away."

"I didn't know about it. I don't disagree with what the First Mother did. They might have betrayed our people, but there was no place for the archivists among the people. With the ability to shape, they deserved more than they were allowed."

"Is that why you have granted them such freedom now?"

She glanced over at him. "They pose no risk, especially as we know what they are capable of doing. And they can serve in other ways. You've already found a way to use them. What other uses do you think we might come across? The People have maintained much knowledge over the years."

"There is something else we may need of them."

She arched a brow at him. "What?"

"I haven't thought it through completely yet."

She laughed softly and Alanna glanced back at them, the snake creature pulling its head away from her body and fixing both Tan and Amia with its bright, almost knowing, eyes. "You have some idea. I know you too well, Tannen. Whatever you're thinking about makes you uncomfortable."

"It makes the elementals uncomfortable as well."

"Then that should be answer enough of the reason that you should not do this thing, whatever it is."

"When I faced Marin, I faced someone connected to a dark power more strongly than anything that I have ever encountered. Even able to use the bonds that I am, even able to summon the elementals, there was still a part of me that suspected that we wouldn't be able to finish her. If she succeeded in trapping me"—and she very nearly had, something that Tan didn't know what would have happened to him if it had—"there wouldn't have been anyone left who could use the true connections to the elementals to defeat her." And maybe they still couldn't, but he had to use everything that he could think about that might give them the *chance* to defeat her.

"You think there's a way for others to use some of the same power that you can reach." When Tan nodded, she continued. "Spirit lets me connect to you and know what you know, often letting me connect as if I were there in person, but I have to be receptive. I don't know everything that you know, and I don't know that you would *want* me to know everything."

"There are no secrets from you."

"Not secrets, but there are things you would prefer to think through before sharing them. This, I can tell, is one of them."

He sighed. "I started thinking about Asboel."

"You think of him often."

Tan smiled sadly. "I do."

"You've told me that he's back with fire. That you've spoken to him *in* fire."

"I have. And Asgar tells me that fire will be reborn, so I have hope that Asboel will return, at least a memory of him. But that's not what I'm thinking of. When we first discovered him, he had been bound in ice. We had always assumed the people of that time had frozen him to protect the artifact because it was too powerful for anyone to possess."

"We saw that with Althem. He wanted to use it for power."

"He did, but we haven't really spent any time trying to understand *why* they had created the artifact. Why would they risk that much power?"

"You think it has something to do with this darkness?"

"I don't know if it did, but I recognized that when I held it, I was able to use power of the Mother almost like nothing else

I've ever encountered. That kind of power *could* have been used to help restrain this darkness."

Amia pulled in a sharp breath. "They were powerful shapers, but they didn't have your ability to reach the bonds, did they?"

"I don't think they did."

"And you… you would recreate it? Would you make more of these artifacts so that others would be able to counter what Marin can do?"

"I think we need to consider it."

Alanna had come over to them and looked up at her mother, holding her arms outward. The snake had climbed off her and curled around a vase near the fire. Amia lifted her and she wrapped her arms around her neck. When they were together, Tan detected a surge of spirit, a shaping such that he wondered if either of them recognized what the other did. Maybe they did. Maybe that was how the Aeta communicated with others able to shape spirit, using a shaping that washed over the other person, much like the fire shaping used within Incendin.

"What do the elementals think of your suggestion?" Amia asked over Alanna's shoulder.

"They worry about the wisdom of it."

"I would share their concern. We know what was done the last time when the artifact existed, what extent others went to in order to acquire it."

Tan patted his daughter on the head and she giggled at him. Normally, he loved that sound, but now it only made him worry. Everything that he did was for her, to ensure that she had the future she needed. Really, when it came to the darkness, any future. If he *didn't* fight, there would be the

Undoing, and if he didn't find a way to stop Marin, and to suppress the darkness entirely, more than an island would suffer. The next time, they would face a challenge where people were at risk as well, where everything that they had would be unmade.

"I'm not even sure that I can figure out *how* to make these things. I think the elementals went into their creation the last time, and I'm not willing to do that to the elementals. Anything that we do needs to be to protect them."

"We'll find a way, Tan. We always do."

He forced a smile, suspecting Amia knew he did. It was more for Alanna than for Amia, though he began to wonder how much she could be convinced by a fake smile. With her connection to spirit, she would likely know as easily as her mother.

His daughter watched him, an intensity in her eyes that made him nervous. The fact that she could connect to the elementals and seemed able to speak to them made him proud, but there was the ongoing worry that Asgar might be right, and that he might be forced into letting her be a part of the fight with Marin and the disciples.

Light appeared on the hearth, and he wondered if she had been hiding in the lower level. She could have been studying there, gaining knowledge the way she knew how, licking everything. What did it mean that she had been down there with the snake?

She is so young.

As am I.

Tan looked over at his bonded. She was a mixture of fire and spirit, but mostly spirit. She was barely older than Alanna, and she had already saved his life at least once. And Tan hadn't hesitated to involve Light in the fight before. Was that the point that Asgar was trying to get across?

She is but a child.

Perhaps to you. You need to see her the way the Mother sees her, Maelen. In that way, she has already grown wise.

Tan looked upon his daughter, noting the long blond hair, the chubby cheeks, and the glitter to her blue eyes, one that was so much like her mother's. She *was* only a child… wasn't she?

He'd avoided reaching through the bonds to her, much like he had avoided listening to conversations with the elementals through the bonds, but maybe it was time.

She watched him, as if expecting him to do something, when a voice intruded in his mind.

Maelen.

What is it, Honl?

The Undoing. You should come.

Tan glanced over at Light, then at his daughter, and nodded. He would reach for Alanna another time.

I will come.

5

UNDERSTANDING THE CYCLE

The air north of the kingdoms had a hint of cold to it, the same cold northern wind that gusted through Par, though this had less of the crispness to it and more of the slimy and foul notes that he'd detected in Xsa. They were in a part of the kingdoms Tan had never set foot in, a long finger of land that stretched into the sea as part of Vatten. He didn't know what it had once been like, but with the Undoing, the land had a rocky and angry appearance.

Honl floated above the ground, his form almost as solid as Light's, who draped around his neck. She hadn't wanted him to come alone, worried about what he might face, and the draasin hadn't been willing to enter the area where the Undoing had begun taking hold. Tan was thankful for her presence.

"This is *wrong*, Maelen."

"This is Marin and the disciples," Tan said. "I've encountered it earlier on Xsa."

Honl looked over at him, the gesture slightly unnatural. "Were you able to counter it?"

"Can't you detect what I was able to do?" Usually, Honl would remain connected to him, not only through their bonding but through the connection they now shared through the wind bond. Why *wouldn't* Honl know what he had done?

"There was... something. Then there was not. I do not know what it meant."

The wind elemental soared across the ground. He had appeared in a form of a man, this time an older man with dark gray eyes the color of storm clouds and a face that reminded Tan of his father. He wondered if Honl had done that intentionally. His father had broader shoulders, and he had been more heavily muscled than the appearance Honl created, but they had a similar height and the same grizzled beard and concerned expression.

Tan remained stationary over the ground, not wanting to get too close. He still didn't know what would happen were the Undoing to touch him, but feared that it might begin unraveling his connections. When he'd faced Marin, she had nearly over-whelmed him and the bonds had begun to separate. Would that happen here, even if she were not present?

But *someone* had to be here for this to work, didn't they?

That meant the disciples.

Tan knew there were Disciples of Darkness somewhere, but he hadn't been able to learn where they studied. If he could find them, if he could trace them back to Marin, he might be able to bring the fight to her, though he wasn't sure that he wanted to.

"Have you noticed anyone here?" Tan asked.

Honl shook his head, a strange gesture for an elemental, and one that looked so... human. Each time Tan saw Honl, the elemental had become more and more solid. Even his form—the man who looked to be about the same age as Roine—had barely changed the last few times Tan had seen him. Perhaps the beard was longer, but that shouldn't matter, not since Honl could take on any shape that he wanted.

"From what I can tell, there is no one else here. There is nothing. The land is broken," Honl said.

Light perched on Tan's shoulder, wrapping her tail around his neck for support, and swiveled her head around as she studied the ground. Tan was surprised to note that she didn't jump from his shoulders as she often would. She remained where she was, stationed atop him, unmoving. If anything, she was rigid, her body tensed. The Undoing unsettled even her. That said quite a bit, considering the way that she had often thrown herself into situations before.

"Marin is using the darkness to unmake the work of the Mother," Tan said.

"She should not be able to unmake it," Honl said. "The element bonds power the world, and the rest of the elementals and human connections join together, binding creation."

Tan glanced over at Honl. "That's an interesting turn of phrase. Did you use binding intentionally?"

"It's not a binding the same as what you have made, Maelen. This is..." He shook his head and took something that resembled a breath. That was a new gesture for him; the wind elemental should have no need to actually breathe. "Finding the words is difficult. The knowledge is there, but it changes on me."

"Why would it change?"

49

Honl took a step away, walking on a cloud of air, keeping himself above the ground. Since rescuing him from Jorma, Honl had remained distant, though that wasn't unusual. He had been distant in the time before his capture as well, something that was tied to trying to understand the darkness and how to bind it.

"Much has changed for me. Since my capture, I was reminded of the fact that I am an elemental."

"You had forgotten that?" Tan shaped himself toward Honl and reached him, failing to anticipate a measure of angst on his face.

"As I took on this form... I think in some ways, I became more like a man."

"Is that what you want?"

Honl smiled slightly. "I do not know what I want. Perhaps in some ways, I am like you, Maelen."

"Are you saying I don't know what I want?" Tan asked with a laugh. In this place, with the Undoing wiping away everything the Mother had created and leaving a foul taint overtop of the world, the laughter died off quickly.

Honl turned to him. "You would have your life, Maelen. That is all I meant."

"For me to have what I want, I can't remain silent when I'm needed. The Mother gifted me with these abilities for a reason. I believe that. And so I need to use them."

"You are the Shaper of Light."

"That's what I hear."

"You do not believe that to be true?" Honl asked.

"I believe that I connect to the great powers of the world in a way others cannot. I believe that gives me an advantage, but I'm not certain that it's enough of an advantage that I will be able to defeat Marin, especially as she continues to connect to Voidan."

"The longer that she acts, the more that power slips into the world."

Tan looked around, feeling the weight of the Undoing. He shaped a binding and layered it on the ground beneath him, forcing back the Undoing. The shaping drained him briefly, but color began to return to the earth.

"It reminds me of what happened when Par-shon attacked," he said.

Tan lowered himself to the ground and walked to the edge of the circle, where the rim of Undoing pressed against his binding. He added another binding, this one angled in such a way that it pressed against the Undoing again, pushing it back. He would have to keep at this, and continually force back the Undoing, but how many bindings would he need to place? What effect did that have on the rest of the world? Perhaps none, but were these bindings any different than what the Order of Warrior had placed all across Norilan? They had forced the elementals to remain tied to the land. The bindings here didn't do that, but there were similarities he couldn't easily move past.

"They are the same, in some ways," Honl said. He joined Tan on the ground, not floating, but seeming to walk. A binding of wind appeared, touched with a hint of spirit, and it pressed back the Undoing again.

Tan looked over at him. The elementals had been unwilling to work with the bindings, fearful that they would be either harmed or touched by the Undoing, but Honl had simply created one. He *had* changed—and more than any other elemental.

Light licked his cheek and scampered down, sitting on the reclaimed ground. She had been silent, seeming to recognize that Honl needed Tan's attention for now.

"I remember how bleak Doma looked when the elementals had been pressed away," Tan said. It had not only been Doma, but Incendin as well. Their particular type of shaping had changed the Sunlands. They were already a dark and dangerous place, but by using fire in the way that they had, they had tormented the elementals in some unintended ways. That, combined with the barrier that prevented the elementals from easily passing between the two lands, had changed them for the worse. "That was how I knew I needed to intervene."

"And Chenir," Honl reminded him.

"And Chenir," Tan agreed. In Chenir, they had withdrawn the elementals intentionally, hoping to save them from the Parshon attack. That had made the lands nearly as bleak as this, though still not *quite* as tainted. Here, the land had an appearance of a place that had been ravaged, that life had abandoned it, and there was the foul sense over everything.

Strange that the Utu Tonah had been involved in that, especially as he had sought to become a Shaper of Light, as if to claim a title through forced bonds.

"What have you learned about Voidan?" Tan asked as they walked forward, both of them placing bindings as they went.

Honl's were simply wind and spirit, and though of wind, and though they should dissipate as soon as he created them, spirit seemed to hold them, to twist them into creation so that they held, allowing the Undoing to be pressed back. With each step, Tan felt a return of life around him. Elementals would eventually return as well, and then the land would be back to normal, other than for the bindings that now covered everything.

"This is not the first time he has escaped," Honl said.

"I didn't think it was. Those ancient shapers wouldn't have needed the protections they placed if this was the first time."

Honl frowned. "I don't think that was the first time, either. Records are sparse, though we do have them from a thousand years ago."

"And before that?"

"There are others, remnants that I can find. They are difficult because they are fragmented. It seems that this darkness bubbles up every so often and men are forced to face it. I have found records of a time before the last, during something the people referred to as an endless war, but have not found anything more than that."

"How would the darkness bubble up every so often? If the bindings are solid enough—"

"They are never solid enough. That's part of the problem, Maelen. Think of what we know of this darkness. When you've faced it, there is destruction to it. Even the bindings, the seals placed, will erode over time. I think that's the only way it *can* be."

Tan paused as he finished placing another binding. Blackened grass began to take on a hint of brown, enough that Tan could detect the life within it once more. "Are you saying this is part of a cycle?"

"It seems that way."

"How are we to know what we can do to stop it?"

"I think," Honl began, turning toward the south. "I think places like Alast and like the tower in Par were meant for us to remember. The Records in Par would seem to indicate that they wanted to share what they knew about this so that those who came after would be able to defeat it."

If that were the case, then the Records had failed. Language had changed over time, and the people had changed. Fear and urgency had faded as this darkness faded, to the point where no one knew how to face it.

Could that be why the elementals had been bound?

They would have known the darkness and would have been tied to it, but Asboel had not seemed to remember. Tan hadn't taken the time to speak to Sashari or to Enya, but he didn't think either of them had remembered, either. Why would that be?

They reached the end of the peninsula and both he and Honl placed the final bindings. They still hadn't come across any of the disciples, though they hadn't fully cleansed the land. There would be more time needed to finish.

And now Tan had new questions.

Sashari. Enya.

He sent the summons through the fire bond. If they heard— and he had little reason to doubt that they would—he would have them join him here.

"You wonder whether the others would have known about it," Honl noted.

"They were from that time. I've been wondering about the artifact they protected, thinking that maybe the ancients knew more than I have been giving them credit for. If they did, and if they faced the same thing that we face now, then it only makes sense that the elementals of that time would have known something as well, don't you think?"

Honl stared out over the sea. His eyes narrowed, the hollows

seeming to deepen as he stared across the ocean. White-capped
swells rose and fell, the water catching the reflection of the sun,
sending streaks of color across the water. A few gulls cawed as
they circled. Distantly, Tan felt the pull of udilm, the elemental
of the sea, but even that had retreated from the shores when the
Undoing had been placed.

Why here? What was it about this land that made Marin and
her disciples want to place it here? The one in Xsa could simply
have been a test, but this one… this seemed something else,
almost as if she expected to find something here.

"Time passes to the elementals the same as it does to man,"
Honl finally said. "Many live for centuries, longer than you
would believe, but even their lives are not limitless. They return
to the bond and are born again."

"You said theirs," Tan noted.

Honl turned to him, frowning.

"You mean your lives?"

Honl tipped his head. "I have changed enough that I no
longer know whether I can claim to be an elemental, Maelen.
Then again, does it matter? If we are all part of the Mother, if we
all exist to serve her creation, it might not matter what I am and
what you are."

Tan wondered if that were true or not. There were plenty of
people with no ability to shape, or even to sense. Were they
connected to the Mother the same as everyone else, or was their
connection somehow lessened?

"You think they would have forgotten over time?"

Honl appeared to shrug. "It's possible that they did. Much is
possible, Maelen."

Was that why Sashari and Enya hadn't mentioned anything

since the darkness had returned? Was that why Asboel had never said anything to him? He knew memories had faded for the draasin, and that over time, much that they had known had changed. In that way, the memories of man had been better. They remembered the draasin, and still feared them, even though they had been effectively gone from the world for nearly a thousand years.

They reached the place where they had begun placing the bindings. Tan noticed something that he hadn't before, and maybe he wouldn't have been able to notice before the bindings were placed. He hadn't been able—or willing—to step foot on the ground. Now that he was, he saw a pile of rock that he had assumed nothing more than rock, but renewed sensation through the earth bond shared with him an opening deep beneath the ground, stretching away from the sea.

Tan motioned toward the rock with Honl. "There's something we need to evaluate."

"Is that safe to do alone?"

"I won't be alone. You'll come with me. And Light."

Honl glanced at the lizard. "I will not have the same power beneath the ground."

"Wind blows underground. There is often a breeze in the tunnels beneath Ethea."

"A breeze, but I am descended from ashi. I think I will be diminished as we descend."

"If you'd rather not go…"

Honl shook his head. "I will accompany you, but I wanted you to be aware that I might not be able to offer as much help as you might need."

Light surprised him by scurrying over to Honl and climbing

up his shoulders. She situated herself there and ran her tongue along Honl's face. It seemed strange to Tan that she would even be able to do that, that Honl could exist in a form that was solid enough for Light to climb, but then, Honl *was* different. Perhaps he really no longer was an elemental.

If that were the case, what did that mean for their bond?

Tan pushed the thoughts away as they approached the tunnel hidden by the rock.

As they did, stone exploded out from it.

6

DISCIPLES ATTACK

Tan caught the first attack in a shaping of wind, throwing debris back toward the tunnel. The shaping slipped over something—the darkness, he realized—and he maintained it, continuing to press.

Next to him, he detected Honl using a similar shaping. Why should he be aware of Honl using his connection to wind? Was it the wind bond that allowed it, or was it the changes to Honl that made it more likely?

Tan didn't allow himself the time to consider for long. Five dark-cloaked shapers strode free from the tunnel, each of them drawing on the power of the darkness. None of them were Marin.

Where was she?

Would she trust an attack on him to her disciples?

Likely, she would. He suspected that she would *prefer* her

disciples be the ones to attack, especially as they could weaken him.

Tan took a moment to study the men and women appearing before him. He did not recognize any of them. Three were men of varying ages. One had a beard much like what Honl now preferred, and two had clean-shaven faces. Those two were also completely bald, and one of them had a healed scar running across the top of this head, as if he had long ago been attacked. The women were both dark haired and had youthful faces. All five summoned the darkness.

Pulling on spirit, he began a shaping that would bind them, but didn't have enough time to complete it.

One of the women sent a streamer of darkness toward Honl.

He stood there, motionless.

Tan shaped the earth, sending her flying, and Light seemed to push Honl down.

Watch him, Light.

I will keep him safe, Maelen.

Turning back to the attack, Tan discovered that the three men had split off and surrounded him. He placed a binding around himself, much as he had with Marin. Using that, he maintained his connection to the element bonds and to the power of the elementals. Tan used neither.

Instead, he opted for a different approach. Shaping hadn't defeated Marin before. The darkness was powerful, and Tan wasn't entirely certain that he had enough strength to stop all of them using shaping alone. Sealed in his binding, there was another thing he could try, and he suspected it would surprise them.

Tan unsheathed his sword.

The warrior sword bore runes down the blade, and he pulled on a shaping of each of the elements. The blade glowed with a bright white light, almost blindingly so. He pointed the sword at the nearest of the disciples, and the man smiled.

"You intend to shape me?" he asked in a hoarse voice. "She has given me power over shapers. I see how you fear it!"

"Not shape you," Tan said.

He lunged forward.

The tip of the blade sank into the man's stomach, and his eyes widened. Tan pushed the shaping he'd drawn through the blade out and into the man. Darkness shattered, and he sank.

Tan spun, remaining in his binding.

The element of surprise was gone. The other disciples backed away from him.

Remaining in the confines of the binding, he could direct his shaping outside of it, but that didn't allow him to help Honl. The wind elemental—or whatever he now was—sent swirling gusts of wind at the dark disciples, but they managed to deflect them, sending them back down and into the sky. Honl was forced back under the attack of the two women.

Tan would have to help him. It didn't appear that Honl could help himself.

He focused a shaping on the ground in front of him, nearest the closest disciple. As he set it, he surged forward, slashing with his sword. The binding held the disciple inside, and Tan needed only a moment to finish him. The man sank to the ground, blood spilling from the sword wound in his chest.

Could he confine the disciples within the bindings?

That wasn't something he had considered before, but it had seemed to hold the other man. If he could, then he could take the time he needed, and maybe even get answers. A part of him even hoped that he would be able to heal them, prevent them from reaching the darkness again. Wasn't that what the Mother expected of him?

Tan created another binding, this one narrow in focus, and shaped it beneath the other man. As it took hold, the man was trapped, sealed inside.

You can bind them, he told Honl.

The wind elemental shifted his approach as well and sent a shaping directed at the ground, catching one of the women. The other seemed to recognize what they intended and started to take off.

Tan didn't want her to escape. He couldn't risk Marin learning that he had discovered some way to confine her disciples, a way that would prevent the darkness from attacking. When she learned, she would come up with some way to counter, and he needed the advantage for now.

With a lancing shot of fire, he knocked the woman out of the sky.

When she landed, he quickly formed a shaping, circling it around her, and drew it tight.

She struggled, writhing within the shaping, but he held onto it.

Tan sighed. They had them. The bindings worked for another purpose.

"What will you do with them now that you've captured them?" Honl asked. His gaze went from the fallen disciples to the bloody sword Tan held.

"We need answers from them," he said. "They might not want to share with us, but they will."

He knelt before the woman lying on the ground, bound within his shaping. She no longer struggled as she had, and looked up at him with a malevolent darkness within her eyes. Tan sank his sword into the ground near her, and her gaze drifted over to it.

"You should kill me as you killed the others," she spat.

"What were you doing there?" he asked.

Her gaze remained fixed on his sword. He maintained a steady shaping through it, enough to keep the blade glowing with a steady white light. Even better if it upset her.

"Kill us now or release us. You will not be able to hold us for long."

"I think I've proven I can hold you."

She drew upon her dark power and it surged against the binding. Tan had to redouble his efforts to maintain it, and the glow to the sword faded as he did.

"As I said, you will not be able to hold us for long."

"Maelen!"

Tan spun, grabbing his sword. Honl's binding began to falter under the strength of the dark disciple continuing to shape within it. Before it had a chance to fail completely, Tan stabbed him with the sword, sending light coursing through him. Darkness exploded from him.

He turned to the other man and did the same, stabbing into him with his sword, pulsing a bright shaping of each element through him until darkness exploded and the man collapsed.

Finally, he turned his attention back to the woman.

A smile crossed her face. "As I said, kill us or release us. If you kill us all, you are nothing more than us."

Tan knelt next to her again. He could feel the power she

summoned and the way it pounded at his binding. She was powerful, perhaps the strongest of all who had attacked. "Who said I need to kill?"

With that, he slipped his sword beneath the binding and into her shoulder. She stared at him, hatred deep in her eyes, and he sent a combined shaping of each element through the sword, adding spirit last. This took more strength than the others, but finally the darkness erupted from her as well, falling the same way as it had with the others.

Tan remained in front of her, watching. "You see? I don't have to kill."

"What did you do?"

"I should thank you for attacking. You showed me something I might not have learned otherwise. The darkness inside you can be destroyed. I don't *have* to kill."

"And if you release me, I will return to the Mistress and she will grant me the ability once more. You will suffer more than you do now—"

"Who said I would release you?"

He struck her on the top of her head and she collapsed to the ground, unmoving. Tan wrapped her in wind and earth shapings, preventing her from moving. He didn't want to risk her escape.

Then he stood and turned to the other two still living and bound within the shaping he'd used to prevent them from attacking. Both watched him. The man grabbed at his shoulder where he'd been cut and the woman clutched her stomach. Neither spoke.

Using wind and earth, Tan wrapped both of them in shapings and released the binding. He pulled them toward him, dragging the other woman with him. He stood in the center of the original binding, studying them for a moment.

What should we do with them? he asked Light.

You were right not to destroy them.

I killed two.

The Mother understands, Maelen, Light told him.

He wasn't certain that she did. How could she understand? Had he known another way—had he known that he could use the sword to disperse the darkness from them—he would have done that from the beginning, but he was still learning how to face the darkness. It was the reason he needed answers; he needed something to help him understand the best way to face this kind of shaper, especially with Marin able to counter his shaping as well as she had managed so far.

"What were you doing here?" he asked.

Neither of the two still alert answered.

"I don't have to leave you alive," he said.

The man sneered at him. "You've shown too often your compassion, *Maelen*. It's how the Utu Tonah nearly defeated you."

There was something in the way the man spoke that struck a chord within Tan. "You're from Par."

"Par. Is that what you would call it now?"

Tan wondered if Elanne would know this man. With his deep eyes the color of a storm and bald, and scarred, head, he seemed as if he would be recognizable. "It has always been Par. The Utu Tonah thought to turn the people into something else."

"Yes. He thought himself a Shaper of Light."

Tan blinked. "How is it that you know that term?" When the

man didn't answer, Tan lifted him with a shaping of earth so that he hovered in front of him. "How close to him *were* you?"

And how had he survived the purging of the bonds? Most had perished, tied to the defeat of the Utu Tonah and the rest of Par-shon as Tan had cast aside the bonds, freeing the elementals. He'd seen children within Par who had suffered because their parents had been taken from them by Tan's shaping, and it was something that had driven him to help them, to teach them *why* he had needed to stop the Utu Tonah, to help them understand a better way to serve the elementals.

"Close enough to know that he was a fool."

Tan nodded. "Did you know he came from Norilan?" The corners of his eyes barely moved, but enough to show Tan that he *had* known. "Is that why Marin came?"

"The Mistress went to Norilan to reveal the night," the other woman said.

Tan looked over to her. She was younger than the man and must have joined Marin more recently, unless the binding to the darkness had changed something about the shaper. "Your darkness is confined."

"For now," she said with a dark smile.

Tan glanced back to the man from Par. He fought against the bindings, his arms moving more than they should if the wind and earth shapings remained stout.

"You're a shaper," he said. "Of each element. Why would you do this? Why allow her to taint you like this?"

Tan called the elementals to assist, asking for them to help hold the man in place. Both ara and a surprising earth elemental, one he discovered was called linad, joined the shaping, holding the man in place. He stopped fighting, looking up at Tan defiantly.

"You can keep holding me, but I *will* find a way free."

"No," Tan said, "you won't. I will hold you, or the elementals will hold you. Either way, without the darkness, there is nothing you will be able to do to get free." The man glared at him before his back sagged slightly. "Now. Tell me what you knew of the Utu Tonah."

"Figure it out yourself if you are so wise, *Maelen*."

Light jumped from Honl's shoulders and raced over to the man. She took a seat on his chest. He struggled again, his eyes wide as he stared at the strange lizard, and she licked his face.

He spat, trying to turn away, but Light held him down as she licked again.

"She's heavier than she appears," Tan said with a smile. "You can share it with me, or you can have her discover it in her way. Or I could simply force you to do what I need with spirit." That was the last thing he wanted to do. The moment he started shaping spirit, the moment he started using it against his enemies like that, was the moment he became something like them. This man didn't need to know. Let him believe that Tan would do it.

"Tell it to stop," the man begged.

Maybe don't show him quite as much affection.

I have discovered much, Maelen. Would you prefer I share?

Yes.

Images flickered through his mind, those of the man and his time serving the Utu Tonah. He had been heavily bonded, carrying nearly twenty different elemental bonds, and had not cared that he tormented the elementals as he did. He was powerful then, able to use his ability as a shaper to augment his connections to the elementals. Combined as he was, he had quickly gained favor with the Utu Tonah… but had been held back because he was *too* interested in power.

If the Utu Tonah feared his ambition, how had he gained favor with Marin?

Tan shaped spirit, layering it over the man. He'd already seen how Marin had used people who had served the Utu Tonah, and had twisted them to do what she wanted of them in service of her dark plans. Was this man somehow used in the same way?

As spirit settled into the man, he resisted.

Not as a spirit shaper. Had that been the case, Tan might not have been able to shape him at all. This was resistance created by his shaping ability. Using a combination of elements, he cut the man off from his connection, and then probed deeper.

Beneath the surface of his mind was a subtle shaping.

Amia…

She joined him as he began peeling away the layers of the shaping. It was delicate work, and something made with skill he'd only seen a few times. If Marin were this talented with spirit, had he made a mistake not searching through the rest of Par to see who else she might have touched? A shaping like this would be difficult to detect, even for him, without reaching in and making the connection.

Slowly, they peeled the shaping away.

Once freed, he detected the person beneath the shaping.

Tan almost recoiled.

What he detected was in many ways worse. Marin had softened his hatred and his anger, so that without the shaping, it surged from him, a darkness that boiled within him.

Replace it, Amia urged.

It is unnatural. He should not be shaped like this.

I think... I think she did him a favor placing it. Maybe she truly served the people of Par for a time before she was tainted, using her shapings to soften those like him.

Do you do the same?

The First Mother fills many roles.

Tan detected that she hid something from him, but decided not to worry about it. Could Amia use shapings like this on her people or others?

If I replace it, is there a way to... soften... him more?

Like this...

The shaping appeared in his mind and he slowly created it, wrapping the man's mind in a new shaping, one that changed what Marin had done. Without the touch of the darkness, and with the modification Tan used on him, he saw the man change as he did. With a soft inhalation, he shivered and his eyes blinked open.

Tan could see the hatred that had burned in them was gone, but at what cost?

He had shaped a man to become something he was not. He had *changed* him in a way that turned him into someone else. How was that any different than what the archivists had attempted all those years ago? Tan had rebelled against that then, and now he was the one doing it.

It is different, Amia said.

I don't see it that way.

He can find happiness this way, if you let him. He can discover his connection to the Mother. He would never have been able to do that before.

Tan pulled away from the connection with Amia. Light watched him, seeming to recognize his difficulty. She slithered over to him and brushed against his legs, nearly knocking him over, and then licked him.

"All men change, Maelen."

Tan almost jumped as Honl spoke. The elemental had been silent, letting Tan work, knowing from their shared connection what he did.

"Even the elementals change. What you did for him is no different than what you did for me."

Tan took a deep breath. Could that be all that it was? Could it really be no different than what he'd done for Honl, or kaas, or even for Fur and the rest of the lisincend? Hadn't he made similar changes over and over? He'd been troubled by *some* of them, but not all. Pushing Fur and the lisincend into the fire bond had been the right thing, as had saving the hounds. Even with what happened to Honl, it was hard to see what he had become as anything other than greater than what he had been.

The Mother gave you your gifts for this reason, Maelen. You need to embrace them. It is why she lets you do what you do.

By setting apart the changes to a person, he made them somehow more important when that wasn't necessarily the truth.

He felt Amia's agreement through their bond.

Help me with this other? he asked.

Together, they sent a shaping over the woman as well, discovering that she had been shaped much like the man. They peeled the shaping away, and then changed it. He could see how it would affect her, and what it would mean for her. Her eyes fluttered back in her head, and then fell closed.

Tan turned to the man. Touching him with a hint of spirit, he looked up at Tan.

"What were you doing beneath the ground?"

Changing the shaping had distorted his ability to reach into the man's mind, and Tan needed him to answer. He had a growing fear that whatever they had planned meant something more dangerous than he realized, especially if Marin would risk them coming here, risk leaving them here.

"We..." He looked from Tan to Light and then to Honl. His eyes remained fixed on Honl the longest. "She had us pushing away the elementals," he said. "We should not have, but we did. I see that now."

"Why push the elementals away?" Honl asked.

Tan stared at the opening to the tunnel. The nervousness that he'd been feeling began to surge within him. Using earth, he traced the connection of the tunnel. It went down and down, descending deep beneath the earth, and headed both south and east.

Toward Ethea.

He began to understand why Marin intended to push away the elementals.

She couldn't actually do that, could she? he asked Light.

Has it not been done before? Light asked.

What is it? Amia asked.

The place of convergence. Ethea is one, and if she moves the elementals, she could shift the place of convergence.

You could simply shift it back, she said.

That's not the issue. The convergences connect to the bindings.

Ethea to the Temple of Alast. He began to understand what she must have been doing in Xsa. The isles were close enough to Par for it to make sense. *There must be one in Par and Norilan. If she shifts the convergences—*

The bindings fail, Light said.

7

THE ATHAN RETURNS

A shaping of lightning brought Tan back to Ethea, where he hovered above the city, choosing not to return to the shaper circle as he normally did. Before landing, he wanted to take stock of the city and understand if there was something he might have missed, something that placed the city in danger.

Could Marin really have shifted the convergence?

He didn't detect anything yet, but if she had, it might have been subtle. What she attempted would not necessarily require great strength, just enough to disrupt the flows of power.

As he hovered in the air, focused on the city, he realized that each time he returned, the city felt less and less like home. There was a brief time after he'd first come to Ethea, and then in the time after Althem's defeat, where the city had felt comfortable enough to let him feel rooted to it. It wasn't the same kind of comfort and familiarity he had known in Nor, but then again, there was something special about a childhood home. Even memories that had not necessarily been good at the time had softened, the edges removed, so that he no longer looked upon the torment in the way he had when he'd been there.

Thinking of Nor brought back memories, and the more that he sorted through them, the more he realized that not everything was as he had remembered. Not all of the memories were good. He'd lost his father in Nor. He'd lost almost everyone he'd ever known there. And he never would have discovered his potential had he remained there.

In that regard, Ethea had been a part of him during a pivotal time. He had learned he could shape here. Not only shape, but that he could be a warrior shaper, something not seen in the kingdoms in a generation. He had continued his romance with Amia here. They had made a home and found a place in the world for themselves. And he had begun to understand his bonds within the city. Those bonds were as much a part of him as shaping.

Yet… returning no longer felt the same. The city felt different, and it was more than the way the skyline had changed. The university now towered on the western side of the city, built solidly by earth shapers and augmented by the elementals. The archives were not as impressive as they once had been, the squat, aged building still amazing for its age, but he had seen equally amazing things in his time outside the city. Even the palace, the garden once shaped in ways the warriors of today couldn't understand, had been destroyed, and none had bothered to repair it. Those shaping were no longer quite as impressive now that he had gained his broader, deeper understanding of the elements.

Tan realized why the thoughts troubled him as they did. The kingdoms and Ethea were a place of his childhood, but they were not home now. The stone ring in his pocket, the marker of his position as Athan, weighed heavily. He rarely wore it, though did keep it with him, simply because it was a way for Roine to summon were he to have the need. The title was no longer necessary; Tan had a greater title, and one he was equally uncertain he wanted.

While hovering, he tried reaching through the element bonds to a few of the shapers, but there was no response. That was not unusual, only unfortunate, especially given what they faced.

Asgar flew next to him, along with Wasina and one of the hatchlings. When he'd left Vatten and the three remaining disciples, he'd called them to him, needing their sensitive connection to the fire bond to help him determine if anything had changed. He'd called to the hounds and detected a pack roaming outside the city. The nymid should be strong here as well, and he could reach golud when he needed. Each elemental would be able to help him know what risks they faced.

Wait for me, he sent to the draasin and the hounds.

Landing in the courtyard of the palace, he hurried inside.

When a white-robed servant stopped him, his young face scanning Tan and his gaze seeming to linger on his sword, he almost smiled. When had he last been here? Long enough that he was no longer recognized as he once would have been.

"Can I help you?" the man asked. He had a high voice, one that warbled slightly. He clutched a stack of linens against his chest and motioned to other servants behind him.

"I had hoped to see Theondar and Zephra," he said. Had he said *Roine*, he doubted the man would know who he meant. Tan might be one of the few who still called him the name he'd chosen while hiding.

"The king is very busy, even for the shapers. You should request a visit through the Master Scholar."

Tan nodded. "I should, but I was thinking I might visit with my mother."

The man blinked. "Your mother… Oh." He clasped a hand to his mouth and his gaze went back to Tan's sword before sliding up to his face. "That would make you… Please forgive me, Athan. You will find them in their quarters. They had a long night following the celebration."

"Celebration?"

The man's head bobbed in a nod. "Of course. Last evening was the Maureen Festival. As you know, most are up far too long."

"Of course," Tan said.

Had he been gone so long that he no longer remembered festivals? The Maureen in particular was a special day of celebration, a day to honor the Great Mother, to celebrate the harvest and prepare for the winter.

As he realized that, he wondered—had Marin timed the attack in the north to the festival intentionally? There was nothing particularly powerful about the festival. Tan detected nothing different from the elementals, but she could have used the celebration to mask her movements. It was a typical time of merriment, one that would distract people… and might prevent them from realizing that anything had changed.

"Would you do me a favor, master…"

"Norman, Athan."

Tan nodded politely. "Master Norman, would you be able to

summon Shapers Ciara, Ferran, and Wallyn?" He tried thinking of who else he could ask, but the three were connected to the elementals. With his mother, they would have every element covered.

"Certainly, Athan. Is there any particular message I should send?"

Tan debated how much information to send in a message. "Tell them the convergence is at risk."

Norman hurried off, leaving Tan standing by himself in the doorway of the palace.

He sighed and started up the stairs to the quarters Roine and his mother shared, trying to think when he'd last been here. Had it been their wedding? It couldn't have been that long ago, could it?

But it must have been. When he'd gone to Norilan, he'd summoned them and they had come. There hadn't been the time needed to come to Ethea and chase after the shapers. They had recognized the danger and most had come willingly. He had not expected anything else.

At the top of the stairs, he paused.

The palace was so much *more* than what he had in Par. There was extravagance here, and he could imagine Althem spending to build it up, to make it into this place of opulence. It was quite different than the estate he called home in Par. That was much fancier than any home he'd ever possessed, but it didn't have the same air to it that the palace possessed.

As he stood there, Tan pressed through his summoning coin, giving Roine a warning that he was here.

Then he waited.

He didn't have to wait long.

A door opened and Roine stood with a jacket unbuttoned, his silver hair grown long and his face with the first hint of a beard. Perhaps Honl modeled himself after Roine. He was in the process of strapping his warrior sword around his waist when he saw Tan. His mouth twitched, almost starting to smile, before fading into a frown.

"Tannen. It is good to see you, but you would not be here if all was well."

"I'm sorry to come at you like this."

"You are Athan; you are welcome in the palace anytime."

Tan resisted the urge to pull the ring from his pocket and return it. "I am not such a good Athan."

"As you've reminded me, I was not either."

Tan smiled. "You didn't have another nation to rule."

"I thought you didn't rule in Par." He finished buckling on his sword and adjusted his jacket, buttoning it closed. As he did, something about him changed, and Tan saw what others must see when looking at him—King Theondar.

"I try not to rule, but they keep demanding Maelen assist."

"Much like the elementals."

Tan nodded. "That's why I'm here today."

"Not to help me with my headache? I think a shaping of water might cure me of the wine I drank at last night's celebration."

"I'm sorry I missed it."

Roine grunted. "Don't be. The Maureen Fest is certainly fun, but the next day is not."

Tan used a quick shaping of water touched with spirit and settled it over Roine. It was a subtle shaping, one where he called upon the elementals to guide him. Roine jerked, blinking softly, and pulled in a sharp breath.

"That… was not necessary. You don't need to shape away my foolishness."

"I need you thinking clearly. I need"—he looked past Roine and toward the bedroom—"my mother as well. Where is she?"

"She is not suffering nearly as much as this old fool."

Tan turned and saw his mother striding up the stairs. She wore a simple gown of white, but somehow made it more formal than it should be. Her black hair, streaked with gray, was pulled back in an elegant bun, much less severe than she'd once worn it. Her eyes flashed a brief annoyance as she looked at Roine—an expression Tan had known well while growing up—before softening as she looked over at him.

"Tannen. Why have you come?"

Tan laughed and hugged his mother. "It's good to see you as well."

She waved him off. "You know I enjoy your visits, but you're not here to see us. If you were, you would have brought my granddaughter. Since you came alone, there is something amiss. What is it?"

"Can we talk more privately?"

Zephra looked over at Roine. "What is it you don't want others to hear?"

"Not others. Only those who won't be able to understand what I need to share with you. Can we go to the throne room? I've summoned Ciara, Ferran, and Wallyn as well."

His mother's eyes widened and he suspected she made the connection to the elements. She tipped her head to the side, likely listening to her bonded wind elemental, Aric. "Oh," she whispered.

"What is it?" Roine asked.

"Tannen is right. Not here."

Roine frowned at both of them as they made their way down the hall and to a private stair leading into the throne room. Two shapers stood guard at the bottom of the stair. Tan didn't recognize either, but from the shapings they maintained, could tell they had some talent. One seemed an earth shaper. The other had bright red hair much like Ciara, and he suspected the man shaped fire.

They stepped aside for Roine and Zephra, glancing at Tan. The fire shaper blinked and grinned as Tan passed. He heard an excited whispering after they went by.

"That was the *Athan*."

"Athan? He doesn't come to Ethea," said a deeper voice.

"I'd recognize him anywhere. I remember seeing him when he visited Master Ferran one time. I bet he's speaking to the elementals now…"

Their voices faded away as the door into the throne room closed behind them. Had it reached that point? Was *he* now the person other shapers looked up to?

"Now that we're here, what aren't you wanting to share?" Roine asked.

"I'd rather wait so I only have to explain it once."

Roine shot him an annoyed expression. "You *do* realize I'm your king, right?"

"Not king regent anymore?" Tan asked, grinning.

Roine waved his hand. "You're as stubborn as her, you know that?"

Tan glanced at his mother. "When you put it that way, I'm not sure it's a compliment."

Roine threw up his hands. "Not a compliment? I've never met two people so persistent! She keeps pushing on me to build the university, to keep teaching even though I have other pressures on my time. I think I'm the most accessible king the kingdoms has ever seen. And you're about the same, always pushing me to serve the elementals first."

"Have we steered you wrong?" Zephra asked. There was a hint of an accusation in her voice, and it mixed with amusement. Tan might not feel Ethea was home anymore, but he'd known his mother long enough to recognize the way she needled Roine. It was the same as she'd often done to his father.

Roine stared at her and shook his head. "You're going to kill me is what you're doing."

"And then I will rule. I think the kingdoms will win either way," Zephra said.

Tan coughed to hide his laughter.

"You don't want that. Then you'd have to teach the students."

"I do my share," his mother said.

"You do. And you spend almost as much time in Par with the students there."

"Because I've asked it of her," Tan said.

His mother turned her hard-eyed stare on him. "Asked? I think you gave me little choice, don't you, Tannen? I would say coerced might be a better way of putting it."

This time, Roine laughed. "At least someone can get you to do what they want. I sure can't."

Tan sensed the warmth between them with the banter. His

mother had a vibrancy to her, as did Roine, that neither had when they'd been apart. "You're teaching, then?" he asked Roine.

His friend nodded. "They need warriors to instruct. There are at least two who will be warriors. Possibly another three more. All these years without warrior shapers, and now they've begun to return."

"We have several in Par as well," Tan noted.

"They should study together," Roine said. "You could send them here, to the university—"

"And we could send the students from the university to Par," Tan reminded him.

"You are *both* foolish," his mother interrupted. "But both right. We need them to work together, much like the Order once worked together."

"Like when they hid in Norilan and became corrupted by the darkness?" Roine asked.

"They were not all corrupted, and those who remain would have much to teach. They had shapings I suspect even Tan would be able to learn from."

He nodded. There *had* been shapings that he could have learned from them. They had been the most skilled shapers he had ever met, and he had understood how those ancient shapers had essentially created what appeared to be life out of nothing, but they had been misguided as well. All that knowledge hadn't made them any better connected to the elementals.

In that, his mother might be right. Maybe he should be getting the remnants of the Order to teach the students. They could do so under the guidance of the shapers of the kingdoms and those of Par, and they might learn much more than they would otherwise. Both nations needed shapers that were more skilled.

"That's a great idea, Mother. When I get through this, I will see what I can do."

"What is *this*?" Roine asked.

Ciara entered the throne room, tight red leathers clinging to her body. Her bright hair was brushed neatly, and she wore two blue ribbons in it. She looked at Tan, a wide smile on her face. "You didn't need to summon. The draasin told me you were here."

"I tried reaching you through the fire bond, but you ignored me," Tan said.

"We can't all sit around waiting on the great Maelen to summon us," she said. "Some of us have other responsibilities, and those we don't ignore."

Tan shook his head and didn't get a chance to retort. Ferran and Wallyn entered then, both fixing their gaze on him.

"Even in my throne room I'm ignored," Roine said.

"You're not ignored," Zephra chided softly. "They just haven't seen Tan in a while. Maybe if he'd come around Ethea a little more often, his visits wouldn't be so eventful."

"It does seem that something terrible happens each time he visits," Roine said.

"Would you both stop?" he said.

Ciara laughed. "They aren't wrong. What terrible thing prompted your visit this time? What was this about the convergence?"

"Convergence?" All amusement faded from Roine with the question. "What is this about the convergence?"

Tan took a deep breath. Everyone other than Roine had a

connection to the elementals, so they would know more about what he was about to share, but it was Roine who might understand it best. He had been the one to explain the places of convergence to Tan in the first place.

"Convergences are places where the elementals are drawn, where there is great power, and a connection to spirit."

"We know this, Tan," Roine reminded him.

He nodded. "And we know that Ethea sits over a place of convergence. That's why Althem chose to attack here."

"Why does this matter now?" Zephra asked.

"Because this convergence grants strength to the temple. The temple is a binding, a way of securing the darkness that Marin thinks to release. And now she attempts to move it."

"Move it? She wouldn't be able to move it," Ciara said.

"Because this wasn't always the place of convergence. The land was changed over time by those ancient shapers. They moved things, drawing the elementals in ways they had not been drawn before, essentially creating the convergence. And now if she moves it, everything that powers the temple, that holds the binding in place, will fail."

His mother closed her eyes and listened to the wind. Tan could almost hear her within the wind bond and chose not to listen too closely. When she opened her eyes again, she shook her head. "Ara tells me nothing has changed."

"I detect nothing either," Ciara said.

Ferran and Wallyn both nodded agreement.

"That's good, because I didn't either, but that doesn't mean she won't try again. I can stop her, but I don't know that I can stop every attempt she makes. She has attacked in Xsa—"

"Why Xsa?" Zephra asked.

"Because I suspect it or Par is also a place a convergence."

"And Norilan?" Roine asked.

"I don't know. When we were there, the elementals had been forced in a different way. I hadn't expected it to be one, but it would explain why there were so many and why they would have the strength they did to create that barrier."

"What do you intend to do, then?" Zephra asked.

"I need you to pay attention to the elementals. If anything changes here, I need to know. I will check in Xsa and in Norilan."

"You should have help," his mother said. She turned to Roine. "You should go with him."

"You want to get rid of me?" he asked. "You really *do* want to rule, don't you?"

"Only because I think I'll do a better job of it." When he smiled, she touched his arm gently. "You know all about the convergences. You were the one Althem sent searching in the first place. And you are a warrior. You should go and see what the two of you can learn."

"I could go to Xsa with him. That's close enough for me to shape my way there and back, but I don't know if Tannen wants an old warrior coming with him."

"Old warrior? I'd be happy to have my friend with me on another journey," Tan said.

"But you have to realize that this time, I lead."

Roine laughed. "I think you've always led, Tannen. You just didn't recognize it until now."

8

A PLACE OF CONVERGENCE

A shaping carried Tan and Roine to the Xsa Isles on a flurry of wind. Tan refrained from adding spirit to the shaping, needing to travel the same way that Roine would be able to travel, and felt the sensation of wind gusting, throwing him around. Traveling in this way was violent compared to the gentle shaping when spirit was added.

Asgar and Wasina remained circling in the air. Tan could feel Wasina trailing through the currents, enjoying the way they pressed against her wings and scales. Asgar had a tension about him. He still feared the darkness, in spite of facing it more than once, and in spite of the fact that Tan had shifted the bonds to bring spirit into them so that they could no longer be affected.

Watch over us, he asked the draasin.

First we're horses and now we're watchdogs? Asgar asked.

Even in that, Tan sensed his unease.

You are my friend, and I will protect you as you protect me, he reminded the draasin.

There was a moment of silence before Asgar answered. *We will watch you, Maelen.*

Tan and Roine reached the island where Marin had attacked him. Life had returned, but there was something different about it. Tan focused on the bindings and noted they still held, but there was still something there that was different. Not quite wrong… but off.

"What is it?" Roine asked.

"Do you sense anything amiss here?"

Roine used wind to carry him across the land, keeping just above the surface, his shaping holding him barely over the ground, high enough that he would not touch it until he had determined that it was safe.

"I sense your shaping. I can't tell exactly what the intent of the shaping is, only that it is powerful." He glanced over at Tan. "That's pretty common with you these days. Most of the time, I can tell *what* you're shaping, but I have a hard time understanding *how* you do it." He smiled. "I imagine it was once that way for you."

"We've been through a lot, haven't we?" Tan asked.

"More than I ever would have believed when I first came to your village. All I wanted then was to stop Incendin. I didn't realize there was another entire world waiting for us to conquer."

Tan laughed. "I wish it were so simple."

"Will this be the end?" Roine asked. "When we stop this darkness, will there finally be peace, or will there be another threat beyond the borders of what we've already discovered?"

"I can't answer that," Tan said. "All I know is that this threat is greater than any we've faced, and everything that we've done has seemed to lead up to it, almost as if we've been guided to it."

"You think the Great Mother has trained you to be able to take on this darkness?"

"Maybe not only me," Tan said.

Roine chuckled. "I have never been particularly religious, but seeing the way you've developed, you might be right. Had we faced this after defeating Althem, we would not have been prepared. Had you faced it before stopping the Utu Tonah, we would not have been prepared. Maybe the Great Mother *had* intended you to do this."

Tan lowered himself to the ground with a sigh. He hoped that was the case. If not, why would she torment him in this way? Why not let him have peace? He'd done enough for the elementals, hadn't he?

"I hope that's what she intended," he said. "Otherwise, all of this will have been nothing more than a way of hurting me."

Roine glanced over and chuckled. "I don't detect anything here that seems like it was a place of convergence," he said.

Tan didn't either, but when he was in Ethea, the only way he really knew there was a place of convergence was because of all the elementals bound there. There wasn't anything else about it that he detected easily. It was much the same with the very first place of convergence that he'd known, the one in the mountains of Galen where he'd discovered the artifact. When he'd been there, all he'd known was that the elementals were strong in it.

If they *were* strong, wouldn't there be some connection he

could detect? Wouldn't there be something in the bonds that he could pick up on?

Tan hadn't tried before, but something had to summon the elementals to these places. If it wasn't something within the bonds, then what would it be?

Focusing on the different bonds, he reached through them. After all the time that he'd spent working with the bonds, accessing them was much easier now than it had been when he first discovered the connection. Fire remained the easiest, but wind came naturally to him as well. Earth and water came more slowly, but he was still able to reach through them, to draw from those connections and pull strength from them.

He didn't take energy from them. That wasn't the reason for his connection. His was about touching the power and focusing to see if there might be something more to it, especially in a place where he suspected there was a connection to something deeper.

As he did, he noted the bonds surging against him.

Tan reached into them.

Power flowed there, running over him like a river. Wrapped as he was within the connection of each of the bonds, he felt the power more strongly than he had before. He felt drawn down, as if pulled into the ground.

Spirit swirled around him, though not from the spirit bond. It came from the connection he shared with each of the individual element bonds. Now that he'd shifted them toward spirit, in effect combining them with the spirit bond, he no longer really needed to reach into the spirit bond itself. It came to him easily, and with the augmentation of the different elements swirling together to grant even a greater connection to spirit.

The power of the Mother filled him, overwhelming him.

Tan could almost feel it like a vortex threatening to draw him downward.

If he remained connected to it, he would be overwhelmed. As he stayed here, he felt staggered by the power of the Mother, filled with a certainty that he had been given gifts meant to help the elementals and the world, if only he could use them.

Tan stretched the connection toward Par, reaching for the binding. He felt the connection of the binding and the way it drew from this place, and knew that he'd been right. This was a place of convergence, a place with much power.

How had the ancient shapers *moved* a place like this?

He had thought he understood what they were capable of doing, but maybe he'd been wrong. If they were able to shift the lines of power, the deep connections within the world, then they were more powerful than he'd known.

They would have to have been, in order to understand how to connect the places of convergence to the bindings. Tan barely understood, though the longer he remained connected as he was, the more he *thought* he could understand. The longer he remained here, the more he thought he might be able to counter some of what Marin had done. Maybe he wouldn't even need to use the bindings to restore the land if he could tap into this power.

And connected to it as he was, he could see the connections to the elementals. Some were old—like that of the draasin and to the udilm crashing into the shores of the island—though some were newer connections, those that had been created at a time when the Utu Tonah had forced crossings, creating elementals that never had existed previously.

Within the connection, he detected Honl, another elemental that had never existed, though his connection to this was different, less substantial than some of the others, as if he touched the bonds in a different way. The longer he focused on Honl, the more he thought he could understand him, and perhaps understand what changes had happened to him. Threads of wind and spirit wove together, bridged in a way they had not been prior to his healing.

Honl wasn't the only elemental like that. Drawing on this power, Tan felt a stronger—and closer—presence to him.

Light.

She was of fire and spirit, but wrapped as he was in the bonds, tied to this place as he was, he noted wind and a hint of earth—something that made sense given what he'd seen from her—and even water. In some ways, Light was a strange mixing of each of the elements, some sort of warrior elemental.

He could see all the nearby elementals, could even see how those he detected could be modified, made into something greater, if he were willing to mix the power he drew from here. Not only the elementals could be changed, but many things about this place, many different powers, even the land itself…

Tan caught himself.

That was how the ancients had moved the place of convergence.

They would have tapped into it somehow, and they would have used that power to create.

It would have been dangerous, and it would have risked unsettling other things the Mother had created. Had they known and risked it anyway? Or had they simply touched the source of power and thought that they knew better than the Mother?

Only, why have places like this? Why allow for shapers with power to be able to reach into such a source of power if not for them to use it? He might be the only shaper *now* to be able to touch all the bonds, but he was hardly the only shaper able to reach them. Within Incendin, there were two able to touch the fire bond. It wouldn't surprise him to learn there might be other shapers who were able to reach the other bonds. At least in Incendin, those connections came from shapers with an appreciation of the power of the bonds and an interest in preserving them, of keeping the element bonds protected.

Power surged through him and he held onto it, filled by it.

There was temptation, much like there had been temptation when he'd used the artifact. Then, he'd had Asboel to help guide him. When he'd connected to all the different shapers to defeat the Utu Tonah, he'd possessed a different sort of power, and Asboel had guided him again, that time through the memory of Asboel in the fire bond, warning him away from what he'd been tempted to do. There was no such guidance this time.

It had to come from him.

Tan thought of all the things he could do were he only to risk it… but that was the problem. Doing so *would* be a risk, and he would place the connections he'd made and the people he cared about in danger, all because he thought he knew better.

The Mother had given him access to her power, but not for this purpose. He was meant to protect, to heal, but not to change what she'd created. He'd done enough of that accidentally. He would not make the same mistake again.

Slowly, Tan released his connection, letting it slip from his grasp.

As it did, he shivered with a longing. Were he to have

remained connected, he wondered if he would have been able to withstand the temptation that he'd felt while holding it. Perhaps that was why the ancients had protected the artifact—they had seen how easily it was to be drawn toward that power, to feel compelled to use it, and maybe wanted to prevent others from abusing it.

"What is it?" Roine asked. "You look like you've just seen a friend die."

Tan took a deep breath and looked around. Even though he was no longer connected to the bonds, he still felt the pull, almost as if the act of reaching it had connected him to the place of convergence. He had to force his focus away or risk getting drawn back to it.

"This is a place of convergence."

"How do you know?"

"I know."

Roine studied him. "Is that what you saw? Is that why your face is ashen?"

Tan touched his cheek before scrubbing his hand through his hair, trying to clear the memory of power. Knowing it was there and knowing that he could reach it made that difficult. He didn't *want* the temptation, much like he hadn't wanted the power.

Only... with that kind of power, he wondered if he could trap the darkness. He had used bindings before, but would he be able to trap it completely by reaching the depths of the power he could detect here, or would that be more than even he could manage?

"I saw," he said, shaking his head, "I saw the power of the convergence. The Mother is here." Not only that, but he detected the way this was connected to the bindings. The ancients *had* tried to use the power of the convergence to trap the darkness, and it hadn't worked.

Why hadn't it worked?

Was it only because they had failed to fully secure the third binding? Knowing that he could reach into the convergence, and that there was more power there than he could ever imagine, he wondered if he might be able to use that and finally hold that binding. If he could, and if the flows of power could connect between the different bindings, maybe he *would* be able to accomplish what those ancient shapers had once attempted. He could complete their work.

"Did she do anything to… I don't know, *change* it?"

Tan shook his head. "The power wasn't tainted. With as much power as I can feel here, I don't know if it's even possible for it to *be* tainted." He looked around, scanning the rocks and trees, feeling the wind across his face, and listening to the sound of the waves crashing along the rocks. "There's so much power here, Roine. The Mother shouldn't be able to be corrupted by the darkness."

"Maybe that's not what they're after. They don't want to corrupt the Great Mother, only what she created. If they can destroy those things, then they can destroy her power. You've seen it, Tan. You've seen what happens when the elementals are drawn away from the land, even what happened when we'd made the mistake to create the barrier. That creates a separation that is not meant to exist, and it's one that damages creation."

Striding across the ground, his boots crunching along the soil, Tan wondered if perhaps Roine were right. Would corrupting the Mother's creation disrupt her as well?

If that were the case, and if for some reason he *couldn't* suppress the darkness once more, how would he ever stop it?

Was that even enough?

Stopping the darkness, suppressing it, was what he *thought* he needed to do, but that only delayed the danger. If he was right, and if the ancient shapers had faced it using the artifact, then suppressing the darkness only delayed another attack. Would there be another like him to face it? He could see to it that shapers were trained, leave records like were found in the archives, even leave walls decorated with runes, a way for shapers who came after him to understand the risk and perhaps carry forward the knowledge about how to defeat it, but was there another way?

Would he be able to contain the darkness forever?

If he could, he would truly be able to bring lasting peace. There might be wars between man and shaper, but they wouldn't have to fear a power greater than any of them, and they wouldn't have to fear the corrupting effects of Voidan on the elementals. Maybe they could maintain their connection to the elementals as well.

"What now?" Roine asked. "You wanted to prove that this was a place of convergence and you seem convinced that it is."

"It is."

"Then what now?"

He looked toward the north.

What they had to do next involved understanding whether Norilan possessed a similar place of convergence, but he needed to know more than that. He needed to know what those Order of Warrior knew.

"You said you wanted warriors to teach the students at the university," Tan said.

"Norilan? I can't reach Norilan without help… No." His gaze drifted toward the sky, where the draasin circled. "I don't want to ride them again."

Tell him I don't want him to ride either. Maybe I can carry him in my talons.

Tan smiled at Asgar, the image of Roine clutched in the draasin talons like some prize as they flew across the sea making him almost laugh.

"What?" Roine asked.

Tan shrugged. "The draasin suggested another way to get you there, though I doubt you'll like it any better."

Roine sighed and shook his head. "That damn mother of yours," he muttered under his breath. "I think she knew this would happen."

Tan laughed. Knowing his mother, it was possible that she had.

"Come on. Your steed awaits."

Asgar snorted flames, and this time, Tan did laugh.

9

RETURN TO NORILAN

Norilan maintained an edge of cold, though the shaping that had prevented others from reaching it no longer surrounded the island. The chill came from the north, a deeper cold than Tan felt in Par, and one that spoke of snow and ice. Riding atop Wasina protected him and he leaned into her spikes, enjoying the comfort of her gliding way of flying. Each of her breaths steamed in the air, creating something of a fog as they flew.

Asgar flew with the same grace as he always did, though his was a powerful beating of his wings compared to the steadying gliding that Wasina managed. Tan would never tell his friend, but in that way, he preferred riding with her more than he did with Asgar. In some ways, he preferred it even to riding with Asboel, though there had been something about the brute power that his old bonded had possessed, a strength that even Asgar couldn't replicate.

Light licked his neck, and Tan smiled. She traveled with them, curled around him as she often did, now so comfortable on him that he often forgot that she was there, if not for the constant licking. It had annoyed him at first, but now he only viewed it as something particular to her and nothing more. He suspected there was more to it, another reason that she continued licking him, but he hadn't been able to determine that yet. Eventually she would share.

You could know if you used our connection, she told him.

You think I should delve into your mind to know why you lick me? You mean, there's a reason other than to annoy me?

She squeezed him with her tail and Tan laughed, his breath pluming out in the cold air. As it did, she licked him again, forcing another laugh out of him.

They soared over the flat landscape of Norilan. Beneath him, he could make out the hard rock and detected where the elementals had once been pulled into the bonds, trapped within rock and dirt and used to create. Many of the elementals were still here, though they had retreated. With his return, they perked up, in some ways noticing that he had returned. At least they didn't try to hide from him as they once would have.

"How many times have you been back since…"

"Since we trapped the darkness?" Tan asked.

Roine nodded, careful to clutch Asgar's spikes in a way that wouldn't damage his hands. He was able to shape fire, and so would be protected in some respects, but Tan sensed the shaping of wind and water that he used as well, a barrier of elements to protect his skin.

"Only a few," Tan said. "I've come back to ensure that the barrier holds, and I've returned to check on the people."

"The people?" Roine asked.

Tan shrugged. "Fine. The elementals. Does it matter that I come back to check on them?"

Roine laughed, lines forming in the corners of his eyes as he did. There was joy in him since leaving Ethea, something about venturing away from the city, away from the kingdoms, as if he'd been freed. Tan thought he understood. In many ways, he felt much the same about leaving Par. He was needed in Par, but getting out and getting away was freeing. He didn't have to worry about what the council might do, and he didn't have to worry about how his actions might be perceived. He could act as he thought fit.

That is what kings do, Light said, licking his face.

What do you know about kings?

Your lands have known many. The memory of them is buried in the stones and in the air. You are different than most.

Because I am no king.

She licked him again. *Perhaps not. You are Maelen. That is much different.*

Tan shook his head.

"Only that I'm not surprised that you would return for the elementals," Roine said, oblivious to the thoughts that had gone through Tan's mind. Not only to his thoughts, but to the conversation that he shared with Light.

There were times when he was thankful that no others *could* know about those conversations. If they could, what would they think of some of the things he shared with the elementals? They were more than bonded; the elementals were some of his closest friends. Would they find it strange that he felt that way, often about creatures they wouldn't even be able to see?

"The elementals suffered the most in Norilan."

Roine sighed. "What I wouldn't give to know what you heard when you spoke to them. What's it like knowing these powers?"

"You haven't asked my mother?"

"Zephra doesn't speak about what she knows with ara. I know it makes her powerful, but then your mother was powerful even before she ever made a connection to the wind. She has always been Zephra, a force of nature."

"She's been something," Tan said, laughing.

As they flew toward the valley, where the city would be found far below, Roine glanced over at him again. "Do they still teach you?" he asked.

"The elementals?" Tan asked.

Roine nodded. "You grew more powerful when you began connecting to them. I think of Ferran, and of Wallyn. They have grown since learning to speak to the elementals. It's made them powerful in ways most shapers would never know."

Tan understood where Roine was going with the line of questioning. He was a warrior shaper, and that gave him incredible strength, but he wasn't able to reach the elementals. Roine would never know what it was like to be able to communicate in the way those who *could* reach them. He would never be able to understand why Tan felt so convinced that he connected to the Mother when he spoke to and connected with the elementals. Roine would never have that.

But Tan could give him a hint of it, couldn't he?

Shaping spirit, he sent it to Roine, layering it through him. As he did, he forged a brief connection to Asgar, using the connection of spirit to the fire bond.

Roine gasped.

"I *hear* something."

"You hear the draasin."

Roine's eyes widened. "How? How is it possible for you to do this?"

"I hadn't considered it before, but you're right. You *should* know what it's like to speak to the elementals. You've been involved in seeing them to safety and protected as much as anyone. What's he saying to you?"

Roine laughed. "He's telling me he'd rather eat you than talk to you!"

I wouldn't taste that good, he told Asgar.

No, but then you wouldn't be able to allow him to bother me again.

A man should be able to speak to his horse, don't you think?

Asgar twisted his neck and shot a streamer of flame that parted around him. Tan laughed.

I think you enjoy being the horse more than you let on.

I think you might taste better than you'll admit.

"Is that how you always talk to him?" Roine asked. They circled now, staying above the valley as it dropped off. Tan detected the shapers deep in the valley. None had left and returned to the city in the main part of Norilan. No one had wanted to leave the valley, and the city had changed enough after freeing the elementals that it hadn't been the same.

"With him? Since I named him, he's always been a little too much of a pain," Tan said.

"You named him?"

"It was the only way to save him. When kaas attacked, I had to save him."

Asgar flicked his tail, a movement Tan had learned meant pleasure.

"Kaas," Roine repeated. "I sometimes forget just how much you've done in service of the elementals in the time that I've known you. Probably more than I remember." He tipped his head and Tan could hear the faint edge of a conversation between Roine and Asgar, though he didn't reach toward it to eavesdrop. He would let them have the privacy. It didn't matter to Tan what they talked about, only that they talked, something that Roine had never experienced.

Would he be able to help others in the same way?

Not all would *want* to be able to speak to the elementals, but if they did, why couldn't he help them? It seemed like a reasonable gift to be able to offer, especially to someone like Roine, who had served the elementals. And with the right type of shaping, he could imagine being able to make the communication permanent, but that would put both the shaper and the elemental in danger, in effect forming a bond that hadn't forged naturally. Doing that felt too much like what the Utu Tonah had done. This… this was temporary, and he *knew* Roine, just as he knew Asgar, and both would benefit from the conversation.

You would never force a bond the way the Bonded One did, Light said.

No, but attaching someone to the draasin feels a bit too close for my comfort.

He would not see it that way.

Tan didn't think that Asgar would, which was why he was especially careful not to do it.

Light licked him again and he laughed. *Watch us from up here?* he sent to the draasin.

Both Wasina and Asgar sent agreement, and Tan looked at Roine. "Are you ready?"

"As I can be. Will I still be able to hear him from down there?"

"I don't know why you shouldn't. It's only a temporary connection, but you should be able to hear him from pretty much anywhere. I can hear the elementals from across the world if I really focus," he said.

Roine patted Asgar's side and shaped himself free.

See? A horse, Tan sent with a laugh.

Asgar shot another streamer of flame at him and Tan jumped from Wasina's back, shaping himself to hover next to Roine.

"I'll never get over how fire doesn't harm you."

"I don't know that it would harm you either. You just have to trust that it wouldn't."

"I'm not connected to the elementals in the same way as you. I don't think that I'd be quite as able to withstand the heat in the same way."

Tan wondered if that were true, or whether the fact that he was a fire shaper—and therefore connected to the fire bond, even though he might not fully understand that—would protect him. That was what he suspected, but he understood that Roine wouldn't want to test something that was little more than a theory.

They dropped on their shapings toward the ground below.

As they did, they passed through a cold barrier, and Tan knew the warriors realized they were there. He hadn't intended to hide the fact that they were coming, and waited, holding himself in the air until the members of the Order appeared.

Two men appeared quickly, both faces Tan recognized from previous visits.

"You are the Maelen," the nearest, a man by the name of Tobin, said. He had a wide face and thick shoulders, though with the loose-fitting robe he wore, Tan had a hard time telling whether it was muscle or flab beneath the robe.

"I am Maelen," Tan said.

"Why have you returned? Has Tenebeth been released?"

Tan shook his head. "Wouldn't you know if he had?"

Tobin glanced at the other man, an almost painfully thin man by the name of Jarra. Both had fought by his side when they faced the threat from Marin and her shapers. They had lost friends, but they had proven to be powerful shapers.

"Before, we might have."

"Before what?" Tan asked, before understanding what they meant. "Jorma betrayed you. She's the reason that the darkness spread as far as it did."

Tobin let out an annoyed sigh. "Perhaps. That is what you tell us, Maelen, and with your connection to the elementals, we have no choice but to believe you."

"I think you have any choice you want," Tan said, "but you don't have to rely on what I tell you to know that I speak the truth. There are those among you who know the elementals. They have bonded. Those bonds know that I shared the truth."

"Why have you come here?" Jarra asked. A subtle shaping built from him, one that evolved in layers, one after another, a stacking so subtle that Tan was almost not certain he felt what he thought he did.

Light leapt from his shoulders and landed on the other man.

He panicked, the shaping he had started fizzling out, and she started licking him. Together, the two of them began to tumble toward the valley floor.

Light?

Do not worry, Maelen. This one made a mistake.

So you will crush him?

In answer, the small lizard spread her legs, pulling the thin skin tight, and caught a current of air as she drifted toward the ground, soaring much the way that Wasina did when she caught currents of air.

What did he attempt?

He thought to immobilize you.

Tan looked up to see Tobin with his hand on his sword. He shook his head. "Don't be a fool. We haven't come here to harm you. Had I wanted to do that, do you think I would have come with just the two of us?"

Release him, he said to Light. *They need to know we're not here to attack them.*

Light did, and Jarra shaped himself up and next to Tobin.

Tobin glanced at the other man, a frown furrowing his brow. Something passed between them and Jarra shaped off, disappearing back to the city. "We saw what you were capable of the last time you were here, Maelen. I don't think you would need more than the two of you to destroy the remaining Order."

He wondered if that were true, and decided that he might be able to. From their perspective, he was much more powerful than them, and he was able to use not only the power of shaping and the elementals, but they would have to know that he tapped into something else, greater than them, especially with the way that he had withstood the darkness.

Roine pulled on a shaping, though his was blunt and

powerful compared to the subtle finesse that Jarra had attempted.

"Wait," Tan warned Roine.

He nodded but maintained his connection. Tan was thankful that he *had* brought his friend with him. "I'm searching for answers. Is—or *was*—this a place of convergence?"

Tobin frowned. "I don't know what you mean by this."

"A place where the elementals are drawn. Where you would be able to reach for the power of the Mother if you knew how."

Tobin's eyes widened. "How is it that you know of this?"

"Just know that I do. Is it?"

Tobin glanced at the floor of the valley before drawing his gaze back up to Tan. "What you ask about is sacred to the Order, a place where warriors go when they demonstrate their abilities with the elements. We do not know it as a place of convergence, but what you describe is the same."

Tan glanced at Roine before turning his attention back to Tobin. "Take us there."

10

A SHAPERS GARDEN

Tan was surprised to learn it was buried within a cave, and immediately began thinking of the convergence within the mountains of Galen. He suspected that had been an original place of convergence, one that had formed naturally, and would have been the main focus before the ancient warriors shifted it by changing the contour of the land. What did it mean that he would find another similar place here?

Did it mean that the one in Xsa should have been somewhere else as well? That hadn't been anywhere below ground. It had been out in the open, exposed, where anyone would have been able to reach. He just happened to be the one who *had* reached it.

They made their way through the tunnel, damp rock pressing all around him. From his connection to earth, he could tell it stretched deep into the earth, strange rock laden with elementals surrounding him. Tan reached toward the elementals, trying to detect whether there would be anything different to them, using them to help draw him to toward the convergence.

Roine remained silent as they went.

Tan reflected on his past journeys with Roine, thinking back to the very first time that they'd traveled together, when Roine had come to his village and when he'd discovered the lisincend —and the hounds. They had made their way through a tunnel somewhat like this, though perhaps one that was better appointed. In that tunnel, the ancient shapers had set lanterns that Roine had lit along the way, casting a soft light to guide them. This time, it was Tan who shaped and Light who guided them, her wide body glowing as she walked through the tunnel. This time, the mission was for Tan, and in some ways, Roine was the one who was dragged along with him.

"How much farther?" Roine asked.

Tobin nodded. "It is not much farther. We will progress beneath the rock and enter the Sacred Pool."

Roine glanced over at him. "Pool?"

"You will see," Tobin promised.

Would they find something like the connection to the Mother, a pool of spirit much like they'd found in the mountains? If they did, how was it possible for Jorma to have been tainted? Wouldn't the pool of spirit have washed away any taint?

A low stone archway loomed in front of them. Tan had to duck to enter and once he did, his eyes took a moment to adjust. Roine's must have adjust much more quickly; he gasped.

Power radiated from here.

It was a wide chamber, and one that looked nothing like the other side of the archway. There, it had been rugged rock, stone that had been left untouched other than as an access to this place. Within this chamber... he felt the power that had been shaped, the power created by shapers with more skill than any alive today.

A sea of trees spread around them, reminding him of what had once existed in the other place of convergence. Flowers bloomed on the trees, flowers that should not exist, but did, shaped into creation and somehow held in place, though not by forcing any elementals here, not the way that they had shaped the city into existence. Distantly, Tan could almost hear the sound of the sea, a steady lapping of waves along the shore, and smelled a mixture of salt and the fragrance of the flowers in the air.

"Did you create this?" Tan asked. "Was this members of the Order?"

Tobin laughed softly. "The Order can shape many things, Maelen, but this?" He shook his head. "We tried to replicate this. You saw our attempts above."

"The city?"

Tobin nodded. "We used the elementals there."

"There are no elementals trapped here," Tan noted. "This is simply shaped power."

Much like there had been in the place of convergence in the mountains, and even in the kingdoms, with Ethea having something resembling this in the courtyard of the palace, destroyed during the attacks on the city.

Light wiggled up to one of the trees and ran her tongue along the trunk.

It flashed, glowing brightly for a moment. Tan expected the tree to disappear, much like the buildings and everything in them had disappeared in the city when she had licked them, but this only surged with color before fading.

That wasn't quite right. Where her tongue had touched the bark, a single line of power remained, glowing softly.

What had she done to it?

Testing, Maelen. You can see.

With that, he had a surge of understanding that came from Light.

She focused it, only allowing him what he could understand, but a shaping came to him, one that was complex and layered, much like what he'd almost experienced when Jarra had attempted to attack. Tan could see the work that had gone into creating the tree, the steady, careful shaping that had been drawn from the ground, not destroying what the Mother had made, but changing it, making it into something else.

He looked up at the top of the chamber, thinking that he understood. All of this stone had been drawn into the shaping, taking earth, compressing it, and creating the life that he saw around him. This would have been a slow shaping, one that would have required weeks and months of steady work, and that for only *one* of the trees. There were hundreds here.

Tan felt awed by what these shapers had done.

The work was not something beyond him, not as he had believed, but the patience required to build it might be. He never took the time to simply sit and shape, to build upon the gifts given to him by the Mother and explore the limits of his power. That was what he detected from Light, the type of shaping that he sensed here.

Are they all like that?

This is the work of an earth shaper. There are others here, Maelen.

Only earth. Would there be wind shaping that could match something like this?

But he knew the answer even without asking. He could *feel* the pull of the breeze upon his cheeks, even without a source. Mixed within it were fragrances, those he had attributed to the trees or the flowers, but they weren't capable of emitting those fragrances without the aid of the wind. Focusing on the wind and letting it swirl around him, he detected a similar layering on it, much like there had been with the tree. The work was subtle, and required him to touch the wind bond to fully understand how it was mixed together, but it was there, and the answers came to him. It would likely be the same with the water he heard.

What of fire?

Tan didn't detect any shaping of fire here, but suspected there would be one somewhere in the chamber. He could wander here for days, letting the awareness of the shapings wash over him, trying to gain understanding, and even then he didn't know if he would ever really be able to appreciate all that had gone into creating this.

"This is a special place for the Order," Tobin said. "We come here with each new warrior, showing them what is possible with shaping, even if the techniques for creating it have been lost to time. We remember much shaping, but this... this is beyond us."

Tobin rested his hand on the trunk, tipping his head toward it until his ear settled upon the rough wood. He closed his eyes, letting them linger for a while, his breathing steady. Moments passed before he opened them and forced a smile. "Some of us continue to return, thinking that we will understand in time."

"What do you hope to understand?" Roine asked. He had

rested his hand on another trunk, and rubbed along it. He didn't seem quite as impressed, but he would if Tan described everything that had gone into the creation here. There was no way *not* to be impressed by the time and power that had been required to make these shapings.

Had it been the same in the other cavern?

Tan had thought the shapings crumbled after the elementals departed, after the convergence faded, but maybe that wasn't the case. Maybe his presence, and his shaping, had destroyed them. How many countless hours had gone into the shapings, only to fail because of what he had done?

"These are a monument to the shapers who came before us," Tobin said. "They were the first of the Order, men and women who had abilities beyond what we possess."

Tan shook his head. "They weren't beyond you," he told Tobin.

The warrior sniffed. "The remnants of the Order have survived in this land for countless years, Maelen. We have protected it from Tenebeth, but we have studied as well, searching for answers and understanding. Were we able to do what these shapers were capable of doing, we would be able to close the seal around Tenebeth for good. We would finally be able to destroy him."

"There is no destroying," Tan said. He knelt in front of the ground and started shaping earth. He started slowly, building a layer that he drew from the stone that formed the archway and diverted it toward his cupped hands. Tan kept them in place, using them something like a sculptor would as he drew the earth between them. It rose, climbing between them.

Not like that, Light said.

An image, or a memory, flowed into him from his bonded, and Tan realized he couldn't move the shaping quickly. He had been trying to force it, but that wasn't the key, not with what he needed to do. It was patience. He had seen that when she had first demonstrated the shaping to him, and though he didn't have time for much patience, he *did* have time to begin.

Strangely, he sensed the shaping had to create life the same way a seed would.

He settled the shaping again, preparing to start over.

This time, he started small and opened his hand, letting the beginning of the shaping grow. He felt what needed to be done and felt that he couldn't rush it. Life—even shaped life—couldn't be rushed.

"Tan?" Roine asked.

He ignored him, keeping his focus on the shaping of earth.

"Tannen?" Roine repeated.

A sprig of what seemed like a tree sprouted between his hands. It was small, barely more than a sapling, but he sensed the start of it.

Tan stepped back.

Tobin knelt next to him and reached tentatively toward the shaping. His mouth worked wordlessly as he fingered the slender sapling that resembled one of the oak trees Tan had known as a child in the mountains of Galen.

"How is it that you knew to do this, Maelen?"

Tan sighed. "As I said, the shaping is not beyond what you're able to do. I don't think it's beyond what *any* shaper is able to do. It takes time, and patience, and a certain type of layering of the element."

Tobin looked over at him. "We have tried what you call

layering, Maelen. That is how most great shapings occur. But even our greatest has never managed to so much as start something like this." He stood. "It is less than these, but I can see the technique would be similar."

"Less only because it would take weeks—or longer—to make anything like these," Tan said.

"You think you could recreate what the ancients made?"

Tan shrugged. "With time. The tree has to grow, Tobin. All the shaper is doing is helping it along."

Roine had moved away from the tree and now knelt much like Tan had. He cupped his hands together and Tan detected the shaping building from him. There was power and control to it, almost more than even what Tan possessed. Roine was an incredibly skilled shaper.

As he worked, a shoot sprang from the ground.

Roine's eyes widened and he held his hands in place, continuing to feed energy into the creation. As he did, Tan detected where the shaping drew from, noted that he pulled from the tunnel, much like Tan had. His shaping layered, moving more quickly than Tan's, but with somewhat less strength. As he worked, the sprout became a sapling, and then became a little taller. Branches started to spread, leaves sprouting on them.

Roine sighed and settled back on his heels. "I'd do more, but even that much has taxed me. I can see how this would take them weeks to shape."

Tan nodded toward one of the larger trees within the cavern. "Some might even have been longer," he said.

Tobin looked between the two of them before attempting it himself. Much like the others, his shaping came slowly, but of the three of them, Tobin had the most control. His shaping layered neatly, building with such skill that Tan could almost not see how he managed it, forcing him into the earth bond to watch. He marveled at Tobin's skill, impressed by how he was able to shape. How had they not managed to do this before? How had they needed Tan to demonstrate, when these shapers so clearly had the necessary level of skill?

They thought only to force it, not build it, Light said. *This shaping you use does not destroy, and it does not create. It only changes what has already been made. The Mother does not frown on something like that.*

Tobin's shaping continued, and he stopped when it had reached a similar height to Roine's. The trees each of them had created were different, but they were recognizable as trees. Tan's had been an oak, Roine's appeared to be the beginning of a maple, the wide leaves already forming, and Tobin started with a pine, sharp needles emerging from it. All they needed was the pine scent.

Tan considered how to create something like that and attempted a layering of the wind. He started with the idea, little more than that, and added shapings over and over. There came a flash of pine scent, but it faded.

He shook his head. "That will have to take more time," he said.

Tobin sighed. "I have tried my entire life to create what we see here, and you come in and demonstrate it in an afternoon. I can see how the shaping will form, and how I will need to keep adding to it, just as I can see that it is not beyond our weakest shaper." He studied the ground, shaking his head a moment. "Incredible. This is not what you came here for, so come with me."

The warrior started away from them, disappearing through the trees. Tan followed with Roine at his side, uncertain what they might find. Tobin made his way with a determined stride, hurrying between the trees, not giving Tan much of a chance to enjoy the work that had gone into shaping them. They were all impressive, each of the trees well crafted, shaped in such a way that he enjoyed the majesty and the sense of power radiating from them. They contained something of the shaper who had created them, as if they had given of themselves in the creation.

Light licked him.

The trees began to thin, and as they did, Tan noted the water he'd heard before. It crashed with a little more strength, waves that he understood were shaped, a miniature sea within the cavern.

"Does this connect to the ocean?" Roine asked.

"We thought the same thing," Tobin said. "Through the years, shapers have searched for where the water would come in, as the level rises and falls, much like the tide. None have managed to detect it, leaving us to believe that much like the trees, the sea here is shaped."

"Everything down here is shaped," Tan said. "Even the breeze. I can't tell where it all comes from, but it's all shaped."

Tobin nodded and continued on, leading them along the edge of the shore.

Roine hesitated, staring out at the water, watching the waves rolling up. "He's right, you know."

"About what?"

"That you come in here and demonstrate skills these warriors could not discover, even with all of their knowledge. I think of the warriors in the university I once knew, some who were among the most skilled in generations, and they would not have been able to come up with what you simply know. It's impressive, Tannen." He stared at the water and a hint of a smile played on his lips.

"What is it?"

Roine laughed. "I still hear him. He tells me not to give you a big head, but in the next breath, he tells me that with a bigger head you would make a tastier snack."

Tan laughed. *You would be afraid of how bitter I would be,* he sent to Asgar.

I am draasin. I fear nothing.

Tan withdrew, wishing that were true for him. Asboel *had* feared nothing, not even death, though now that Tan knew that fire cycled and would one day return, perhaps death didn't have the same finality to the draasin. Asgar *did* fear. He had experienced the pain of the darkness tainting him, and he feared it happening again. And Tan didn't blame him; it was something he feared as well.

Making their way after Tobin, they found him on the edge of a flow of orange fire. Lava poured out, though there was no real heat to it. Tan reached toward it but Tobin grabbed his arm, pulling him back.

"It might not seem hot, but men have lost themselves to fire here, Maelen."

Tan smiled. "I am not most men."

Tobin chuckled. "Perhaps not, but I still think you should not risk burning your hand off like a child near a flame. Come. You have not seen everything yet."

"What more is there?" Roine asked.

"The Sacred Pool," Tan reminded him. If his suspicion was

right, then the Sacred Pool would be spirit. He had only known liquid spirit in one place and had not detected it in any of the other places of convergence.

They reached a series of boulders, each one larger than the next, the boulders creating a circle. Tobin started climbing, grabbing invisible handholds as he made his way up the nearest rock. He stood atop it with his neck craned, looking down at something below.

"Do you think it's in there?" Roine asked.

"This is too much like the other place of convergence for it to be anything else," Tan said.

"That was what I was thinking as well."

They climbed the rock and when Tan reached the top, his breath caught.

Beneath him stretched a massive pool of silver liquid, much like what he'd seen in the other place of convergence and pretty much what he'd expected to find here. Within that pool of spirit, he felt its reflected power. Now that he was here, he could feel how the spirit in this pool matched that of the spirit bond and might even be the source of it.

Memories flooded into him, those from when Amia had climbed into the pool and he'd been unable to take his eyes off her. He had known the strength of her ability then and had realized how powerful she truly was.

Even that didn't keep his attention.

Within the pool, suspended over the middle, was a long cylinder.

An artifact.

"Great Mother," Roine breathed. "There is another."

11

THE SACRED POOL

"Y ou know of it?" Tobin asked.

Roine glanced at Tan, who answered. "We have seen something like it."

Tobin nodded. "When you weren't surprised by the shaping within the Cavern of the Sacred Pool, I suspected you had seen something similar. I would not have expected the ancients to have left another."

Tan sighed. "I hadn't either."

"We call it the Warrior's Pride," Tobin said. "None have ever managed to reach it. We have tried shaping ourselves to the device, but anything we use to shape ourselves over the surface fails. It is as if the shaping fizzles out."

"It would. The pool is spirit."

"Spirit?"

Tan nodded. "There are few places like this, Tobin. This is a pool of spirit. It would take someone able to shape spirit to reach the device."

"We have shapers able to reach spirit, and they have not managed to shape themselves to it."

Tan stared at the artifact. There was another. Knowing it existed worried him. If there was one here, and there had been one in the kingdoms, did that mean there had been a third?

What would happen if Marin were allowed to reach it?

Tan didn't have to think long to come up with what she might do with it. If she could corrupt it, she might be able to reach power she would not be able to otherwise. She was a shaper, so there was nothing that would stop her from using it, and if she did… he imagined that she would be even more destructive. The tainting that she'd managed so far would be nothing compared to what she would be able to accomplish with it.

"It's not a shaping," he said.

He sighed and started taking off his cloak and jacket, moving next to unbuckle his sword.

"Tan," Roine started, "it's safer here. Think of the last time. We won't be able to keep it as safe as it would be here."

Tan shook his head. "That's not true. If Marin somehow manages to discover this is here, she could reach it. She has a connection to spirit and she would be able to do the same as Amia when we found the last. I can't let that happen."

"And you think she would be able to get through the Order and reach it?"

Tan shot him a hard look. "She uses the darkness, Roine. She has disciples. And she's growing stronger. I don't know what she's capable of doing, but I do know that she can't be allowed to reach this."

As Tan stepped out of his pants, Tobin watched, a strange expression on the man's face. "Maelen?"

Tan walked to the edge of the rock and prepared to jump, steeling himself for what he might experience as soon as he touched the liquid. Would it freeze him in some way? He didn't think it would hurt him—he hadn't been hurt the last time that he'd gone into the spirit—but it was possible that this time would be different. The device looked different than the first artifact they'd recovered. It was possible that even the pool was different.

Tobin grabbed his arm. "Maelen, this is even worse than fools who attempted to touch the lava. Men who have stepped into this have died, consumed by it."

"I've told you before, I'm not most men," Tan said.

He stood, naked atop the rock, hesitating. The last time he'd come to a pool of spirit, he'd been able to wade in. This appeared different—deeper.

Then he jumped.

He was surprised when Light jumped as well, joining him in the pool of spirit.

When Tan struck, his breath was sucked out of him, and he sank.

Tan tried swimming, sweeping his arms, but it was like swimming through mud and he couldn't get anywhere. Instead, he continued to sink, deeper and deeper, pressure building around him.

Light?

Trust the Mother, Maelen.

He trusted, but he hadn't expected the pool to be so deep. The last time, they had waded into it and been able to wade back out. There would be no wading out this time, and he wondered if he should not have avoided jumping in until he knew how deep it was. Even were he to reach the surface, he didn't know if he would be able to swim out.

And Tan kept sinking.

The pressure became pain. His chest burned and he realized it came from an inability to breathe. Would the Mother have brought him here, allowed him to come so far, only to die here? That didn't seem right, and that didn't seem like anything that she would do, especially with Light somewhere near him, but without being able to swim, there was nothing he *could* do.

The pain became too much. Without wanting to, he sucked in a deep breath, filling his lungs with the liquid. It went into his throat, his nose, his belly, and pooled, growing thicker, seeming to push him down even more.

He felt a growing certainty of his own death.

The pain faded.

He seemed to stop sinking.

Tan floated.

As he did, he noted a surge of light, that of color and brightness. Through it, he saw Light, her form long and snakelike, different than she had been before. She swam through the liquid and reached him, brightness all around him.

Light?

You are safe, Maelen.

I can't move.

Only because you choose not to move. You are safe, Maelen.

How am I able to live?

You breathe in the Mother. She is life.

All elementals think they're life.

They are, because they are all a part of the Mother. She is life.

What now?

You wait.

For what?

For the Mother to tell you what must be done.

Tan floated. Time passed, an unknowable amount of time. He was disconnected from his bonds and could not hear any of the elementals other than Light. It was as if only the two of them existed.

That wasn't quite true.

There was a distant flickering in his mind, like a tapping. When he traced it, he found Amia and smiled, relieved that he had not lost that connection. From there, he detected another, a brightness that rivaled Light, and discovered it was Alanna.

How?

She was powerful here, as bright as an elemental.

As he focused on her, he discovered something else. She had aspects of the elementals. In some way, because of him and his bonds, she *was* an elemental.

How had he never seen it before?

How is it possible?

You serve the Mother, Maelen, and she knows what is needed. Trust.

He began to understand why the elementals thought that she should be a part of whatever he planned. She was more like them than he had realized. He thought of his daughter like a child, and she was, but she was something greater than a child.

Has there ever been anything like this before?

The Mother creates what is needed, Maelen.

And she had created Alanna.

What did that mean? How was she intended to help them?

Would those answers come to him while he was here?

Tan tried, reaching for her, trying to gain that awareness, but felt only the connection to his daughter. It filled him in a way that he hadn't been connected to her before, a sense of warmth and love that radiated from her. Tan radiated it back to her, hoping that he offered her nearly as much as she offered him, but thinking that what he was able to show her was a pale reflection.

He pulled Amia into the sense and felt her on a different level than he normally did. She was there, practically with him. He detected the bond between them, the one that she had forged so long ago, and fed this power into it, welcoming it. They would remain bonded, and because of that bond, they had created Alanna.

Together, they embraced their daughter.

Power surged from them, a bright light that together matched what Alanna was able to show them. She burned more brightly back to them, a flash of the sun, a brightness that could not be denied.

He stayed there, connected to his family.

From there, he began to feel other connections. They trailed away from him, not as strong as his connection to Amia. That wasn't quite right, he decided. They were strong, only different.

The bonds to the elementals.

There was Light, so close to him that he could touch her. There was the bond to Honl, and he pressed the power of the Mother through it, solidifying it. The nymid had bonded him as well, and he touched upon that. Kota, the hound watching his family while he was away, came to him as well.

Lastly, there was Asboel.

The bond remained, and Tan was surprised to note that awareness of his first bond filled him. Touching upon it, he felt the connection stretch to the fire bond, and into fire itself. As he did, awareness of Asboel—not only the draasin, but of all the lives he'd lived and would live—came to him.

How is this possible?

The Mother, Maelen.

It was Asboel, speaking to him, not only through the fire bond, but speaking to him as he once had spoken to him. In this place, Asboel had not died—would not die. He lived on through Tan, and would be born again to fire. Tan could see it, and knew that he would, as well as *when* he would. Asboel would always live.

My friend, he said to Asboel.

Within his mind, he felt a huff of fire. Warmth surged through him and he glowed.

He understood why he had never felt compelled to bond another fire elemental. He had not needed to. The bond had not disappeared. Death did not separate them, much as it wouldn't between him and the other elementals, much as it wouldn't between him and Amia, or Alanna. They were connected.

The only thing that can separate us is Voidan, Asboel said. *It can destroy, That is what it wants. You must serve the Mother. Serve creation.*

I do serve.

That is why she chose you, Maelen. She chose well.

Awareness of Asboel, mixed with the other bonds, left him practically glowing.

As he focused, he realized that he *was* glowing.

Tan smiled. He would keep this connection and use the power he felt around him, the power within the pool, to hold it steadfast within his mind. Asboel might not live, not in the same form, but he still lived.

Now, Maelen.

Light intruded upon his sense, and he knew what was expected of him. It was time for him to leave the pool of spirit.

He didn't know what he had accomplished, and maybe there was nothing other than to know his bonds, to understand that they were the reason he served the Mother, but he would take the message the Mother had given him, and he would continue to do what was needed.

Light swirled around him, creating something of a vortex within the liquid.

Tan slowly eased toward the surface and added a shaping, mixing each of the elements to it as he went. He lost track of how he shaped, knowing only that power flowed from him. In this place, each of the elements was the same. Each meant power, each meant life, much as Tan was meant to use them.

It carried him to the surface.

His head appeared above the top of the silver liquid.

Above him, he saw the artifact, the ancient device created to summon the Mother. He hadn't taken the time to try and under-stand why, but knew that he should possess it, and that he needed to prevent Marin from reaching it.

Tan reached for the device. When his hand gripped it, the pool of silver liquid, that of the Mother, began to recede.

He continued his shaping and managed to elevate above the surface. Once there, he hovered, the liquid dripping from him. Using wind and fire, he shaped himself to the rocks.

"Tan?"

He reached for his clothes and started dressing, pulling on his pants and then shirt before covering himself with the cloak. Lastly, he strapped on his sword.

"Tan?" Roine repeated.

He looked up at his friend. "What is it?"

"What is it? It's *you*."

Tan paused and looked down at his arms. They had taken on a translucent tint, and he glowed softly. Was he shaping and didn't know it?

Light climbed out of the pool then and shook herself. In the pool, she had been a long, snakelike lizard, but on the surface, she was back in her usual form. Tan had learned that Light could *change* her form, but had thought that she would have been more changed from jumping into the spirit pool.

Am I shaping?

Light licked him and he heard something that seemed like a laugh from within his mind.

Do you not know when you shape?

I don't think I'm shaping, but this...

You have always been touched by the Mother, Maelen. This is just an extension of that.

What does it mean?

It means it is time for us to depart.

For where?

Only you can answer that, Maelen.

"We should return," he said to Roine.

"I think that's probably a good idea. We can get you back to Ethea, and—"

"Not Ethea. I need to go to Par and get my daughter."

"Alanna? What do you intend for her?"

She was somehow key to what was happening. First the elementals showed him, and then the Mother. Whatever role she would play was important. He just had to be willing to let her.

"She will help us fight this darkness."

12

FILLED WITH THE MOTHER

Back in the city within the valley, Tobin continued staring at Tan as if he didn't know what to say. Tan held onto the artifact, and stuffed it into his pocket as he ran his finger along the runes carved into the sides. Power thrummed through it, and there was a distant part of him tempted to draw upon that power, but he knew not to let himself. It was the reason he knew he needed to protect it. Others might not have the same control and might let themselves get overwhelmed by the desire to pull on that power.

Tobin's gaze continued drifting toward Tan's pocket. Would he try to take it from him? Would he be so overwhelmed by desire to hold the artifact and call upon the power of the Mother that he would attempt to harm Tan?

Now that Tan had been in the pool and practically drowned in the connection, he wasn't certain whether Tobin *could* harm him.

He felt different, but found it difficult to describe why, even to himself. There was the sense of power, but it was not the same sort of power that he'd been able to draw before. This was a vague sense, almost a blurring of power, one where he wondered if perhaps his connection to the elements had changed again.

Had the Mother made it so that he no longer shaped?

"How do you feel?" Roine asked as they approached the city. People within it began to come out, making their way toward the doors or pausing in the street. They all looked in their direction.

"I feel the same as I always feel," he said. "Has more than my skin changed?"

He'd been changed by the elements before. When he had nearly pulled on fire and had practically become one of the lisincend, he had changed, so he knew the power of the elements. This didn't *feel* the same, but then, he hadn't been aware of what he had been doing, either. He had tried to help the Aeta and taken the power of fire into himself. Had he not done something similar with spirit now?

You haven't been changed that way, Maelen, Light shared with him.

Not in that way, but he *had* been changed. He didn't know what it would mean for him in the long term, but for now, it meant that his skin glowed and that he had some difference to his shaping, but not one that seemed like it would cause him any real problems.

They reached the city. It was more like a town, not nearly the size of Par or Ethea, but there were enough people, especially those that had come out of their homes, almost as if they had known where Tan had been.

Had they?

Did they recognize that he had been to the Sacred Pool and returned?

When he had emerged from it, it wasn't like when he'd left the place of convergence in the mountains. Then, there had been violence and an attack, as the lisincend had followed him when Fur still wanted him dead. Now that he was an ally, Tan couldn't imagine the anger the creature had when he'd chased him.

"Why are they all watching us?" Roine asked.

Tobin glanced back. "They know that the Shaper of Light went to the Sacred Pool. They might not know what it means, but they know that he went. I suspect they hope to learn that you have failed as so many have failed before you."

"Failed?" Roine asked. "You don't think they will hope that he succeeds?"

"We are a proud people. For Maelen to have come, and for an outsider to be the Shaper of Light, that was bad enough. And now for him to claim the prize, that will be worse. The pool is a special place for the Order."

"You can demonstrate to them how to shape the forest," Roine suggested.

Tobin cocked his head, a hint of a smile coming to his lips. "Yes. That might help."

"You could even claim to have discovered it," Roine suggested.

"I think most will know that I would not have. They will see the Shaper of Light return. Some might even visit the Sacred Pool and discover the prize is missing. All will have seen the way his skin burns with the light of the Mother. They will know who rediscovered the key to the forest, which is probably how it should be."

As they entered the village, Roine grabbed Tan's arm. "How much longer do you want to stay here?" he asked.

"There's another reason for us to be here," Tan reminded him. "It's not only about the convergence."

"After this," Roine said, motioning to Tan with a sweep from his head down to his toes, "you still want to see if the Order will help teach? Does that even matter anymore? Look at everything you can do, Tan! We need only *you* to teach."

Tan shook his head. If he were gone, he wanted to ensure that the shapers continued to have a way to protect their homes. He wanted to make sure that Par was safe, and that Ethea was safe. Tan didn't think he could even teach them what they needed to know. His connections had always been different enough that it made it more difficult for him to explain to another shaper *how* he did what he did. If nothing else, the failings of the past proved that even the best documentation would eventually fail.

"I think it's important for us to know what they know. If they'll be willing to work with our shapers, then we will have another way to ensure the safety of all of our people."

Roine sighed. "I suppose you're right. It would be much easier if you could just shape that knowledge from them."

Tan smiled. "I could, but where is the experience in that?"

They reached the inside of the city. People continued watching them, but none followed. For that, Tan was thankful. He didn't want to have to chase the people away, but then again, he could simply shape them away if it came to it.

They reached a long two-story building that had been formed by a powerful earth shaping. Tan could feel the power within the shaping and could detect the way they had moved the earth to pull it from the ground. In that way, it was something like the way the university had been built, though with the university, the elementals worked with it, holding the stone in place. There was more grace in this shaping than any that he'd seen in Ethea, even from the original university. As old as it was, it hadn't the same skill these shapers possessed.

"What is this?" Roine asked.

"This is the Seat of the Order," Tobin said. "It's not the same as what the seat once had been. Our records describe a place of great power, a massive tower like a monument to the Great Mother, but this is what we have today."

A tower? Could it be a coincidence that Par had a tower? He didn't think that the tower in Par was a Seat of the Order, but there was little doubt that they had been a part of its construction. Those shapers would *have* to have been much the same. The markings that spread throughout the city, those that held the Records of Par, had been much more refined than anything that could be made today, so he suspected that the ancients were involved.

Maybe there was another relic of that time to find. If he could discover the ancient seat of the order of warriors, they might be able to find answers—and they might be able to understand what they had once known.

The inside of the building was exquisitely decorated. Everything was shaped. There were sculptures that represented the elementals, all of a smooth white stone streaked with black lines. There were other carvings made of wood, though they seemed to have been hardened, as the shaping of earth had not only created them, but had modified them so that the wood looked more like rock. There were plants that grew where plants should not, blooms of color from flowers that he suspected were fed by shapings.

A massive fireplace ran along one wall, and the fire dancing within cast much warmth. Unlike in Par, where saa would be drawn to such a fire, there was nothing drawn here. There was a sense of the flame, but no elementals were pulled toward it.

The crafting of the mantle above the hearth looked equally impressive. He couldn't help but note the detail and the tight carving that worked figures into its surface.

Not figures, but runes.

Tan made his way to the hearth and stared at it. The runes exuded power, though he didn't know why. It wasn't that the elementals were trapped within them, but that the *elements* were, as if a shaping were held confined by the rune.

How was that possible?

Could he recreate it? Were he to have that ability, he could think of many ways that he could use it. The only other ways he'd seen something similar had been when he'd seen the way that the elementals had been bound, but this didn't seem to be anything that held the them.

"They are called rune traps," Tobin said, watching him as he studied them.

"Rune traps?"

He nodded. "They hold element power. When they're made a different way, they can hold the elementals. These do not."

"I see that, Tobin."

"Good. I don't want you coming in and thinking that you

need to destroy our rune traps. These only grant strength; they are not meant for much else other than decoration. Few even know how to make them anymore."

"Why?"

"They are not considered as useful as many of the other shapings. The traps can hold power, but using the elementals would be more effective and longer lasting."

"And more harmful," Tan said.

A troubled look crossed over his face. "We didn't know that we harmed the elementals by binding them with the runes. They were thought to be nothing more than power to be used."

"You had bonded shapers. You should have known better."

"Those who are bonded cannot explain what they use, Maelen. They are powerful, and others would like to be as powerful as them." He traced one of the runes and a surge of color sprang from it. Tobin seemed not to notice. "Who could blame them for wanting to become powerful enough to stop Tenebeth?"

That was what drove these people, he realized. They wanted power, but they wanted it for a specific reason. They each wanted to be able to do what they could to stop the darkness from spreading. In that way, they were much like Tan.

He could find a common ground. With that, he could work with them, and they could find a way to stop this Tenebeth together.

"We will stop it," he said.

"Now that the Shaper of Light as appeared, I believe that we will," Tobin said.

"I will need help."

"You have the power of the Mother. You need nothing more."

Tan shook his head, thinking of all the bonds that he had seen while within the pool. Connections stretched from him and to others, many different connections that reminded him of the way he'd drawn enough power to defeat the Utu Tonah. Those were what he needed in order to stop this darkness. Without those connections, they would fail.

"Why did you bring us here?" Tan asked.

"I wanted you to see the pride of the Order, Maelen. I wanted you to know that we have value."

"I have always believed that you have value."

"Have you? You come to our land and you demonstrate power unlike anything we have witnessed in centuries. So much changes because of you, Maelen."

Roine covered his mouth and laughed.

Tan shot him a look, but Roine only shrugged.

"He's right, you know. It's that way wherever you go, Tan. You changed the kingdoms, and then you changed Incendin, and Doma and Chenir. You went and changed Par. *You* are the catalyst for change."

"Those were all things that needed to change," Tan said.

Roine laughed and nodded. "That doesn't change the fact that they are changed because of you." He looked over at Tobin. "I understand, even if Tannen here doesn't. Change can be diffi-cult, but trust me when I tell you it's not all bad. In fact, he usually does things for the right reasons. When he does that, then the change is good."

"Usually?"

Roine shrugged. "I don't want you to think you've always been right."

Tobin laughed. "You have changed other places, Maelen?" he asked.

"Other places? He changes every place he's ever gone. There is nothing that he has visited that he hasn't changed. My homeland, for example," Roine said. "The place I knew had a wall between it and another country, a barrier that prevented our peoples from mingling. It stopped a war, but it limited us in ways that we never understood. Tan removed that barrier, and he forced us to see that the other side was not the threat we once thought them to be. Now... now he counts them as friends."

"You could count them as friends as well," Tan said.

"It's harder for me," Roine said. "You changed what we knew, but it's hard to change those memories, Tan. I fought them for most of my life. Giving up on that is easier for you because you never knew it like I did. It would be easier for you to forgive. For me... it will take longer."

"There was a barrier?" Tobin asked.

"One of our people created the barrier, though I think they had the idea from Norilan," Roine said. "He was a great shaper, a man I had misunderstood when I was younger. He had helped create our barrier as a way to stop a war. And it did. Shapers didn't die the way they once did, and we thought that we thrived, but I think we separated ourselves and lost something."

"You lost the elementals," Tan reminded him. "They want no part of a barrier. They're meant to roam the land, holding the connection to the Mother."

Roine sighed. "We know that now. Like I said, there were many things that he changed."

Tobin nodded slowly, running his hand along the mantle. "Why did you come here, Maelen? What would you have change about Norilan?"

"I came because of the convergence," he started, but realized there was another reason that he needed to have been here. A prophecy, one that he had forgotten about. The Order possessed it, and he wondered if it was something the ancient shapers had seen while connected to spirit. Perhaps while he had been in the pool of spirit, *he* would have been able to see it as well, but Tan hadn't gone looking for any prophecy. "You once told me the Order had a promise of the Shaper of Light."

"You are he," Tobin answered. "You are what was foretold."

"What else was foretold?"

Tobin stared at him before turning to a shelf and grabbing a thin leather-bound volume off the shelf. He flipped it open and traced his fingers along the page. "We have records here that stretch back for several thousand years, Maelen. They are shaped to preserve that knowledge, as the pages would other-wise crumble. This is one such volume."

He handed it to Tan, who took it carefully. In a glance, he noted the pages were thicker than any he had seen in the archives within Ethea, even those in the lower archives. The texture of the cover was smooth, and not leather as he had initially believed, but something else. The writing was made in a neat script, and it was one he didn't recognize at first. With a flash of insight—Tan wondered if it came from the connection to the spirit bond—he could read the words.

"This predates the kingdoms," he said, skimming the page.

"Is it *Ishthin?*" Roine asked.

Tan shook his head. "Older. I don't recognize it."

"How are you able to read it?" Roine asked, looking over his shoulder.

Tan glanced at him. "The connection to spirit, I think."

Reading through the pages, he noted a comment about the Shaper of Light. Was this where Honl had discovered the phrase? Tan had never heard of it before Honl and didn't think it came from anything in the archives or even from the records in Par. And Honl had spent time searching through Norilan, which made it possible that he *had* discovered this text. The elemental would have understood what was written here, the same as Tan now did.

Honl?

There came no response through the bond. It was a question he would hold onto and ask later, especially as Tan didn't think he would have time to remain and read everything in the book.

"It predates even the Order as I know it," Tobin answered. "It comes from a different time and a different world, and speaks to an end of the darkness, of a time when the Shaper of Light brings about a change, one where darkness is no longer feared." He nodded to the book, and Tan handed it back to him. "Scholars have argued over the meaning for centuries, and most think it simply a reflection on the time, that the ancients feared the night."

"For good reason, it would seem," Tan said.

Tobin's eyes narrowed. "Perhaps. Regardless, none ever believed that Tenebeth could end. The darkness is as much of the world as the light. But there must be balance, and the darkness must be held in check." He sighed, closing the book. "Or so I thought. So much has changed."

Tan stared at him. "Do you fear change?"

"Too much changes, Maelen. That is all you bring."

"I have changed what needed to be changed," Tan said. "As to the rest, that's not up to me. That's up to the connections you make. That's up to the elementals and the Mother."

Tobin watched him as if he expected Tan to say anything more, but what else was there for him to say? Norilan represented the old way and the old warriors. Tan valued what they had done, and valued the fact that they had been more skilled with actual shaping than he would have been, but they had not known nearly what they should have known. They were not connected to the elementals the same way he was, and because of that, they were not bound to the Mother the same way.

Either Norilan would help, and they would do what they could to be a part of the defenses needed to stop the darkness from spreading, or they would choose to avoid their responsibility and would hide. Tan hoped that they took part, but if they didn't—if they were unwilling to help—then he would still do what *he* needed to do, regardless of whether they participated.

And staying here much longer didn't accomplish anything. Marin and her disciples were still out there, and he needed to discover what she intended so that he could determine what he could do to stop her.

Now that he'd sunk into the pool of spirit and had reconnected to the elementals, he wondered whether he would be able to detect her. Could he use the knowledge of the elementals, of the connections that were formed between he and them, to discover what she might be after?

Tan thought that he might be able to do so, but he needed to get away from here first. There was too much suppression within Norilan, as if the land itself still remembered what had been done to the elementals for all that time.

Still… he detected something, an odd sense that plagued him, leaving him with a vague awareness that something was off. Was that Marin?

It was far from here, if so.

"Roine," he said, looking up, "I think it's time for us to leave."

Roine watched him for a moment, his brow furrowed in such a way that Tan thought he wanted to say something, but he refrained. Instead, he nodded.

As they returned to the doorway leading out from the Seat of the Order, Tan glanced back at Tobin. "There are others who could learn from you. Ethea and Par have students of shaping, and they would value the knowledge of the ancient Order."

"They have no need of the Order. If you offer your services and your lessons, what more can the Order do for them?"

Tan smiled slightly. "You'd be surprised. The Order has more skilled shapers than any found in the kingdoms." He waited for Roine to object, but he didn't. "If you want to ensure the Order lives on, working with the others will be your way to do so. Consider that a positive change."

He had pulled open the door when Tobin caught him with a question. "Does the Shaper of Light command this?"

Tan blinked. He suspected he could tell him that he did, and that the Shaper of Light wanted them to work with the other shapers of the world, but what message did that send? Was it a conciliatory message or one that would only lead the Order to rebel against him? He might need them when he faced Marin. Considering what he had needed when he faced the Utu Tonah, he might need anyone when it came time to contain the darkness. It was much more powerful than anything he'd ever encountered.

"Not the Shaper of Light, and not a command," Tan answered. "Maelen asks. That is all."

As he stepped out into the street, noting the people looking at him, still standing within their homes, hiding but not really hiding, he wondered if that would be enough. The Mother knew he hoped that it would be, but Tan was not certain.

Taking a long look around the city, he shaped himself into the sky and to the draasin.

13

BLESSED BY THE MOTHER

The shaping carried him above the clouds, where he rejoined the draasin. Wasina bowed her head to him. Asgar did the same. Both flicked their tails excitedly as he appeared.

What is it? he asked Asgar.

He focused on the fire bond, but it felt strange doing so. Not because it was difficult to reach, but because he seemed able to reach the bond more easily than he expected. Fire flowed to him as if he were sitting within the bond. All he had to do was reach over to the draasin and he could know their thoughts.

Tan suspected he could reach through the bond and find Ciara with Sashari or Cora with Enya, though Cora sat within the bond more than most shapers. He had always felt connected to the bonds, but this was a greater connection.

And it was changed since he'd gone into the pool of spirit.

He had been less connected before entering spirit. The bonds had been easy enough to reach, but it wasn't the same. It wasn't as if he stayed within it at all times.

The more he focused on fire, the more he became aware of the fact that he was still connected to the other bonds: earth, wind, and water. The sense of them all seemed to fill him.

Had the pool of spirit somehow brought him closer to the bonds themselves?

He knew that it had brought him closer to *his* bonds, those of the elementals as well as his family, but he hadn't expected the same from the element bonds. If he were this connected to them, there would be advantages when facing Marin.

Even spirit… Tan had managed to reach the spirit bond, but that had always seemed a distant sense. This was more acute, more present within his mind.

Why should he feel it now?

Because he was out of the city.

Within the city of the Order was something that prevented him from fully detecting the new connection. Maybe that was intentional, and those of the Order had done it so that they wouldn't risk themselves facing angry and tainted elementals, or maybe it was because he had been closer to the place of convergence and the elementals drawn toward the convergence limited that connection in some way that he didn't fully understand. Or maybe it was nothing like that. It could be only that there *was* such a connection to the Mother while there that he wasn't able to notice the distinct difference to the rest of the element bonds.

Asgar laughed, and it came out as a huff of smoke and fire. *You come looking like this and you question?*

Looking like what?

The draasin let out another streamer of steam and smoke, this time more focused than before. *It is you, Maelen. You have been blessed by the Mother.*

Tan laughed softly. There seemed a hesitancy to Asgar that wasn't normally there. Was it because of what had happened in the pool of spirit, or was there more to it?

Connected as he was, he sensed the issue with Asgar. It was fear, though not the fear that Tan would have expected. He didn't fear Tan, or the shapers in Norilan, or even fear the darkness, in spite of what Tan had thought. He feared disappointing the Mother.

Was he alone with that fear or did other elementals feel the same way?

Tan stretched through the bonds and noted that many of the elementals—at least those he detected close to him—felt much the same. And it wasn't a fear of how the Mother would react, it was that they would fail her in some way.

Pulling from spirit—and Tan didn't know if he drew from his own pool of spirit or the spirit bond or even from the spirit that he'd nearly drowned in—he sent out a reassuring sense to the elementals, letting it course through his connection to all of them. It surged through the bond, streaking away from him, a wave of reassurance that he hoped helped soothe the elementals that thought they might do something that would disappoint the Mother.

Then he retreated and focused on the elementals in front of him, on Asgar in particular. *You won't eat me, then?*

I think the Mother would be angry were I to try.

The Mother would not be angry. Didn't she make you a hunter, Asgar?

All the draasin hunt, Maelen. You know this.

Then you should know that would not anger her if you acted because of how she made you.

Asgar snorted, seemingly amused. *There are times you show real wisdom, Maelen.*

Only because she has helped me see.

Is that what you were doing here? Is that why you disappeared, and then when you appeared again, you were... much brighter than you had been before?

I think she needed me to see certain things.

What sort of things?

The kind that tell me we need to return.

You questioned that?

No, but I think I have a different sense of urgency now than I had before. I know what we risk by not stopping Marin from attacking.

We risk life.

More than life, Asgar. We risk our connections. Those are what brings us life. Without those connections, there is no life. There is nothing to live for.

It started to make sense to him now, though he didn't know why it would have taken him so long to understand.

What bonds?

That was what the Mother had shown him, wasn't it? Even more than the connections that he possessed, she had shown him the connections that were formed by others, that *must* be formed by others. If they didn't have those connections, then there would be no way for them to keep living.

Alanna was a part of it, and one that might be greater than he expected—or would have wanted. She had a connection to the elements and the elementals that he didn't fully understand.

The elementals needed that connection as much as the shapers did. They needed to connect to the life, to help them come closer to it.

Tan had helped encourage it over the last few years, but he hadn't done enough. He had changed the elementals—all of them. He thought of what had happened with first the hounds, and the way that he had brought them back into the fire bond, and with what happened to Honl. He had thought the elemental changed, and he *had* been changed, but not always in the way that Tan realized.

Now that he was better connected to spirit and to the wind bond, he thought he understood, and he began to have an idea of what he might need to do.

Would it be possible?

Asgar looked over at him, his bright yellow eyes full of knowledge and life. Tan suspected that the draasin knew exactly what he was thinking, much as he knew what Tan began to suspect he might have to do.

Is it possible?

Maelen—

Is it possible? Can I shift all those able to shape closer to the bonds? They already reach the bond, even if they aren't aware of it.

You are connected to the Mother in ways that none have ever been connected before. I would think that anything is possible for you, Maelen.

He had to understand more, which meant returning. Now, it was not only because of what he knew Marin would attempt, but because he wanted answers. He could get them, and he could make some changes, but they might be more than what any would have expected.

And yet... hadn't he discovered that the changes he made were the ones that the Mother sanctioned? If he did anything that she *didn't* want done, she wouldn't have given him the power that she had.

You will carry him back?

I will. And what of you?

Wasina will bring me.

That is not an answer.

You can know what I'm doing through the fire bond, Asgar. You will know as soon as the others.

You really intend for this to happen?

He looked over at Roine. The man had remained silent, yet he watched Tan. He probably knew that he was having some conversation with the elementals, but not what he was saying. If Roine did, what would he think?

For us to have the strength to withstand the darkness, I think this is what must happen.

What of the elementals?

You are already connected to the bond. I don't think anything will change for you.

Not at first, Asgar agreed, *but if you really intend to forge a connection between the bonds and all those able to access it, then there will be changes. I don't know what they might be—I don't claim to have the understanding of those things—but I recognize what might happen when the power is changed.*

Everything must change, Asgar.

That seemed to be the problem in the past. That was what Tan wondered. Perhaps the darkness had not been subdued for long because they had *not* changed nearly enough over time. The shapers had maintained their connection to their power, and the elementals had retained their connection, but other than that, nothing else really changed.

Everything has changed, Maelen. When you first appeared, it changed.

Then it must continue to change.

Yes.

You will return him to Ethea?

I will return him, and then I will join you. What you intend should be interesting.

There won't be much of a hunt.

I don't know that you can make a promise like that. When you are involved, there's always a hunt, even if it's not one you intend.

Tan smiled and shaped himself up onto Wasina before turning to Roine. "The draasin will take you back to Ethea."

"That's it? We come here, you go for a swim in spirit, and then we return? What did we accomplish?"

Tan sighed. "I think the swim in spirit is what needed to be accomplished, Roine. I think that was the reason that we came."

"What of the Order?"

Tan shrugged. "They will either help or they won't. It's the same as what happened when we faced the Utu Tonah. I didn't know whether you would help."

"You always knew that I would come."

"I couldn't force you to come. I had asked you to do something you had never imagined doing." Tan hadn't been able to understand that until hearing it from Roine as he described the effect Tan had on him to Tobin, but he got it. "Much as we can't force anything with Tobin. He will either offer his help, or he will not. If he does, we should be prepared to take it. If not, then we continue as we have been."

Roine glanced at the ground with an almost longing in his eyes. "Think of what we could learn from them," he said. "I imagine it would be nearly as much as what you have learned from the elementals."

"We can all learn from the elementals," Tan said.

"Only if you speak to them. The only reason I speak to this elemental is because you have granted it. Without that, I wouldn't have that ability. I'm thankful of that, but I know that those given the chance to communicate with the elementals have a much better understanding of what they can do, and how that power works in the world."

Tan patted Wasina's side. "You're right. Which is why I intend to change that."

14

A DAUGHTER SPEAKS

I t was late. The sun, now set, left only a few streaks of
color in the sky. Wasina remained perched on the top of
the tower, waiting for Tan much like Asgar often did. He
detected her watching, looking around, surveying the city. It
was rare for her to spend time near Par. Most of the time when
she was here, she did so in the caverns, waiting near the eggs
and the ancient records. Tan left her as he returned to his
family.

What would they have detected during the time he was in
the pool of spirit? Would they have known that he was there?
He'd made a point of not communicating with Amia since then,
telling her only that he was well but not wanting to worry her,
and he knew that she *would* worry were she to know what he'd
been through.

Then there was Alanna.

The bond had given him a different insight to her. She was

his child, descended from he and Amia, but she was like the elementals as well.

How?

Tan needed to understand before he was faced with another attack. He knew that they would be faced with another one, and sooner than he wanted. Already he could feel the dragging sense that Marin did something. For the first time, he thought that he could find her, but doing so required Alanna, of that he was now certain.

Would Amia understand?

For that matter, did he?

As he strolled through the halls, the estate felt cooler than usual. None of the servants were out in the hall, and he was thankful for that. Had he passed anyone he recognized, how would he explain what had happened to him? How would he explain that he was still Maelen, and that the change to his skin didn't mean anything?

But that wasn't entirely true. The changes *did* mean something. They meant that he could reach the bonds and that he was better connected to them. They meant that the Mother had wanted him to have the power that he did and she would be fine with him using it. And they meant that he would be the one who had to stop Marin, though he had known that fact before.

"Maelen."

He turned and noted Maclin coming down the hall. The man had refused to abandon his post as household servant even after assuming the title of Master of Souls.

"Maclin. You should be in bed."

The other man scanned Tan a moment, a question lingering in his eyes, but one that he didn't ask. "You should be as well, though I heard you took another trip to Norilan. A dangerous place."

"Not so dangerous now."

"There remain shapers who exceed the ability of Par's." Tan nodded. "Then it remains dangerous. We would work with them, of course, as I suspect you would ask."

"I actually asked them to come to Par to teach."

"Then we should begin to make preparations."

"I got the sense that they weren't interested."

"I will prepare the same. When the Maelen makes a request, most eventually agree to it. I would not be surprised if they arrive soon."

Tan smiled. Maclin started to turn away, but Tan spoke up. "Maclin?"

The other man turned, holding his hands together in front of him. "Yes, Maelen?"

"You haven't said anything about my appearance."

"It is not my place. You are touched by the light, Maelen. I think there is something of the Great Mother in that. You do not need my guidance to understand that."

"I could always use your guidance. I value your opinion, Maclin."

"Less and less than you once would have. When you came to Par, you were arrogant but ignorant. Both have changed. The arrogance turned out to be a deserved confidence. The ignorance has improved the longer that you rule."

"Thanks."

"Your family will be awaiting your return. And the people would be honored if you made an appearance. You are infrequently seen in Par these days. You have much that you can influence simply by who you are."

"I will do what I can, Maclin."

"As you always do, Maelen."

They parted and Tan reached his room. When he pushed the door open, he found Amia resting in a chair, her eyes closed and the reflected light from a fire in the hearth leaving her face practically glowing. Alanna rested on the chair next to her. Even though he hadn't been away from her for very long, she still seemed to have grown. He suspected he would feel that way about her every time he left her.

As he crossed over to them, Alanna opened her eyes.

She didn't giggle, and she didn't smile or speak. She hadn't yet, though he knew she should have. Rather, there was a brightness behind her eyes that he hadn't seen before.

Alanna had always had a certain spark about her, from her giggle to her smile to the way she grabbed at his finger and pulled at it, forcing him to pay attention to her. This was something more. This was intelligence and knowledge.

She spoke to him.

Maelen.

Tan froze.

Should he be surprised that she would speak to him this way first? He didn't think that he should be, but then, he would have expected a different address from her.

Maelen, not Father?

Maelen has a greater meaning than Father, does it not?

Tan marveled at the way she spoke to him, at the intelligence within her words.

But should he?

He had seen the brightness glowing from her when he was in the pool of spirit. And he had seen how she was more like an elemental. Didn't Light speak to him in a similar way?

Maelen is the name the elementals gave me. Is that what you are?

I don't know what I am. I feel the Mother and the connections that are necessary for me to reach the Mother, but I know that I should not be anything more than a child.

You've changed since I left, haven't you?

He had thought that he might have imagined it, but now he no longer knew whether that was the case. The changes *were* real. Alanna had grown.

The Mother has changed me, much as she has changed you.

And your mother?

Alanna gazed upon Amia and warmth radiated from her, a glow that matched what Tan felt coming off himself. It was then that he realized that the warmth was a reflection of what he saw when he had been in the pool of spirit. It was the way the Mother had looked upon him, and the way that he looked upon his daughter.

Strange that she would look on her mother in the same way.

Asgar thinks you need to be a part of what I'm planning.

He didn't bother hiding the elemental's name as he would with others. With Alanna, he had long wondered whether it made a difference. With her connection to spirit, she likely knew the names of the elementals anyway.

I think the Mother intends for me to be used.

Why?

In answer, her gaze flickered to his pocket and the device began to grow warm.

Tan pulled it free and was not surprised to notice that it

glowed, almost matching his skin as it did. The power within it surged, flickering against him. Tan felt a slight stirring of desire to use it, but not as he would have before.

Yet, when he looked on Alanna, he saw that she had no interest in using the device, and the way that she looked at it told him that she understood what it was and how to use it.

He held it out to her.

It floated toward her and she took it.

When she did, the device surged with power, glowing with a blinding yellowish light. With a flash of colors—blue and red and orange and green and more than he could count, more colors than the rainbow—the device simply disappeared.

Tan felt a moment of panic. They needed the device to stop Marin, though he wasn't sure how it would be used. He didn't even know if he could be the one to use it. How much more power could he pull when he was already connected so tightly to the bonds?

What did you do with it?

The Mother wanted the contents returned.

Returned? Did you destroy it? Tan suspected elementals went into making the device, much like they had gone into making the artifact.

There can be no destruction when we use the Mother.

You changed it.

Yes.

How?

The same way you were changed.

I don't understand.

I took the blessing as she instructed.

Tan blinked but thought he understood what she meant. She

had absorbed the device. Which meant that the power within was now *her* power.

What will you become? he asked.

What the Mother intends for me to become, much as you were intended to become the Maelen.

I am still man.

Are you, Maelen? Have you not become something else? What man can withstand the flame of the draasin? What man can survive udilm? What man can endure the Mother when she makes herself known? The elementals understand that you are something more, and have been from the moment you first made your bond to the Eldest.

I only wanted to be Tan.

And I only wanted to be your daughter.

You are still my daughter, he said, picking her up off the chair and holding her close to him. She wrapped her arms around him and he smiled.

And you are still Tan.

There are times when I'm not certain who I am anymore. I am not a shaper, and I don't rely on the elementals as I once did.

As I said, you are Maelen.

Now that you've absorbed the relic, he started, not able to believe that was what she had done. It seemed impossible, but what other explanation was there for it? *Do you know what it is that we're supposed to do?*

You came here with a plan.

I came here to see my family, he said.

That is a plan, isn't it?

Tan laughed and hugged her close.

As he did, he noticed that Amia had stirred and she looked up at him, noting the way that he held onto Alanna. Tan wasn't sure how she would react. Would she blame him for what happened to their daughter? How could he deny that the changes were his fault? He was the reason that she had changed. Because of the connection to the Mother, she had been forced to change. Would they miss her growing up? Would they miss having the opportunity to work with her and teach her, guide her along the way?

Did you miss that with me? Light asked.

I think you missed out on something. Check with Asgar and with Wasina. They had different experiences of their youth.

Is one necessarily better than the other? Because Asgar bonded and gained from that connection doesn't mean that he was lessened by it.

He wasn't bonded.

You gave him a name. To the Mother, that is the same, Light said. *And because Wasina took the time to understand the world on her own before choosing her name doesn't mean that she had a greater experience than Asgar. They were given what they needed.*

Tan looked from his daughter to Amia. Would she see it the same way?

She is the Daughter, Maelen, Light reminded.

"You really have been blessed, haven't you?" Amia asked, sitting up. Her hand went to her necklace and she ran her fingers around the inside of it. Tan knew there were runes engraved on the metal, and that those runes matched the binding that he now used to shape and create the power that would hold the darkness.

"I went into a pool of the Mother."

Amia smiled and joined him, holding Alanna between them. "I know."

"I don't know what I was thinking. I probably shouldn't have gone, but..."

"You went where you were supposed to go, Tan."

"Everything changed after I did," he said.

He'd been the focus of so many people frustrated about the change that he'd brought that he hadn't taken the time to think about what it meant for himself. He was impacted almost as much as the others. Not only what had happened to him, and to the elementals that he had bonded, but to his family and to those he cared about.

"That is the way of the Mother," Amia said, resting her head against him. "It's when we do not change that she grows frustrated. You have been given power to cause that change, Tan. You use your ability to shape to bring things into a different form, taking from one and turning it into another. That is all about the Mother."

He had worried that she might be mad, and that she might be disappointed in what he had done, but then, he should have known better. As Light had reminded him, Amia was the Daughter, gifted of the Mother with great connections to spirit. He'd never really questioned what that meant, but seeing Alanna, and knowing how she had been changed, and how she was more than only a child, he thought he began to understand.

"You know what she is, don't you?" he asked.

Amia laughed softly. "She is my child, Tan, touched by spirit the same as you and I." She looked up and met his eyes. "I have known. From the moment she touched the bond of what had once been a draasin, I have known. She is filled with the power of the Mother."

"The elementals think she can help in the battle that is to come."

"I suspect that she can."

Tan looked from his beloved to his child. "Have you spoken to her?"

Amia touched their daughter's nose, tracing down it. Alanna smiled then, looking like the child that she was, grabbing for her mother's finger. "Every day," she whispered to her.

"Not like that." *Like this*, he said, shifting the form of communication.

Amia smiled. *Every day.*

Tan sighed, wrapping his arms around his family. The glowing to his skin increased, and he realized that it came from Alanna as well. Somehow, Amia added to it, and they all stood there, holding each other, the power of the Mother filling them, and the room, with its light. In that moment, Tan thought he understood their purpose and had a flicker of hope for the future.

RETURN TO THE MOUNTAINS

Tan rode on Wasina as they traveled toward Ethea. The draasin caught currents of air, rising high over the ground as she did, soaring first up and then back down, her massive wings barely beating against the sky.

Two of the hatchlings flew alongside him. They were growing quickly, their bodies growing so that they were nearly the size of Enya when she'd been freed from the ice. In time, Tan could tell that they would be similar in size to Sashari. Not as enormous as Asgar or Asboel, but still giant creatures.

Amia and Alanna rode with him. They were the reason he didn't shape himself toward Ethea, choosing instead to take the draasin, knowing that shaping all three of them would have been possible but it wouldn't have been as interesting a trip. This way, he could see the ground spread beneath him and he could watch as the sea changed over to Incendin and then over to the kingdoms.

As they did, Tan nudged Wasina to turn slightly north.

"I thought we were going back to Ethea," Amia said.

"We will. There's something I want to revisit first," he said as he pointed. The soft glow to his skin had receded. It was still there if he looked, but for the most part, it took someone who knew him well to notice.

They soared ever higher, eventually reaching a series of rising mountain peaks. Green trees rose along the sides, that of pine and oak and some elm, the fragrance filling the air. Tan could almost imagine that all of this had been shaped. Maybe it was the vantage, that of flying near the clouds, but he imagined some great shaper pulling the mountains and trees from the ground, much like he had done with the beginning of the tree in the cavern.

Wasina knew where Tan wanted to go, and she guided him toward one of the peaks. As they flew, Tan felt a strange tingling, one that reminded him of the barrier that once had separated the kingdoms from Incendin. Far below, he could see the glittering water of the lake leading toward the mountain, and he could feel the drawing of the elementals, though they weren't as strong now as they once had been.

The place of convergence had suffered much over the last few years. After centuries left untouched, now it had been tampered with, not only by Tan, but by the lisincend and by the shapers of Par-shon, eventually being left alone. There was still a wildness to it, something unrefined, and in many ways, different than the convergences he'd discovered in other places.

"What is it?" Amia asked.

"This was once a powerful convergence."

"I remember."

"No, before that. When Ethea was first formed, they changed the landscape, and that shifted the convergence, pulling it toward the capital."

Many things have changed, Alanna sent.

I'm not certain this should have changed.

The Mother exists in both places. Nothing was destroyed.

Tan stared at the ground, considering. He had long thought that drawing the convergence away from here had damaged things in some way, but that wasn't the lesson he'd been learning. Hadn't he been seeing that changing what the Mother created was not harmful? Only when there was an attempt to destroy was there a problem.

What about if Marin pulls the convergence away?

Voidan will be released, Alanna said.

Tan found her matter-of-fact comment somewhat disheartening, but then... she also had no fear about it. Alanna—as touched by the Mother as any elemental—did not worry about Voidan getting free.

Why?

How can you not worry about what will happen?

His daughter laughed, the high-pitched giggle so jarring compared to the maturity he heard within his mind. She touched his cheek, trailing her fingers along his jawline. *How can you worry when you've been given so much?*

Because I don't know how to stop her.

You need not worry. She will come, and you will oppose. It is the way the Mother intended.

She intended for me to face Marin?

Alanna giggled again. *Perhaps not her, but she could feel the tremblings. You can too, if you pay attention. The darkness has been gaining strength for many years. It was a matter of time before it escaped. That is the cycle, and you will be the one to end this cycle.*

Images flashed in his mind, images that Alanna as his child should not possess. They were of Doma falling before Incendin. Of the barrier erected between the kingdoms. Of Par becoming Par-shon. They were flashes, barely more than touches of memory, but he knew them, recognizing them for what they were.

If he ever questioned her connection to the elementals, that answered it for him.

Everything that had been occurring for the last century had built up to this.

In that way, perhaps the Mother *had* been planning.

Was that why he had been granted his abilities?

Does it matter, Maelen?

Tan couldn't tell who had asked the question. It could have been Wasina, or his daughter, or any of the elementals he felt through his solidified connection to spirit and the bonds. The source of the question didn't matter. He knew the answer as surely as they did.

He tapped Wasina on the side and she turned, catching another current of air and taking them toward Ethea. Villages occasionally appeared below them, dotting the landscape. Tan had never taken the time to visit the countless villages scattered throughout the kingdoms, villages that were much like the one he had come from. How many people were isolated from the events taking place? How many depended on him doing what he must so that they could continue to have that isolation?

Untold thousands, he knew as he touched upon the spirit bond. They were all there, connected in some way, though more faintly than those who could shape.

As they approached Ethea, Tan sent out a call to those he shared a connection with.

Shapers he had worked with before, shapers who had trained with him, even those who had opposed him. He sent the request through spirit, letting it flow from him.

And realized that they should not meet in Ethea.

Doing so felt… wrong.

Instead, he motioned to Wasina to return, guiding her back toward the mountains.

Where everything had begun for him, it needed to end.

It felt fitting, and he hoped the Mother appreciated the symmetry.

When they reached the mountains again, with the crystal blue waters of the lake below them, Tan stood on Wasina and grabbed Amia and Alanna, shaping them to the ground. He had thought that Wasina would soar above them, but she surprised him by diving toward the lake and plunging deep beneath the surface in a spray of white tinged with a hint of green.

Where are you going?

Memories of the Eldest are here, Maelen. I would see what he knew.

He knew nothing but cold. A darkness for nearly a thousand years.

And I can experience it for a few moments.

They made their way along the shore, and Tan sighed. Such strange memories had been formed here. This was where he had sacrificed himself for Amia, and where he began to learn his connections to the elementals, but this was a place where many lives had been lost.

As the Mother directed, Alanna told him. *Change sometimes requires pain.*

The change that has been here has required destruction.

Not destruction. Lives might have been lost, but they were returned to the Mother. In that way, they served.

How is that different than what Marin intends?

You know that it is different, Maelen. There is nothingness to what she would have. That is not the same as change.

It was hard to feel like there was that much difference. Both were destruction, even though he knew that the destruction that Marin sought was somewhat different than what he suspected Asboel—or even his father—had experienced.

With what Alanna said, he had to wonder—did it mean that his father had returned to the Mother? Would he, like Asboel, live on within the bonds?

And more than that, would Tan be able to reach him if he were to connect deeply to the earth bond?

There was something both reassuring in that… and dangerous. He could continue to strive for the missing relationship he once had with his father, or he could continue to focus on those around him now.

And what would his mother think if she knew she could reach her long-gone husband? What did that mean for her relationship with Roine? Would it change the way she felt?

Perhaps it *was* better to leave those who had gone to rest within the bond and not attempt to dredge them up.

They are with us anyway, Alanna said. *They might seem like memories, but they are the spark that gives us life. I know the way that your father has driven you, Maelen. It is in everything you are.*

How can you know that?

I know you, Maelen. I know what you have done for those you care about.

Tan fell silent, looking around, consumed by memories.

Amia took his hand and squeezed. "It's almost like we were never here," she said.

Tan scanned the shores and saw no sign of the fires that had burned through here once upon a time, but then, there was no sign of the power of the nymid or the sense of the draasin that had once been trapped in the water.

A powerful shaping built, and a shaper exploded to the ground next to them.

Tan wasn't surprised to see Cora appear first. She frowned when she saw Tan holding Alanna.

"What is this, Maelen?"

"A calling to those who might be able to help," he said.

"Including your child?"

"She can help. Ask the draasin. Or Fire."

Cora's frown deepened and her eyes took on a faraway expression. When it cleared, she looked at Alanna with an interested glint in her eyes. "She is connected to Issa. Did you do this?"

"Do you think I would force my daughter into the bond?"

"No, but I think she would be nudged into those connections without your choosing. You are powerful, Maelen, and your offspring would be powerful as well."

"You have no idea," he said.

Other shapings built, and shapers began to appear. First there was Roine and Zephra, who hurried to Alanna and lifted her, spinning her around as she hugged her closely. Tan wondered what Zephra would think were she to know that her granddaughter was much more mature than she ever imagined. Would she clutch her tightly like she now did? Would it even be possible for Zephra to connect to Alanna and understand what had changed with her?

Probably not. She knew about the wind bond, but she was not able to reach it.

That was what Tan needed to change.

He would start with those he was connected to, those he had fought alongside, those who already had some sort of connection to the bond, though many didn't know it.

"What are we doing here?" Roine asked, leaving his mother as she held Alanna.

"This is a follow up to what happened in Norilan," Tan said.

Roine grunted. "I was afraid of that. What do you intend to do?"

"You will have to wait and see like everyone else."

"Great. Why do I have the sense that most of us don't really want to know what you intend?"

Amia squeezed his hand once again.

One by one, other shapers appeared.

There were shapers from all over the kingdoms, at first only those like Ciara and Ferran and Wallyn, those he had worked with before and who knew him well, but over time, others came as well, some Tan had not yet met. They came from Chenir, the Supreme Leader bringing other shapers with them, their strange way of calling to the elementals announcing their arrival. Some tapped on their legs, others move their fingers, and others made movements that Tan didn't yet understand, but they came.

Shapers came from Incendin. Not only Cora, but fire shapers who had never been twisted, and then those like Fur, and others of Incendin. They came from Doman, Elle and Val and a dozen other shapers of varying strength. And they came from Par. There was Elanne, Maclin, even Tolman and his wife Reyelle. Students came with them, and they waited, not surprised by the strange summons Tan had used. He was not surprised by that. The shapers of Par had been quick to adjust to the new strangeness that he had created.

He had hoped there would be shapers from Norilan as well. The call had gone out to all shapers he had once been connected to, which included those of Norilan. None answered.

Tan took a deep breath as he looked at the congregated shapers. There were so many. This would be his legacy, if nothing else. He would see that they worked together for a common purpose, and he would help them find a greater understanding of their abilities than they would have without him.

Thank you for coming, he started, sending it through the sprit bond.

Most blinked, seemingly surprised by the wordless connection. Few were bonded to elementals, so would not have the same understanding of how to communicate without words. Those who *were* bonded to elementals watched him with a firm sort of interest in their eyes.

We all face a threat unlike anything we have faced before. Many of you have fought by my side before, he went on, sending images of both battling Althem and the Utu Tonah, *and some of you have only gained your abilities recently. All of you will be essential to facing the threat we now face. Many have suffered as we have fought, and many more will suffer if we do not oppose this new threat. I under-*

stand that much of the world as we know it has changed, and I come before you promising more change.

He paused. A few murmured softly, and Tan did not attempt to stop them. They needed to have a chance to understand what he would ask of them, even if he could not explain it fully yet. There was no real way to explain it. They would have to experience it.

If you are willing to stand with me, and with those who share the concern for the elementals and for all that the Mother created, I can promise you that you will not fight alone. Many of you have bonded to the elementals, and you in particular know the importance of what we do.

He felt a surge and a building of shaping.

Tan paused and looked around at the faces of the shapers spread around him.

Lighting exploded nearby.

Three shapers appeared.

Tan smiled.

They were of Norilan. He saw Tobin, Jast, and a woman named Erica.

They watched him, and Tobin nodded.

So many places were now represented. That would be the key to survival, and they would all have to learn to work together, much as Tan had learned that he had to work with Incendin, and Doma, and Chenir, and now Par. Norilan was one more place that needed to work with him.

What I must ask of you now will be different. In the past, most of you experienced change as it happened, the same way as I did, forced to respond when we were attacked, or when we escaped a different threat. This will be something else. This will be a change I will place upon you. I will not do so without your willingness. You answered the call, so most of you have chosen to be here in the first place, but for the next part, you will need to agree. I do not know how it will work.

A soft murmuring began again, quietly at first, and one that he wasn't certain he recognized. As it built, he realized that the shapers who had come to him, who had answered the summons, all spoke one word: Maelen.

That was all the agreement he needed, and perhaps it was all that he would get.

Tan closed his eyes, focusing on the connection to spirit, and pulled on that connection, drawing strength from it. From there, he reached toward each of the other bonds, pulling from them as well.

Alanna, please help me.

You do not need my help.

I think that I might. Amia as well.

His family. They would have to help him succeed. They would have to help him forge a different bond, one that had never existed, but one he thought might be crucial moving forward.

Tan started pressing out with spirit first.

To this, he added the laced connection of the other element bonds. They stretched from him, moving away in a smoothing that was like thin tendrils that were pulled toward the shapers, almost as if on their own. Maybe they were. It was possible the element bonds knew where they needed to go and where they should be drawn, and went to the shaper. Some were touched by more than one, and they stayed there.

Reaching these people with the bonds was only a part of

what he wanted to do. He needed to solidify that connection so that they could reach it on their own.

Could he do that?

Can you help? he asked Alanna.

You don't need our help, only our connection.

He sent more spirit through the bond, but that was not what it would take. Forcing the element upon the shapers wouldn't work. He might be able to push enormous amounts of spirit, but that wasn't the way that he'd reach them.

It would take something else, only what? How had *he* reached the bonds?

Looking to Cora—one of the few others he knew with the ability to reach one of the element bonds—he wondered what it had taken for *her* to reach it.

Neither had been given the connection. Tan doubted he would have been able to reach the bonds other than the fact that he knew they were there… and had reached for them himself.

That had to be the key. He could drive the change, but he could not force someone to do it. They had to ask for it. They had to *want* it, much as he had wanted the change that had come to him, change that had given him the strength he had needed.

The only way to do that would involve showing them that the bonds exist, so that the shapers could decide for themselves whether they wanted to reach for it.

Tan drew upon more spirit, this time tapping into it not only through the spirit bond but drawing also through his connection to Alanna and Amia.

With this, he sent a message to the shapers around him.

Power flashed.

And Tan's connection to spirit crumbled.

He sank, hoping he had been strong enough, that he had managed to send enough to those with him that they could make a choice, but he didn't know whether he had. Now he had to wait.

As he did, he felt something else, and something unexpected. Darkness.

16

THE VOICE OF THE MOTHER

The darkness was near Tan, too close to be anywhere but here.

And he had just expended all that strength to attempt to form a bond.

Had he made a mistake?

The shapers collected near the shore of the lake didn't look at him. None spoke. He was drained and couldn't tell if they even attempted to speak in the bonds, or if they were simply dazed from having so much spirit thrown at them. Even Amia seemed stunned, and he wouldn't have expected that considering how they were connected and what she knew of the spirit bond through him.

The only one who didn't seem quite dazed was Cora, but she stood with her eyes closed and rocked in place.

Wasina flew overhead, as did Enya and Sashari, and even Asgar.

Still, Tan detected the darkness.

He staggered forward. Reaching the water, he stepped into it, letting it lap around his ankles. Another step, and he fell forward.

Water swirled around him.

Tan closed his eyes, his breath held, letting the power of water surround him. He knew without straining for it that there was great power here. The nymid occupied these waters, and he was connected to them.

Translucent shapes appeared, tinged with green. How long had it been since he had seen the nymid? Too long.

Come, Maelen, you are needed.

I am weakened, nymid. I need to rest.

There is no rest, Maelen. You must rise. You have the strength. You have always had the strength.

It's not my physical strength, nymid.

You have the strength. You have always had the strength, the nymid repeated.

Something grabbed his hand and Tan looked to see Alanna clutching it. *Stand, Father. You are needed.*

Daughter. What did I do?

What you were asked to do.

Tan stood and took a breath. As he did, he felt a shiver work through him. That shiver was the darkness, he was certain of that. Whatever was near would happen soon.

How had Marin planned this? She would not have known where he was going to be, and she should not have been able to respond this quickly.

Slowly, too slowly, it seemed as if strength returned.

Tan hoped the shapers would begin to come around, but

they didn't. They stood as if in some sort of daze, unable or unwilling to move. Had he more strength, he might use a shaping of spirit to check on them, but that would have to wait. For now, he had to protect them.

A flash of fabric along the edge of the trees caught his attention.

Draasin, he sent, *look for disciples. We must defend the shapers until they come around.*

If they would come around. Had he done something permanent to them? If he changed them in some way that had left them prone to injury, he needed to be there so that they could be kept safe.

We will watch, Maelen.

The answer came from all around him, not only from the draasin but from the nymid and from hounds that now prowled the woods, and even breathed in the wind, from ara. The elementals answered for him, as they so often did. They would be his support.

Tan shaped to the air and surveyed the land around him. There were disciples here, but where? As he hovered, he found a pair of them in the trees.

Tan landed, unsheathing his sword as he did.

He had destroyed the connection to the darkness in others who had been tainted by it. He could do the same again. One of the disciples sent a stream of black toward him, as if the night itself intended to swallow him.

Tan repelled it using a shaping of spirit through his sword, drawing on his own power. When that was not enough, he dipped into the spirit bond again, afraid that by doing so, he would be weakened even more. The shaping deflected the darkness.

He darted toward the man and caught him in the shoulder with his sword, surging spirit though it, much as he had done before. As before, the connection to spirit sent the darkness exploding out of him. Tan shifted the direction of the shaping, turning away from cleansing the man of spirit and instead checking for a spirit shaping that might have been layered atop his mind. When he found it, he peeled it away, working quickly —and, surprisingly, assisted by Alanna.

"You have already failed," the man said as the shaping disappeared.

Another who supported Marin, then. Why the need for the shaping? What did it do... other than ensure they didn't change after she'd granted them power? Marin couldn't have them opposing her, especially when they had power and potential to do so.

"I have already succeeded in freeing you," Tan said.

He spun, jabbing at the woman wearing a heavy black robe who came from between a pair of trees. She carried a long staff and slammed it into the ground. A sickly green light radiated from it as she did.

Tan caught the staff with his sword and she twisted, driving it around.

She was skilled with the staff, where he was only proficient with his sword. He had taken the time to understand how to fight with a sword and had trained with men who had real skill, but he was a shaper first and a swordsman second. The way this woman spun her staff, the controlled way she swung it at him, told him that she had training with it.

She slammed it into the ground again.

As she did, the sickly light trickled out from the staff, filling the air around her.

Tan shaped, sending spirit flowing through his sword. Where it struck the greenish light, there was a flash of brightness before it faded.

The woman prepared to bring her staff back down again.

Tan sensed that she was summoning the darkness the same way that the shapers of Chenir summoned the elementals. If he let her continue to do this, she would remain strong—possibly too strong for him to defeat.

When she raised her staff, he threw his sword.

It was a gamble, but it paid off.

The blade streaked toward her, catching her in the arm. Tan leapt toward her, pushing forward with a shaping of wind, and grabbed the hilt, sending spirit through the blade. Power burst through her and darkness dissipated.

Tan quickly shaped spirit, reaching into her mind and searching for a shaping, but there was none.

Either she wasn't shaped or it had been done more carefully than he could detect.

Rather than risking her coming at him with an attack, he struck her on her neck with the hilt of his sword, pushing enough earth through it to bring her down. She crumpled.

He felt a moment of regret at needing to hit her like that, but it was better to keep her confined while they faced the disciples. Using earth, he wrapped her wrists in tight bindings, drawing strength from the roots of the trees around him so that they held her down.

Keep them here, he said to the hounds prowling in the woods.

There came a soft braying, just enough that he knew they agreed, and he took to the air once more.

His heart sank as he did.

There were over a dozen disciples of the dark making their way toward the place of convergence, and so far, none of the shapers had snapped out of his forced connection to spirit. He didn't want to think about what he might have done and whether he had left permanent damage to them. Spirit could heal if he had, but only if he had the time to reach them. Not only the time, but the strength as well.

Two of the draasin—Wasina and Enya, he realized—fought a pair of the disciples on the far side of the lake. Both twisted and spun in the air, avoiding the attempt at sending shadows their way, narrowly missing them both. Sashari shot from the sky, streaking toward the ground with her wings wrapped around her body, her tail extended behind her and flames shooting from her nostrils. Even the two hatchlings that had dared come, not yet even named, nipped at one of the shapers of the dark.

Only Asgar did not.

You can help, he prompted.

If the darkness reaches me—

A powerful voice interrupted. *You are protected by the Voice of the Mother. You should not fear.*

Asgar breathed out in a powerful streamer of flame and, with a flicker of his tail, shot toward the two shapers Wasina and Enya faced. The three of them dispatched the shapers quickly.

Tan looked around, wondering where the power of that voice had come from. There was a strength to it, and a warmth, and it had seemed someone had just claimed a title.

He found Alanna in the middle of the lake, hovering.

She did not shape, at least not as far as he could tell, but power flowed from her. It streaked from her, touching each of the draasin as they fought. When a strand of dark shaping snuck through, her shaping of spirit—or whatever it was, as Tan wasn't completely convinced it was a shaping—reached out to them and touched them, calling them back to the Mother.

She protected them.

She was the Voice of the Mother.

How long have you known? he asked.

Awareness awoke in me when you reached the pool. You opened it within me, connected as we are. That is my purpose.

What happens if—

He didn't have a chance to finish.

Five shapers converged on her. They hesitated a moment when they realized that she was a child, but then quickly pressed their attack once more.

Alanna barely moved.

Power exploded from her, a ring of light that layered over the dark shapers.

The strange snake that often wound itself around her uncoiled from her body and lashed out in a spiraling motion, striking each of the shapers as it did. That wasn't a spiral—it was a rune. The elemental created a rune as it struck the dark disciples, and drew power as it did.

It made no sense to him. Alanna was somehow almost an elemental, but she had a bonded creature, one that *was* an elemental, only an elemental that was nothing like any that he'd ever experienced. It rarely left Alanna's side and usually couldn't even be seen.

The serpent reached her and quickly coiled around her waist again.

Throughout all of that, Alanna continued to stretch out her power, sending spirit to the draasin and to the hounds in the woods, and even to the nymid and ara. Tan could feel how she drew upon spirit, from some depths of the bond that even he barely understood.

With another explosion of light, spirit washed once more away from her, this time stretching toward the stunned shapers. The connection was nothing more than a touch of spirit, a simple connection, and one that Tan would have been able to do, but it revived them.

The shapers woke and Tan was no longer alone.

Cora joined him first, holding herself in the air on a current of fire that Tan could not see. "She is precocious, Maelen."

"You have no idea."

"With her involvement, I feel like we might have a chance."

Tan had begun thinking the same way.

"What is it like?"

"What?" he asked.

"To finally meet someone who might be more powerful than you?" Cora asked, nothing more than a hint of a smile crossing her lips.

Tan laughed. "At least I know she will do everything she can to help ensure our success."

"She is part elemental," Cora noted. "Enya tells me that she sits within the spirit bond, but she also sits within fire. I suspect she sits in the other bonds as well?"

"I am not certain." Amia came toward him, carried by Roine and Zephra on a current of wind. "She called herself the Voice of the Mother. I don't know what that means, but there is a title there that we have not possessed before."

Amia's eyes narrowed. "You heard that?"

"She told one of the draasin that the Voice of the Mother would protect him when he hesitated. And then she did."

Alanna had returned to the shore and sat, arms resting in her lap with her hands folded together, looking like nothing more than a small child, but inside his mind, he heard her still. The maturity and power she possessed continued to increase, as if she fed upon spirit.

Was that what she did?

Could she feed on spirit?

It would change her, and it would explain the maturity she possessed, but if that were the case, then she would never return to the child he and Amia had wanted. If she was the Voice of the Mother, she would never have a chance to grow and experience the world in the same way that he had.

She will be more than we are, Amia told him. *Isn't that all our parents wanted for us?*

Knowing that did nothing to make him feel better. She would be more than him—she already *was* more than him. And it was possible that she didn't even understand what was changing for her, or what it meant.

"What happened?" Roine asked. "I feel… something. I don't know what it is. You were speaking within our minds like when you allowed me to connect to the draasin, and then you sent a suggestion. Now… now it's like there's a whispering, only it's not the same as when I spoke with the draasin."

"What is it like?" Tan asked.

His mother shook her head. "That's what it is, isn't it? You showed us the bonds. I thought my connection to wind seemed more potent, but didn't know why that should be. Now I feel not only my bonded, but all of the elementals around us." She closed her eyes, turning slowly in place. "There are so many. How is this possible, Tannen?"

"We all will need to be connected to a greater power when we face the disciples. If we are to survive the darkness, and if we are to defeat Marin, we will need the capacity to reach for more than what we had been."

"You let *all* of these shapers reach Issa?" Cora asked.

"Not Issa, at least not for them. Some will reach for wind, some water, some earth, and some—yes—will reach fire. There will be an understanding of the fire bond."

He turned toward Ciara, who had reached Sashari and sat atop her, now leaning toward her neck, pressing her head toward her spikes as if listening—which she probably was. There was no surprise that Ciara would be able to reach the fire bond so quickly; she might have been able to do so even without his intervention. That was what he hoped, that he had only pushed forward what would have happened eventually. He thought about shapers like Ferran, so strong with earth and able to reach golud. He had worked with the elemental well. Tan wouldn't have been surprised that he would reach the bond without him.

"What now?" Zephra asked. "Now that you have shown the bonds, and some appear to have bonded, what will happen with us?"

"I don't know," Tan answered. "The disciples will continue to attack, but I don't know when they will come again. I think they tested us here, thinking that they would have an opportu-

182

nity to hurt us and our shapers. They were not expecting the Voice of the Mother."

"None of us expected that," Amia said.

Tan nodded toward his daughter. She traced in the sand, and it took him a moment to realize that she formed runes of power. How would she know that without being shown? As he watched, he realized that she tapped her feet with a certain rhythm. Had she always done that?

"I think," he started, "that maybe *she* expected it."

AFTER THE ATTACK

The lakeshore had a somber feel to it in spite of the fact that so many now had the ability to reach the element bonds. Tan could feel people flickering into the bond, more with every passing hour. There was a connection, but it was more than that. Those who reached the bond held onto the connection but didn't delve too deeply into it. They didn't pull upon the power of the bonds—though Tan suspected they would in time.

Amia walked with him, holding his hand as if neither of them had a care in the world. Alanna remained with Asgar, the draasin watching over their daughter as if she were one of the hatchlings in the cave. Tan suspected he didn't really *need* to have Asgar watch her, especially if she was as powerful as she seemed, but he felt a parental comfort in allowing it. There was darkness surging; he could practically feel the power of it flowing around him, but for now, he would not fear it.

"I think back to when we first came here," she said after a while. "Those first days."

"We were much younger then," he said.

"Not much."

Tan smiled, squeezing her hand. No, it hadn't been that long ago that they had been here. "I was a different person then."

"As was I."

He glanced over at her, noting the way the sunlight danced off her golden hair, reflecting almost as much from the band around her neck as it did from her hair. Tan could still see the girl he'd been so taken by when they arrived at his village, the one who had caught his attention even before needing to use a shaping to draw him to her. "You've changed somewhat," he decided, "but now that I think of it, not as much as others. I think having you remain so steadfast has allowed me to grow and change."

"You don't think I've changed?" There was a note of disappointment in her voice, and he wondered what bothered her.

"You've grown stronger, more skilled with spirit. You've become the First Mother, and taken on all the leadership that entails. And now you are the mother to our child. I think you were heading toward all of those things regardless of what happened."

"Is that what's bothering you, then? I wouldn't have expected the change you've instigated to trouble you this much."

"I've never had trouble with change. Without it, I would never have become the man I am. But it's transformation we're talking about, not only change." He motioned toward the lake, remembering what it had been like when the northern end had been completely shaped frozen. Maintaining a shaping like that would have been incredibly difficult, and Tan realized now that the elementals had been a part of it, whether or not they had wanted to be. "Freeing Asboel, that was change. Stopping Althem and recognizing Incendin was not our enemy, that was change. Even stopping the Utu Tonah and helping lead their people was a kind of change. This… where I have now shown people the element bonds… this feels different."

Amia pulled him toward her and wrapped her arms around him. "It's not them that you fear, Tan. You forget that we're bonded, and I know you as well as you know yourself."

He arched a brow at her. "If that's not it, then what is it?"

Amia turned him so that he could see the three draasin arranged along the shore. Asgar crouched with Wasina and Enya, all three of them surrounding Alanna, protecting her. "You fear what's happening to her."

Could that be all that it was?

Maybe Amia was right. He *did* fear change to his daughter more than he feared what had happened to himself, but only because he'd had the chance to grow and develop. Alanna had not had that chance, and if these attacks persisted, she might never have the chance.

Yet even that was not what troubled him.

It was that she was forced to develop as quickly as she had been. Now she had demonstrated her connection to the Mother, and if what she had said was true—and he had no reason to believe it wasn't—she was connected to the Mother in ways that even Tan couldn't understand.

"I fear that she hasn't had the choice," he said with a sigh.

"Are you so certain? What I can tell from her is that she *has* had a choice. She is precocious, but she gets that from both of us, as she does the ability to shape." Amia hugged him. "You forget that I was shaping when I was barely four. She started earlier, which tells me that she will be powerful, but that doesn't mean she was not born for this. The rest—the connection to spirit and to the elementals—I think she got from you."

She rested her head upon his chest and he breathed in the scent of her, the comforting awareness of her. She was his home, more than anything else. Through everything, she had been stable.

"I don't want anything to happen to her," Tan said.

"Neither do I. I suspect your mother felt the same, wanting to keep you safe in Nor. My mother wanted the same, which was why we ran from Incendin. Our parents wanted to protect us, much as we want to protect her, but think about how we felt, and think about what we have needed to do. There comes a time when we have to trust that they will be able to take care of themselves."

"I thought it would come a little later than this. She's only two—"

"In human terms, Tan," Amia reminded him, "but she is partly elemental, which makes her… I don't know what it makes her. Something more. I don't think we were ever meant to protect her for long."

"I know. I think I just wanted to hold onto it longer."

"I want the same, but I think the Mother is showing us that we aren't able to hang onto her anymore, much like she showed Zephra that she couldn't hang onto you."

"That was the Mother, and not me?" Tan asked with a smile. "Now I have a different argument to make when she gets angry with how I ignore her."

Amia didn't move, and Tan didn't want to separate from her. He needed the closeness, needed the time with her. It had been so infrequent these days. Even connected as they were, there was a distance that had grown, but maybe it was one that *he* had allowed to grow. Had he only been less focused on chasing Marin and more focused on maintaining his connections, he might have been able to avoid it.

"What now?" Amia asked. "Now that you've changed these shapers, what will happen next?"

Tan closed his eyes, focusing on the bonds. They were there, so close that he could almost reach them, and he trailed his consciousness just over the top of that connection, wanting to listen to the bonds but not wanting to intervene and disrupt the growing connections the shapers were making.

"I don't know what will happen next. It felt like something that needed to be done."

"Then it needed to be done," Amia agreed.

"We have to find where Marin is hiding and what she has planned. She still wants to release Voidan, and has grown enough in power that she might be able to do it, but so far, I've only managed to come across her a few times. Mostly it's her disciples."

"If only there was a way to draw her out," Amia said.

Could there be?

The disciples had come here, as if they had known what Tan planned. He didn't know *how* they would have known, only that Marin must have been able to determine it through her connection to spirit. Did that mean she had some insight as to what he did? Had she been granted a connection to the bonds by what he had done?

If she had, did it matter?

Tan had sealed the element bonds with spirit, protecting them. If one of her dark disciples—or even Marin herself—attempted to reach the bond, they wouldn't be able to taint it, would they?

What he needed was something that would interest Marin.

What would that be?

He thought he knew. Anything that risked drawing out the darkness, or that would allow her to draw out the darkness, would appeal to her. She hadn't attacked the bindings he'd replaced in Norilan. So far, she'd focused on the places of convergence, as if undermining them would undermine the entire suppression of Voidan. And she had sent disciples here when he'd been trying to connect shapers to the bonds, though she must have known that he would succeed—and that her disciples would fail.

Had he made a mistake?

Tan had made plenty, but had he been mistaken in not protecting Norilan more than he had? Or had Marin only been testing him, determining whether he could discover what she attempted?

He didn't have answers and hadn't been able to get them from the shapers they had captured, but he hadn't subjected them to a weapon he doubted Marin even knew about.

It was time. They would get answers, and he would learn what Marin planned.

"You've made a decision," Amia noted. "Why do I get the sense that it troubles you?"

Tan sighed and looked toward his daughter. "Because even though I know what the Mother seems to be telling me, it means bringing her more deeply into this than I want."

QUESTIONING THE DISCIPLE

T he lower chamber within the tower of Par had a dank odor, one that spoke of the power of water and earth mingling here. Heat hung on the air, as did a slight flickering of wind, all shaped. This was a place of power, a place Tan had created to prevent the captured disciples from escaping, protected by elements and the elementals that the shapers would not be able to reach.

Tan walked through the invisible barrier without lowering it, Alanna clinging to him. She had been silent on the return to Par and had not questioned him when he told her what he needed.

They had gone to three different enclosures without answers. None of the shapers would answer, and when Alanna had used her ability with spirit on them, she had not discovered anything, either. Now they were at the one disciple who had challenged him while facing them in Vatten, and Tan didn't think he would get anywhere with her either, but he had to try. They needed answers, even if he was no longer certain what they might be.

Elanne had come with him. Tan could feel her within the wind bond, a soft whispering within his mind. She had embraced the connection quickly, understanding exactly what it was and what it meant for her. The connection gave him a surprising benefit, one that he had realized extended to all who joined the bond.

Careful, Maelen. I know this one from when she served the Mistress of Souls. She was hard even then, Elanne told him.

He nodded. These were spirit shapers. That was why Marin preferred them. With spirit, even Tan would not be able to reach beyond their defenses, not without dipping heavily into the spirit bond to draw out the answers. He had a growing sense that Alanna would not have such limitations.

One of the disciples, a dark-haired young woman, watched his approach with a dark smile on her face. She crouched on the ground, his earth shaping holding her. Though he had cast out the darkness from her, that hadn't changed her attitude. In fact, it might have strengthened it, making her opposition to him even bolder.

"Maelen. You come before me with a child? I knew you to be arrogant, but I thought even you had limits to your arrogance," she said.

"Do you think I should fear you would harm this child?" Tan asked.

"You would deny that she's yours?" the disciple asked.

Tan looked at Alanna, a smile coming to his face as he noted her soft cheeks and the deep blue eyes that reminded him of Amia. "I would never deny that." He looked up. "But do you really believe that I cannot hold you confined with element power?"

The woman stood. Then she took a step.

Had he misjudged her ability?

She smiled and tapped her hand on her leg. Darkness swirled around her.

No, he hadn't misjudged her ability, only neglected to account for the fact that she could somehow summon the darkness, much like the shapers of Chenir could summon the elementals. He had seen her do it and thought that he had her confined so she couldn't recreate the summons, but somehow she had still managed.

Tan didn't bother stopping her.

It was a risk, but the disciple needed to understand that she would fail.

Maelen?

We are fine, Elanne. I won't let her harm you.

I'm not worried about me. I'm worried about that little girl of yours.

Tan sniffed, sensing the way Alanna had already started drawing on a steady spirit shaping. She allowed him to know how she created it, and he knew it would be a powerful shaping, one that he probably would not have been able to counter.

I would worry about what Alanna intends to do to her.

"Your powers aren't limitless, Maelen," the disciple said, oblivious to Tan's conversation with Elanne and with the shaping Alanna built. "There are powers that are beyond you, powers that you fail to recognize."

"I recognize those powers," he said.

She took another step toward him. With each step, he noted a rhythm to the way she moved, and the tapping on her leg increased. Tan could almost make out the pattern before deciding that he didn't *want* to make it out. Doing so risked understanding the darkness, but more than that, it risked him opening himself up to it.

"No. You only think you understand. Tenebeth is greater than all of us. The mistress has shown this truth to me, as she would show it to you were you willing. Once you touch this power, you will see how powerful you could be. You could remake the world—"

"Not remake. Destroy," Tan said. She hesitated, watching him. "The power of the Great Mother allows you to remake, were you to want to, but that's not what you want at all. That's not what any of you want. You think only to destroy."

The disciple smiled. "I am surprised, Maelen. You are more small-minded than I would have expected. I thought that one such as you would see the appeal of Tenebeth."

"One such as me?" he asked.

She cocked her head to the side. "You've taken power wherever you've gone. Don't deny it. We've seen what you did in the kingdoms, and then in the Sunlands, and now in Par. You pretend you do it for noble reasons, but you want power and to inflict your vision of the way the world should work."

"Not my vision. The Mother's."

"And who is to say that she is right?"

The disciple brought her hands together, and darkness surged between them.

Tan felt it flow around him, a power that he did not understand.

He shaped, pressing back with each of the elements, drawing

through the bonds to protect himself, Alanna, and Elanne, and pushed back.

The darkness continued to press, now collapsing around him.

Had he made a mistake?

He had thought that he would bring Alanna here, and could use her to help him understand what Marin intended when she attacked, but he began to wonder if that had been an error. As he tapped into the spirit bond, pressing back against the shadows, he felt a surge of power, but it was the power of the darkness, and a power that his connection to spirit failed to stop.

Reaching into the spirit bond, Tan discovered he was not there alone.

The sense of Alanna filled it.

She wriggled free of his arms.

Light and warmth burned from her, exploding from her, dispersing the darkness.

The disciple stood frozen, the movement she attempted to make, the summons she attempted, stuck in place.

You will speak for me, Maelen?

You can't speak for yourself?

There are limitations to my body. Perhaps one day, she said, though there was something in the way she said it that made him wonder.

I will speak for you.

The message flooded into him and Tan almost staggered back under the weight of it.

Are you certain this is what you want to convey?

This is what you must tell her, Maelen.

Tan stared at the disciple, still not certain that he should say what Alanna wanted him to say, but he couldn't deny that she was the one more powerful with spirit. She was connected to the Mother in ways that he was not. If this was what the Mother wanted...

"You are mistaken in thinking Voidan can bring the power you seek. There is only one power, and that comes through understanding," he said. "Believing there is an easier way will only lead to failure. Believing you have control will only lead to destruction. You will be granted this opportunity to disperse the darkness, but it will be your last."

Only her mouth moved. "Release me."

Tan shook his head.

"You will not be able to hold me indefinitely. I have proven that I can escape from your torture once before, and I will do so again. And now I know your daughter has power. She will be brought to the mistress and shown the power of—"

Alanna didn't allow her to finish.

Light surged from her, arcing across the distance between them. Where it connected with the disciple, there came a flash of greenish darkness before it burned away, leaving a brilliant white light, bright as the sun. It continued to burn, forcing Tan to look away, spirit surging brighter than any shaping he could manage.

Then it faded.

Tan looked over to the disciple and saw that she was gone.

"What did you do?" Elanne asked

She is returned to the Mother. She will be shown the power she seeks then.

Alanna—is that what the Mother wants of you? You are to destroy?

His daughter turned to him and looked at him with her knowing eyes. *Do you believe that death is destruction, Maelen, or is it only a continuation of life? Have you not seen how your bonded are returned to you?*

People are not elementals.

What are people but fragments of spirit, all parts of the Mother?

Tan blinked. *Even those with no abilities?*

All is life. All come from the Mother, Maelen.

I needed her so we could know what Marin planned. With her gone—

There are other ways to determine what she planned. Her physical form might be gone, but as I said, she has returned to the Mother.

Won't her darkness taint the Mother? Doesn't her presence there disturb what the Mother is?

Can you be cold beneath the sun?

What does that have to do with anything?

Can you be thirsty standing in a river?

You're saying the power of the Mother overwhelms everything else she might have attempted.

Now you understand, Maelen.

And there's some way for us to reach that power?

As you have learned, there is no destruction, only change. She exists with the Mother, much as everyone who came before exists with the Mother.

Can I reach it through the connection to spirit?

It is possible that you could, Maelen, but finding it would be like searching for a grain of sand in a desert. You would need guidance.

You?

I have the Mother for guidance.

What did she know? Tan asked.

He wasn't sure what to expect, but a series of images came to him. Some he recognized—like the building darkness in the place of convergence near Xsa and where he'd stopped the disciples while facing them in Vatten—but there were others he didn't recognize. Flashes of mountains he at first thought indicated the mountains near Galen where he had summoned the shapers, but were not. There were massive crashing waves, slamming into shores he had never seen. Dry and arid air, that of a desert of flowing sand, nothing like he would find in Incendin.

Where is that? he asked.

I can show you what she knew, but nothing more than that, Alanna answered.

She smiled at him and plopped onto the ground and curled up, falling quickly asleep.

Tan stared at her, at first surprised that she would be able to sleep here before realizing that she must be as exhausted as he usually got after shaping spirit and connecting to the spirit bond. In that way, maybe they weren't so different.

"What was this, Maelen?" Elanne asked, making her way over to him. "What happened here?"

Tan had forgotten that she was here. She'd been so silent during the attack of darkness, and then had remained quiet while he had been speaking to Alanna, that he had not remembered her presence. Tan scooped Alanna off the ground and held her against his chest. She writhed a moment and he realized that it wasn't her at all but the elemental she had bonded slithering around her. It felt strange holding her like this.

"Where did she go?"

198

"She's gone," Tan said. "The Voice of the Mother claimed her."

"The Voice? That's your daughter, Maelen!"

Tan looked down to Alanna and brushed her blond hair back from her head. She snuggled up against him and for that moment, he could imagine her being the little girl she was supposed to be. "She's my daughter, and she's so much more."

"What of discovering what Marin intends? How can we do that if the Hand destroys those who might know anything?"

"She didn't destroy. I don't think she would be allowed to destroy," Tan said. "And she was able to give us the insight about where Marin has gone."

"Where is it?"

"I don't know," he answered. "She showed it to me in visions, so I don't know where it is. But we will find it."

Elanne sighed. "You intend to visit the others as well?"

There were several other disciples remaining, but what would it serve to continue bringing Alanna in front of them? Elanne was right—if Alanna *did* wake to help, would she only bring them back to the Mother, essentially killing them, regardless of what she claimed?

"No. I think it's time for her to rest. I have another place I need to visit."

"Will you need my help, Maelen?"

He smiled at her and shook his head. "This is one I must do myself."

THE MISTRESS'S PLAN

Wind whipped around him, cold and biting, with a hint of snow and ice from the north. Tan stood on a shaping of wind and earth, studying the bindings that held back the darkness within Norilan. He had come with Alanna, knowing that her connection to spirit—if she *were* the Voice of the Mother—would grant a greater understanding of what they were to do. When she'd fallen asleep, he had intended to leave her behind, but Alanna had woken before his departure, almost as if knowing his intent.

He still didn't know what to make of what she'd done to the disciple. Amia hadn't either. Perhaps traveling together would help him begin to understand better.

Tan feared that the binding had been released, but the binding remained as stout as it had been when he first placed it. Perhaps even stronger, as several of the Order had come and continued placing bindings around it, holding the seal in place.

Marin had attacked here once, but he didn't think she would be able to attack again. There had been too much strength placed here, enough that she would not be able to destroy it without a significant battle. Even the elementals within this land assisted, helping to hold the binding in place, something that they didn't do in the other places of convergence. Then again, the elementals of this land had suffered in a different way than those elementals had, struggling with the forced connection to the land that the others—save for those in Galen that Tan had first freed—did not have.

The wind shifted, blowing warm for a moment. Tan looked over to see Honl appear. His weathered features were more drawn than before, as if he really had suffered under the weight of some great worry. The hair that he now created was a more uniform gray, and hung wavy and long down to his shoulders. Somehow, he even made it appear to flutter in the breeze, matching the long gray cloak he wore.

"You should not have come here alone, Maelen," Honl said.

"This place is as safe as any, I think." He glanced to Alanna, who seemed to be playing near the rocks. Now that he understood what she had become, he doubted that she actually played. She sat quietly, as if she simply surveyed the land around her.

"You didn't know."

"No. But I thought I should determine whether there was anything she could do to free him from here."

Honl floated around. That wasn't quite right, Tan realized. He appeared to walk, actually touching the rock, his boots crunching with each step. Why would he choose to make the illusion so complete?

"You have sealed this place well. It holds," Honl said.

"It holds," Tan agreed.

"Why have you returned to these lands?" Honl asked. "Have you not gained what you needed here? What more do you want?"

Tan looked around. As much as he would like to press the sense of Voidan back and complete the seal, he could not do that himself. He became less and less certain that he was intended to do that himself. The bindings that had restrained Voidan had been placed long ago, and though stout and even though they had held for all that time, they still failed eventually. Would anything he could place do any better?

"Understanding, I think," Tan said. He looked up at Honl, thinking back to the book the Order possessed. "You came through here more than once, didn't you?"

"The barrier made it difficult."

"You passed through it. When you returned to help me face the darkness and rescue Amia the first time, you had already found the Order."

Honl looked away, the embarrassment on his face almost human. "I had discovered them. I still wasn't certain what to make of them. They were... destructive. They had a secret, and I was determined to know what it was before I shared with you. With the barrier in place, I didn't think there was any harm in waiting."

"Until you were captured."

"Until then," Honl said softly.

"You found their prophecy?" Tan asked.

"Is that what they would call it?"

"A foretelling. Prophecy. Tobin has used both terms during

my talks with him."

"A glimpse of the Mother would be more fitting, Maelen. You have had a similar glimpse."

"I wasn't focused on seeing what would be."

Honl smiled at him, wrinkles forming at the corners of his eyes. "It's not as simple as that, Maelen. There is nothing quite as certain as what will or will not be, only what could be. That is what the ancient order mistook. They saw a Shaper of Light and claimed a prophecy of one, which led to the Utu Tonah and suffering of a people."

"As well as to the Mistress of Dark. They are related," Tan said.

"They are, and more than the Order would recognize. I suspect those who *were* able to reach the Mother did not know what it was, and did not know how to handle what they were seeing. Their minds processed it as a certainty."

"What if my mind also couldn't handle it?" Tan asked.

Honl smiled again. "You have been trained over the years, prepared to handle your exposure to the Mother. Do you think that she would have shown you what she has without your being ready?"

"I don't think I can be ready for what she has shown me. Can anyone?"

"You mean can your daughter."

Tan swallowed and nodded as he looked back at her. She had moved farther away from him, but he could still feel her in the bond. "I changed Alanna. Stepping into the pool of spirit—"

"Is that when you think you changed her, Maelen?"

Tan frowned. "That wasn't it?"

Honl shook his head. "She has been connected to the Mother

since before birth."

With a terrifying understanding, Tan knew what Honl meant.

Amia's attack.

Alanna had been shaped with spirit, and connected to spirit, long before she had been born, before he had even known Amia was pregnant. In order to save her from the darkness, in order to protect her before he had understood what they were facing, Tan had connected to spirit, and had bound that to her.

He had changed his daughter, but not when he had thought.

She would have been conceived by then, but might not have been anything more than a tiny glimmer of life, nothing more than a spark.

"You must accept change the same as the rest of us, Maelen," Honl said gently.

"I thought that I was. I thought..." What had he thought? That he could bring change to others and not have the same occur to him? His actions influenced everything around him, including his family. And now he couldn't even object to what had happened. Without Alanna and her connection to the Mother, he wasn't certain they would have survived the last attack from the disciples. He was beginning to think they wouldn't survive Marin without her.

"I don't know that I can suppress Tenebeth, Honl," he said.

"Is that what you intend to do?"

"Isn't that what I'm supposed to do?"

His bonded elemental shook his head, wind playing through his hair, blowing it back from his neck. He took a step toward Tan, boots crunching again, the only other sound. "I can't say I know what you're supposed to do. Only you can know that."

"The prophesy—"

"Means nothing, really. It was one possibility among many."

"But I am the Shaper of Light."

Honl nodded. "That much has come true."

"Then the others might be equally true."

"Or they might be equally wrong. You will do what you need, Tan. You always have."

Tan hesitated. "Tan this time, not Maelen?"

"You were Tan first. I think this more… intimate."

Tan took a deep breath. "You're nearly human now, aren't you?"

Honl frowned. "Not human, but not elemental. Parts of both, I think. Interesting that spirt would change me in this way."

"Amia claims humans all have a spark of spirit and that they all are connected to the Mother."

"Perhaps," Honl agreed.

"You don't think so?"

"I am still searching for understanding. As I begin to think I understand, something else changes and I realize that I do not know what I thought I knew."

Tan looked at the remnants of the city and the tower that had been built to confine Tenebeth. Through the bindings, the edges of it appeared blurred, as if it were not real. Tan could feel it through his connection to earth, but it was a vague sense, one that he wasn't certain he really detected. Passing through the binding proved difficult, and he didn't dare risk it. Were there any way to convert the barrier he'd created and use the tower as the ancient shapers had intended, tying it to the place of convergence, he would do so. It had to be a stronger seal than what they had created.

Or did it?

Marin didn't attack here, though she had attacked in other places.

Was that because the bindings were stronger here? Or did the fact that they were newer matter?

Maybe the answer wasn't finding a way to finish the work of those ancient shapers, but to attempt something new and different. And then he would have to create a record of it for the generations to follow. That was the failing this time. None other than the Order had known to fear Tenebeth, and by the time they had learned, it had almost been too late.

Tan shaped a connection to the binding, feeling the power residing within it. The power pushed against him, forcing him back, just as he suspected it would force the darkness back on the other side. It would be so much easier if there could be some sort of natural balance, one where there didn't have to be a separation, but that risked allowing Voidan too much power over the world. He'd seen what had happened when Marin and her disciples allowed themselves to be corrupted. What would happen if others allowed the same? How much would the world suffer then?

"I think," Tan began, "that we need to reconsider how we hold him in check."

"You can never expect to truly hold the darkness in check, Maelen. Whatever you think you can do, others before you have tried. How many cycles do you think this has occurred?"

"How many times has Voidan been freed?"

"More than I know," Honl answered. "When I was better connected to the bond, I think I understood, but that connection has faded somewhat. I still can reach the bond, but the connec-

tion, that power that I once was a part of is… lessened somewhat." He scanned the area around him and smiled. "Yet I feel
as if I have gained something as well. Losing my connection to
the bond has given me an understanding of the life you live. I
think that has been a reasonable exchange."

Tan sighed. If Voidan had been freed many times before,
what hope did he have to fully contain him? The ancient shapers
had been powerful, and many seemed as if they had a greater
knowledge than he possessed. More than that, there were
simply *more* shapers, some so talented that they had understood
how to create things like the artifact, or how to move the places
of convergence. What hope did *he* have of succeeding when they
had failed?

And not only once, they had failed more than once. There
was evidence of the bindings and of the places of convergence,
but if there had been more than the single failing, that meant
that the darkness had been suppressed more than once.

How?

And where was the evidence of it?

Time might have taken it away, or it might be that what Tan
thought was a single attempt to confine Tenebeth had been more
than that. If the tower in Par had been part of more than one
attempt to trap it, would he even know? What of the kingdoms
and what he'd seen in Ethea? Would Tan know if there was
something there?

Probably not. There had been so many changes over the
years, shapings that had been added and modified in ways that
he probably *wouldn't* know, as they were layered atop each
other.

Yet… if he could understand what had been attempted, if he

could learn how they had secured Voidan in those previous attempts, he might be able to find a different way, one that might trap him more effectively.

"Honl, can you help me find—"

Tan didn't have a chance to finish. Standing on the plains of Norilan, with the barrier he'd created to contain the darkness so near to him, he felt pressure build against him.

Not from the other side of the barrier, though he hoped he would detect that if it occurred. This came from somewhere else in Norilan, near enough for him to detect the way it pressed upon him.

Maelen!

It was a cry for help from Alanna.

Tan exploded into the air and surveyed the land, but saw nothing.

Where was she? Where had his daughter gone?

When he'd detected her last, she'd been wandering through the city, riding along one of the elementals found within Norilan. With his connection to her, he should be able to find her easily, but he couldn't detect her as he thought he should be able to.

Alanna?

The Mistress. She is here.

Tan unsheathed his sword and sent spirit flowing through it.

Next to him, Honl hovered. Tan noted how substantial he appeared, even now and in this form. "What is it, Maelen?"

"She's here," he said to Honl.

"Where? I do not sense anything."

Neither did Tan, which troubled him. Shouldn't he be able to detect something?

Alanna?

When she didn't answer, his heart fluttered.

Alanna? Help me find you.

There was no answer.

Tan raced higher into the sky and called to Wasina as he did. She had been circling, but with his summons, she shot toward him, flapping her wings in the incredibly precise way that she had.

She was here, Wasina. Help me.

I detect nothing.

Tan closed his eyes, focusing on spirit and on the spirit bond. He should be able to reach Alanna through the bond, at least to know whether she was harmed, but he didn't even detect her within it.

Help me.

Tan sent the request to all the elementals in Norilan. Most were elementals he had freed, and he hoped they would be able to help him identify what had happened to Alanna. Had he made a mistake not remaining with her? With the maturity she'd demonstrated, it was easy to get lost in the idea that she would be fine on her own, but she *was* still a child in physical form. It wouldn't take nearly as much to overwhelm her as it would him.

The elementals had no answer for him.

His connection to spirit gave him nothing.

Panic surged through him as he lowered himself back to the ground.

He'd lost his daughter. He'd lost the Voice of the Mother. And the worst part was he had no idea how it had happened.

20

A DAUGHTER, LOST

A mia reached Tan quickly even though she was riding atop Asgar. The draasin was flying as fast as Tan had ever experienced. He streaked toward the draasin, the sense of the fire elemental drawing closer so fast that Asgar practically seemed to be shaped. He landed in a flurry of wind and a flap of his massive wings, steam rising off his body.

Amia jumped down and ran to Tan. "Where is she?"

"I don't know what happened. We were here... and then she was gone."

"You weren't attacked?" Amia asked.

"There was no sense of attack," he said. "I detected a hint of darkness and knew that Marin must be here, but I never saw her. The sense happened so fast that I could almost have imagined it. How could she have gained such power? It was more than she'd possessed the last time I faced her."

Amia's eyes were closed and she rocked in place. Power

from a spirit shaping surged from her, radiating away. She didn't need the connection to the spirit bond to use it to detect their daughter. Her technique was more refined, tied to the ways the Aeta had long remained connected.

"She's gone," she said, opening her eyes. "I don't even detect her anymore. How is it possible?"

Tan could only shake his head. He had no idea how it had happened, had no idea how Marin would have been able to sneak in without him knowing. And he had thought she hadn't attacked Norilan. She did—only she did it in a way that he would never have expected.

"She should be connected to spirit," Amia said. "I should be able to feel *something*, but it's as if she is not there."

"Darkness shields the light," Honl said.

"That should not be possible with her," Amia said.

His eyes wrinkled and he shook his head. "It should not. It means the mistress has grown stronger than before."

"She was already stronger than before," Tan said. "When I faced her the last time, I barely survived. Even her disciples have become incredibly strong."

"That should not be possible unless she has freed even more of Voidan than we know," Honl said. "The bindings should hold him."

"What if there are bindings we don't understand?" Tan asked.

"There are only the three. That is all I have discovered. They were meant to connect, but they hold even without that connection."

Tan remembered how they were supposed to connect. When he'd been in the Temple of Alast, he had seen how they were supposed to combine, to use spirit together, flowing from one place to the other on a shaping more complex than those he'd seen from the Order. He had felt how that would have been effective, and how if it had taken hold, it would have bound the darkness.

"There has to be another," Tan said.

"There are not," Honl said. "Even the records here only speak of three."

"You told me that there have been cycles. If there *have* been cycles, it means the darkness has escaped more than once, and it means that it has been suppressed more than once. What if one of those other seals failed?"

Honl started away from him, crossing his arms over his chest. The sound of his boots crunching off the rock seemed louder than it should. "It is possible, but I have gone through every known record," he said. He scratched his chin, staring at the barrier that prevented Voidan from escaping in Norilan. "There is nothing other than these three."

"Which means there are records we haven't discovered," Tan said. "Were Alanna here, she would be able to help me find it."

"She is not, Maelen," Honl said softly.

"She is not, but there is a place where I might be able to help me find what we need."

21

RETURN TO THE POOL

T he return to the Sacred Pool came on a shaping rather than with the draasin. Tan needed to travel quickly, and he didn't worry about weakness or fatigue. Every moment that he delayed finding Alanna meant something worse could be happening to her.

As much as he hated to admit it, of greater concern was what they might be able to learn from Alanna and how Marin might be able to use—and abuse—Alanna's connection to spirit. If that were to happen, Tan wondered if he would be strong enough, if those he had brought to the element bonds would be strong enough.

Answers.

That was why he had come. Amia had insisted on coming with him this time, knowing what he intended. It was only fitting that she would.

They reached the cavern floor and Tan veered away from the

city, avoiding Tobin and the others of the Order. He would visit with them when he had found his daughter. He could take that time and see if he could convince them to work with the shapers of Par and Ethea, especially now that some of them had willingly responded to his summons.

Neither of them spoke. They didn't need to. Both of them were focused on what it would take to find Alanna.

Even Light, wrapped around his neck as she so often was, sensed his unease, though he didn't know if that was more because she recognized how he felt or if she shared it. The elementals worried about Alanna's safety, but they did so for different reasons.

When they reached the entrance to the cavern, Tan hurried inside, shaping a soft glow that hovered in front of them to light his way. He doubted that he would need it, but Amia would. At the archway that would bring them back into the Cavern of the Elements and to the Sacred Pool, he hesitated.

You must continue, Maelen, Light urged.

I know.

The longer she is gone, the greater the risk the Mistress will—

Will what? he asked, looking down at the lizard. *That she will corrupt her and use that power to free Tenebeth?*

She does not seek to corrupt, Maelen. Your child is the Voice of the Mother. There is no corruption possible.

Then why did she take her?

She seeks to destroy, Maelen. That is what she is after. If she can destroy the Voice, there will be less to oppose her when she continues with her plan.

Tan took a deep breath, pushing down the anger that rose into him each time he thought about what Marin intended. First she had taken his wife, and now she took his daughter. It would end. All of it would end.

He ducked into the chamber.

A quick glance showed him that shapers had been here since his last visit. Tan wasn't surprised. Revealing the secret to growing the garden had seemed the most exciting part of the visit for Tobin. Tan wondered why before remembering that ancient shapers of the order had done something similar, almost as if they did it as a way of leaving something of themselves upon the world.

"Beautiful," Amia whispered.

Tan pointed to the sapling that he had started. "That one was mine."

"An oak tree. Fitting for you."

"They're common in Nor. It felt right."

"And they're stout and sturdy. Like you."

Tan nodded to her and continued deeper into the cavern. As he passed the water and the desert, Amia whistled softly to herself. Then they reached the stones overlooking the pool of spirit.

Two shapers stood on the stones. Both were wrapped in shapings of what appeared to be spirit, but connected in ways Tan had not experienced before. They wore dark maroon robes that were nearly black, reminding him of the clothing the lisincend once had worn.

"You may not enter," the nearest said. He had a shaved head and sun-darkened skin.

"Are you with the Order?" Amia asked.

The other shaper stepped forward. She had jet black hair that barely moved as she walked. Her robe shifted slightly, but it seemed *wrong*. "This way is forbidden," she said. Even her words were accented strangely.

Tan glanced at Amia. *They are not from the Order,* he said.

They are not human, Light added.

Tan blinked. *What are they? Elementals?*

Not elementals, at least not yet. They are... constructs. Like the beginning of elementals. They should not be here.

Why should they not be here?

They are not from the Mother.

Light leapt from his shoulders and scrambled up the rock.

As she did, the nearest shaper—or whatever he was—pointed at Light. A streamer of color burst from the tip of his finger and struck the lizard, holding him in place. The other shaper approached and crouched next to him. For a moment, Tan noted a surge of blackness behind her eyes, but then it was gone.

He unsheathed his sword, but he was too slow.

A dark shaping built from the female shaper and streaked toward Light.

It struck her in the side. A hole began forming, created out of the blackest night, oozing through her.

"No!" Tan shouted.

The shapers looked up at him and stood. "You should not be here," the man said again.

This time, he pointed his finger at Tan. When color spilled from it, a mixture of sickly green and red that swirled toward him, Tan was ready and sent a shaping of spirit through his sword that caught the color, where it disappeared in a burst.

Brightness exploded from Light and she slithered forward.

The female shaper reached toward her, grabbing at her tail.

Tan shaped spirit at her, striking the shaper in the arm, freeing Light. She disappeared over the edge of the rock. A soft splash told him that she'd reached the pool of spirit.

He had a moment of concern, worried that the darkness within her might taint the pool of spirit.

It will not, Maelen, Light sent.

At least he knew she was unharmed. The spirit pool would heal her. It had to.

"Tan!"

He jerked his attention around in time to see the two shapers directing their attention to Amia.

He brought his sword up, connecting with the surge of color coming from both. Where their strange shaping met his spirit shaping, there was a flash and then both dissipated.

Rather than pointing his sword at them and shaping, he slid forward on a connection of wind and earth, slashing at the nearest shaper. Where his sword connected with the man's arm, light trickled free. Tan swung again, spinning, and caught the man in the stomach.

He disappeared in a flash of light.

That left only the woman.

As Tan jumped toward her, he realized that she fought differently.

When he attempted to catch her on the arm, slicing as he did with the man, she jumped, making him miss. Tan stabbed and this time she *folded*, moving in ways that no person could move, but then, she was not a person. She was some sort of twisted elemental.

He hesitated. If they were elementals—and if they were twisted—he couldn't harm them. Had he already made a mistake fighting the one? He was meant to help the elementals, not destroy them.

Not an elemental, Amia sent. *That's what I've been trying to understand. These are physical creations out of darkness.*

Marin is creating her own elementals? How? Marin had been a powerful shaper, but this was an order of magnitude more. What had changed with her to allow this? What had she discovered?

Something like it. This would be no different than fighting Marin or her disciples.

It might not seem like it, but it was. At least with them, he had known how to fight them. Spirit worked against them, and he could touch them with his sword. Their bodies didn't contort in ways that bodies should not. Facing this, he would have to attempt a different approach.

Spirit.

It was the only thing that he'd found that was effective against the darkness. As often as he had faced the dark, it had remained effective. That would be how he would hold her.

Not him. Amia.

Shape her, he sent.

Amia nodded her understanding. Tan shaped with spirit, sending it through his sword, drawing her attention. As he attacked, she folded again, bending out of the way. This time, she bent into Amia's shaping.

She spun toward Amia, but Amia held her with a powerful band of spirit, wrapping it around the dark woman from her head to her feet.

Tan sliced through the shaping and struck her with the sword, driving it through the spot her heart should have been.

The woman disappeared in a flash of color.

Tan sighed. "How was that possible?" he asked. "Voidan doesn't create. It destroys."

"I don't know," Amia answered. Her eyes narrowed in a troubled expression. "But you're right. That shouldn't have been possible." She looked at the rock. "What happened to Light?"

Tan jumped to the top of the rock in time to see Light slithering free from the pool below. Was it his imagination, or was the pool not as deep as it had been?

Maelen, they siphoned off spirit to mix with the darkness. This gave them form. There will be others.

Others?

Tan barely had time to question.

There was a sense of darkness mixed with something familiar—spirit, he decided—that suddenly surged around him. Now five wispy forms appeared, each in the shape of a man or a woman. He wondered why those shapes, and what they meant, but would have to question it later, if he survived.

They pulled on power—were consumed by power—and Tan questioned whether he would be able to defeat them the way he had defeated the other two. Amia could shape, and she could draw upon enough spirit to hold one or maybe even two of them, but all five? That would be too much.

Darkness reached toward them in strands so thick that Tan could think of only one way to protect them. He grabbed Amia's hand and jumped.

They plunged into the pool of spirit.

The last time he'd been here—and when he'd had gone in before—he had taken the time to remove his clothing. In a flash, it disappeared, only his sword remaining.

Light jumped in, joining them.

As Tan and Amia sank, they held hands. Power surged around them.

Tan felt filled by the connection to spirit, filled by the power that was all around him. All he had to do was reach for it... and he was not alone.

Amia was there, shaping with him, drawing more than he could draw on his own. They were filled by spirit. Tan had an awareness of everything around him and he drew upon it, casting away the power the five dark shapers used as they created their physical forms. Surrounded by the power of spirit as he was, he could feel it as they disappeared, no longer connected to this place, no longer real.

Tan sighed, letting the sense of spirit surround him.

Understanding flowed into him, and he noted the warmth and brightness of Amia next to him. They shaped together, the interconnectedness of it binding them, and he felt a certain relief. In that moment, he felt as if things *might* work out.

Where is Alanna?

He sent the question out to the brightness, to the source of spirit, knowing that in this place, all knowledge could be had.

Tan waited, expecting a voice, or a vision, but none came.

Where is the Voice of the Mother?

Through the bond he shared with Amia, he could feel her unease. He shared it.

There came no answer.

There was another question he needed to ask, but didn't *want* to ask. Only, it was one he needed to have answered. For him to be able to keep fighting, and for him to keep doing what must be done, he needed to know.

Does she still live?

This time, light surged around him. Within the light, there was awareness of those who had come before. Tan detected people he'd known and cared about—his father, Lacertin, other shapers who had fallen fighting with him—but there was no sense of Alanna.

She lived.

But the Mother shared with him something more alarming, and something that shook him: she didn't know how to find Alanna either.

Could Marin have discovered some way to obscure her from the Mother?

How could she hide from spirit? Tan hadn't realized that such a thing was even possible, but then Marin had attacked without him knowing, had grabbed him with his barely having a sense that she was there. There would have to be some way for her to do that.

If the Mother couldn't help him find her, was there another way?

How has Voidan been suppressed before?

There was emptiness for a moment, and then visions came to him of the Temple of Alast, of Par, and of Norilan. They faded, and were replaced with other images, a different set of three constructs, and a different set of bindings. In this vision, he saw draasin fighting alongside men, working together, dark shapers consumed by Tenebeth opposing them, and the brightness that glowed from the center, a creature that reminded him far too much of Light.

Nobelas.

The name filled him.

Light swirled around him. Her form shifted again as it had been the last time they had come to the pool of spirit.

You are nobelas?

I am spirit, Maelen. You have always known that. But if you were to have a name, those you refer to as the ancients knew my kind as nobelas.

Your kind?

There have always been nobelas. We appear when needed, when the darkness approaches. That is the only time we are needed.

You were the key to stopping Voidan before.

Once. There were others when nobelas was not needed, when it was the power of the shapers who managed to stop Voidan.

More visions came to him, one after another. In each of them, shapers—men and women so much like himself—fought against the darkness. There was one where the artifacts were created, used to seal the darkness. There was one where men were the seals, binding themselves to the earth, drawing upon the power of the shapers. There were others when the elementals formed the bond, creating it in a way that had required they willfully sacrifice themselves, letting themselves be destroyed to hold back the darkness.

They flickered through his mind.

When Honl had called it a cycle, he had been right. There were dozens of times that Voidan had been stopped, the cycle repeating. Each time, the world changed slightly, and each time the Mother had to rebuild, as if starting anew.

The visions stopped.

There was only a piece of land. Nothing else.

Beneath it, there was darkness.

Tan could *feel* it, almost as if he could feel a sense of cold, but he should not detect that here. There should be only warmth when this close to the Mother. There should be only the connection to spirit.

In that place, darkness bubbled up, much like spirit did here.

Tan thought he understood. That was a source of Tenebeth, much like this was a source of the Mother. Marin would be there.

It matched what he'd seen when facing Marin's disciple. If they had seen this, then he was even more certain this was the place he needed to go.

Where is it?

Another image came to him.

It took his breath away.

Tan had thought that the pool of Tenebeth would be in some distant and remote place, but that was not where he would find it at all. This was nearby—at least it would be when he was closer to Ethea, and near enough that he should have seen it before now.

Why hadn't he?

The only answer he could come up with was that the entire island had been masked from him. Maybe it had been masked from everyone, using the effect of the bindings, closing it off so that others couldn't—and wouldn't—reach it.

He needed landmarks so that he could find it, and the Mother provided them as well.

The Voice is in danger, Maelen. You must hurry.

Tan didn't know whether this came from Light, from the pool of spirit, or from the Mother herself.

It didn't matter. All that mattered was reaching Alanna and stopping Marin.

22

UNDERSTANDING THE SEALS

"Why here, Tan?"

Honl walked across the narrow strip of land as it stretched out into the sea. On either side, waves crashed along the rock, sending spray into the air.

Tan turned to his bonded elemental. Maybe that wasn't the right way to describe him anymore. Honl might be bonded to him, but he was something other than an elemental. Tan no longer knew *quite* what that was, but maybe that didn't matter. Honl was Honl, and that was enough.

"We're here because of something I saw in the vision given to me by the Mother."

"I thought we needed to find the island."

He nodded. "We do, and I think I have an idea of *how* to find it, but there's something that's been troubling me over the last year."

"What is it?"

"Marin has been gaining in power and her strength has been increasing, this in spite of the seals we placed. I thought there were only three places where the bindings have held, but I think she's discovered others."

Honl was shaking his head, making him appear so human as he did. "There were no other bonds, Maelen. I studied the records the Order possessed. There's nothing there but the three, and the third they weren't able to secure."

"I don't think the third matters nearly as much as we think it does," he said.

"Why wouldn't it matter? The three bindings confine Voidan in place, holding him from this world."

"And they do, yet she has still grown stronger. How is that possible?"

A troubled expression crossed Honl's face before fading. "You think there were others."

"I know there were others. The Mother showed them to me. From what I saw, Voidan has been released countless times over the years. Each time, shapers have succeeded in suppressing it once more."

"Why should this be different?"

Tan shook his head. "I don't know why it should be, only that it is." The more he thought about it, the more certain he was that there was something different this time. Not only with Marin and the effort she had gone through to free Voidan, but in the power that he had been given. The flashes of memory the Mother had given him had shown him something else—that he was the first given the powers that he had been given. That meant something—if only he could understand what it was.

They reached a tall pillar of stone and on it, Tan noted the faded image of runes. They were faint and barely recognizable, but they were there.

And damaged.

Something had been done to this pillar. He had a flash of memory and recognized the pillar though he also knew he had never seen it before. The pillar was older than any other structure that he'd ever come across, but the damage to it was new.

A binding, and now broken.

Was this how Marin had grown more powerful?

Could she have found the other bindings and attacked them?

It was possible that she had. He didn't know how she would have learned of them—he only knew they existed because the Mother had shown them to him.

Had Voidan shown them to Marin?

It was possible that enough of Voidan had escaped that he had been able to guide her.

It would explain how she had gained so much strength over the last few months. These seals—seals that had been in place each other time Voidan had escaped—had been released.

They wouldn't be able to confine Voidan again without help.

Which meant they had to seal off all these other bindings.

If they didn't, then Voidan would continue to leak out, giving Marin or someone like her more power.

Maybe that was the issue that had happened in the past.

Could it really be that the new seals didn't completely confine Voidan?

Tan studied the pillar, realizing how the damage had occurred. With a shaping that required each of the element bonds mixed with spirit, he repaired it. The shaping drained him, but he quickly felt his strength return.

Even if he wanted help, others wouldn't be able to repair the previous seals. That was the reason the Mother had given him his ability, and the reason that she had shown him the seals that had been placed over the years.

He had to replace them.

"How many?" Honl asked.

Tan shook his head. "Too many."

"We could trap Voidan and rescue Alanna before we do this," Honl suggested.

"I don't think that's what I'm meant to do. I think the Mother intended for me to repair them now."

"What of Alanna?"

Tan swallowed. "I hope…"

Honl rested his hand on Tan's arm. "I hope as well. The Mother would not put you through this only to take her from you."

"I don't know that the Mother is the only one with power in this situation."

23

RESTORING THE SEALS

They reached three more seals, repairing them without any additional issues. Two were pillars, and Tan realized that they were partnered with the first pillar he had come across. Had the old shapers used trios of shapings much like they had used the last time? Was there something about three that gave power? It seemed to Tan that five would be more important, one for each element, but then those who had placed these seals had probably known nearly as much as him—possibly more. They were shapers of power. Shapers who had studied the elements for far longer than he had known them.

As they approached the next image that the Mother had given him—this one in a clearing near Chenir where a circle of boulders surrounded what looked like a small pond—Tan hesitated.

It wasn't a pond at all.

What they came across was a pool of the Mother.

Tan frowned. How would there be a pool of the Mother here? How would others not have known?

And, as he looked around the boulders, he decided it was possible that they had known. There were markings on the rock, and from the vague feeling Tan had as he neared, he realized the runes were intended to obscure this place, hide it from the outside world. Had Tan not had the image from the Mother, he would not have found it.

But now the runes hiding it were damaged, much like they had been in the other places they had come across.

Tan started shaping, drawing on the runes, adding the power of the elements, when he detected a building power. This was not the power of shaping as he knew it; this was the power that came from Voidan.

Tan looked up. Seven disciples appeared atop the rock. The grinned when they saw Tan, as if they had been waiting for him.

Not waiting for him. They had been trying to create the constructs of darkness.

Had they succeeded yet?

"Maelen." It was a petite woman with dark hair. Tan realized they all had dark hair, as if their connection to Voidan changed that about them. Even those with the pale complexions of someone who should not have such dark hair now did. "We have expected you."

"You think the seven of you can stop me?"

The woman grinned darkly. "Not stop. Delay."

Delay. That meant they wanted to give others a chance to destroy more of the seals. Or they hoped to create the darkness. Either way, he couldn't let them succeed.

Tan pulled on his connection to the bonds, to spirit, and repaired the runes.

Turning to the disciples, he sent spirit at them, directing it through his sword. Two fell quickly before they found a way to circle him. They used shapings of dark energy and surrounded him.

Tan pulled on spirit, sending it surging, exploding outward.

It wasn't enough. Their dark energy was too much.

Tan had another source; this close to the pool of spirit, he pulled on that power and sent it through his sword, through the disciples. As one, they froze.

Tan sent another shaping and this time, it knocked them all back.

He wrapped them in earth and used a quick shaping of spirit to remove any shaping that had been placed on them. Only two had any real shaping for him to counter. That troubled him.

"Maelen."

He turned to Honl, who stood near the pool of spirit.

Tan realized the pool had been drained.

Had he done that while trying to stop them? Could he have *spent* the source of spirit?

That left him with an uneasy sensation. If he could, and if the source of the Mother could be drained, then there was another reason for the disciples to test him like this. If they could force him to drain spirit, and if they could force him to expend energy like that, then they would weaken him.

As he stood there, he realized that the pool gradually filled once more.

Tan breathed out a sigh of relief.

"The Mother returns," Honl said softly.

"I thought that they—"

He hesitated.

One of the disciples laughed softly.

Tan turned and saw it was the lead woman. She watched Tan, her eyes dancing with a dark energy. Even as he had shaped her with spirit, freeing her from Voidan, she had summoned it back to her.

Would he be able to stop them for good?

In the past when he'd exiled Voidan, he had been able to keep it at bay. If they were able to be restored as quickly as this, did it mean that Voidan had grown in power?

"You know what it means, don't you, Maelen?" the woman asked.

She stood facing him, breaking free from his shaping of earth.

Tan wrapped her in another shaping of earth, this time adding wind and water.

She remained confined, but Tan could feel her resisting, could feel the way her resistance bulged against his shaping. Much longer and he wouldn't be able to hold her.

Hating what he had to do, he darted toward her, sword outstretched, and plunged it into her chest. As blood bloomed around the end of his blade, a wicked smile crossed her face.

Had he done what she wanted?

"Why?" Tan demanded, withdrawing his sword and slamming it into his sheath. "Why force this? What do you think you can accomplish?"

She laughed at him and met his eyes with defiance.

"Where is my daughter?"

"Maelen," Honl whispered.

When she didn't answer, Tan leaned into her. "Why?" he demanded again. He pressed with his sword. It felt *right* destroying the darkness—destroying her.

Her eyes glazed closed and she didn't answer.

"Where is Alanna?" he demanded.

Honl pulled him away. "You can't let Voidan destroy you."

"How?" Tan asked, turning away from the fallen disciple. His breaths came raggedly and the anger he felt still coursed through him. "How do I do that when they want only to destroy, and I'm forced to destroy to stop them?"

"There is but one way, Tan. You have to keep the light inside you when it is darkest."

"I don't know if I can," Tan said.

"You can. That's why the Mother chose you."

Tan swallowed. Chose. The Mother chose him, and his daughter was the Voice of the Mother. He needed to honor her, not do something that would shame her.

"Come, Honl. Let's repair the remaining seals. Then we will rescue my daughter."

24

TENEBETH

The air whipped below him as he circled on Wasina's back. Far below, Tan saw the distant form of the island. It was massive and scarred, the surface resembling what Marin had tried achieving when she'd attacked in Xsa and in Vatten. The blackened surface was barren, even the sense of earth absent from it. Surprisingly, he felt the way the sea attempted to avoid it, waves moving around it, as if to touch the land as little as possible. The wind avoided it as well, steering clear so that no elementals were placed in danger by the emptiness that would be found there.

That is where I must go, he told Wasina.

Not alone, Maelen. You cannot do this alone. You have done what is needed alone; now you can have help.

He had repaired all the seals alone, facing only a few more disciples, but he didn't think he could bring others with him either. It risked too much.

They will come to your aid regardless of whether you are willing to accept it, Wasina said.

She was probably right. Which made what he needed to do all that much harder.

If this fails, they will have to seal me to the island.

Maelen —

This is the source, Wasina. If I fail, and if I can't rescue Alanna, they will have to do it. He opened his mind—and his connections —up to his other bonds. Not only to those bonded to him, but to the elementals that were nearby. *The darkness cannot be allowed to escape. We have to do whatever it takes to suppress it.*

And we can't lose you, Maelen.

He realized something with her comment that he'd never comprehended before. The elementals feared for him the way that he feared for them. *You will not lose me. Haven't you and Asgar shown me that everything returns to the Mother?*

There are some things you cannot return from.

Tan swallowed. He was ready to die if needed to save his daughter. He would sacrifice himself to save his family and those he cared about. But he wanted to believe there was something else for him, that his death would mean something were he to make that sacrifice. Falling and not having anything after… there was a certain terror to that.

Then I will make certain I return.

Wasina circled, making her way back to the tower in Par where Amia waited. He could sense her within his mind and knew that she felt much of the same determination that he did.

When they landed atop the tower and he climbed down, she met him, her hands clasped behind her back. "Did you find it?"

Tan nodded. "It's where we were shown."

"What now?"

He could tell she asked in spite of knowing how he would answer. That was one of the downfalls of the connection they shared. There were no surprises, not when it came to what they shared between themselves.

"Now I intend to go get her."

"By yourself."

"I've already asked the draasin to seal off the island if I fail."

"And if they can't do that? If they won't?"

Tan looked over at Wasina. She watched him with her large golden eyes. He had only to touch upon the fire bond and he would know her thoughts. Even as he did, he still didn't know whether she would do as he asked. Would the other elementals?

There was another way he could see his request completed.

Tan focused on each of the element bonds. *Shapers. I call upon your help. I go to face Marin, the Mistress of the Dark. She has abducted my daughter and seeks to free the darkness. This cannot happen. If I fail in my task, I ask that you place this binding*—he sent an image of the binding that would seal not only him to the island, but Marin as well—*over this place. With enough of you, there should be no way that she can escape. Please help with this. Help the elementals. Help the Mother. Help me.*

All the potentially connected shapers would now know what he wanted of them. If the rescue were to fail, he would see to it that they assisted him and did what they could to prevent Marin from freeing Voidan.

"Tan," Amia said, taking his hand. "I heard what you sent, but you will not be going alone. I won't let you go alone." When he started to object, she stood on her toes and kissed him softly on the lips. "She is my daughter as well, and I am going with you. We're stronger together."

There was no use in objecting. Tan didn't even disagree with her. He was a powerful shaper and connected to the element bonds, but he was even stronger when connected to her. "I'm afraid," he said.

"So am I."

"Not for me. For her."

"So am I," Amia said again.

25

MAELEN'S CALL

They reached the island atop Wasina. As they did, Tan noted the building pressure of shaping, the soft sensation in his ears. It was rare he noticed it these days. When he'd first been learning of his ability, he had noticed the sense of pressure constantly, that of shapers working around him, especially when he'd studied in the university. These days, he no longer detected it in the same way, either because he had grown accustomed to shaping around him or because it was overwhelmed by the power he was able to draw. That he could feel it now made him wonder.

Scanning the area around the sea, he realized the reason.

Dozens of shapers had appeared.

Not dozens, hundreds. Power surged from them, many with more than he'd ever detected. Elementals joined him as well, circling around the island, creating something of a buffer, pushing back the sense of the darkness that he detected.

"They came for you," Amia said.

"I hope not."

"Why? You don't want the help?"

It wasn't about help, not for him. This was about not wanting his friends and the other shapers to risk themselves on his behalf. "I hope they came for the elementals, and because their connection through the bond told them they should."

Wasina caught a current of wind and circled, soaring above the ground. As she did, Tan looked at each of the people who had come to help, each one a shaper he shared some sort of connection with. There were those from the kingdoms—Ciara along with her bonded draasin Sashari, Ferran with the earth elemental he had connected to, Wallyn with water, even Seanan and the other shapers who had been at the university with him. He saw representatives from Doma—Elle and a trio of water shapers. Chenir used their strange summoning shaping, tapping a call to the elementals, one that reminded him so much of how the disciple had called on the darkness when she had been captured, using that to free herself from the shaping he'd used to trap her. Incendin and dozens of lisincend, along with Cora and her shapers. So many, more than he would have expected to answer his call, though why should he not have expected otherwise? They had come to help the elementals. Even from Par, he counted the shapers who joined him, Elanne and Maclin and Tolman and Reyelle. All of them came, joining him. There were students scattered among them as well, though Tan didn't know them as he did the other shapers. He could feel their connection to him and could feel the way they touched upon the bond.

"They might understand how the elementals need them, but

I think they came for you. You have saved them—all of them, Tan. That is your legacy."

There were elementals here as well, and not only the draasin. Wind and earth and water all joined with fire, the connection growing strong.

Maybe they had come for him. Would that be so bad?

If Marin succeeded—if Tan failed—then everyone would suffer. If the darkness were freed, if it were released upon the world, then everyone would suffer. What did it matter *why* they had come, only that they had. Perhaps that was the only thing that *did* matter.

She will fight what I do here, Tan started, sending it through the connection of each bond. *She will oppose this work. With your help, you can help contain her.*

What do you need from us?

The question came through the bond, though Tan didn't know who asked. It could have been any of them. Now that he'd connected the shapers to the element bonds, how would he know who he spoke to? And did it matter? They all wanted to help, and they all *could* help, if only he knew how.

The memories that he'd been given, gifted to him from his time wading into the pool of spirit, told him what had been tried before. There had been many attempts to stop the darkness, many times where it had been suppressed, only to get released once more. Tan wished there was some way to suppress it for good, for them not to have to fear its release again. That was the peace he wanted not only for himself, but for Alanna, and for those who would come after him. They deserved that peace.

The memories told him nothing about how to stop Voidan, only that it *had* been stopped in the past. There had been other shapers, and some with incredible skill, who had helped. He had detected those shapings when he had gone to the temple and when he had gone to the convergence in Par, and he had detected those shapings when he had been in Norilan, using his shaping to help bind the darkness.

In that way, with the memories and the remnants of shapings that had lingered across the land, he realized that these shapings were something like what Incendin used, the massive fire shaping that he had once been a part of. Each shaper had had added their voice to the seals over the years, giving them more and more strength, until now the seals were something else.

Much like with the fire shaping in Incendin, which Tan didn't think that he would be able to recreate, that even with the skills he possessed, he wouldn't have the time or patience to make what those shapers had done, he didn't think he would have the ability to do anything more than what the ancient shapers had accomplished when it came to the seals. So much had already been tried. He might be a different shaper, and he might be connected to the bonds, but he didn't necessarily know more than those shapers.

Tan realized that he would not be able to do anything more than those shapers either.

It had been arrogance for him to believe that he might be able to do anything more than suppress the darkness. Even the elementals had been trying to tell him that he would be able to suppress it, but nothing more than that. Why would he think that he *could* do anything more?

He'd been foolish, that was why. Overly confident in not only his ability, but in how he was different to the Mother. Wouldn't she have shown him a way to stop the darkness if that was the intent? It *wasn't* the intent. That was what he had to know.

He might not be able to defeat the darkness, but he could defeat Marin. He could keep her from hurting others. And he *could* rescue his daughter. Those were the things he would do.

Form this, he sent through the bonds.

Tan created the image of the bindings, only this time, he added a piece to it, one that hinted at the elementals and gave a hint of the power that his friends possessed. He wasn't certain whether the knowledge was his or borrowed from the Mother, only that it felt right.

Taking Amia's hand, he jumped from Wasina's back. *Be strong, friends.*

The draasin snorted, flames leaping across the sky. Water and wind splattered him. Deep below the water, the earth rumbled. And shapers pulled on the power they possessed.

Tan and Amia streaked toward the ground. This would be their fight, but they were not alone. Tan didn't think he'd ever been alone, not really, when facing off against the various forces he had opposed over the years. This felt different, though. There was a sense of finality to this, in that if he managed to succeed, they would finally be able to rest, and that those he cared about would know true peace. The world had changed and he had been the harbinger of it, guiding it, something that he felt a certain pride in.

He took a breath, and power filled him.

It felt willingly given, the elementals and the element bonds surging power through him. Tan leaned on the connections to the bonds, reaching through them, letting that awareness fill him. Power and light exploded from him, and through him, out of Amia.

They landed.

The ground here was hard and hurt even through his boots. With each step, he pressed shapings out, driving them through his boots, forming a binding with each step. Tan feared that if he didn't, he would be subjected to the pain of whatever strange darkness that Voidan wanted to push upon the world.

"It feels… like Norilan," Amia said. Her words were muted, almost hollow, as if the absence of shaping sucked everything from them. Likely it did, including the life from her.

"Norilan had a memory of what it had been," Tan said. "This is everything missing. This is more like what had happened in Chenir when they called the elementals away."

"There is still life here," Amia said. "They may have wanted to pull life away, but they can't do that, not when the Mother lives so strongly. Feel the earth. It's still there, beneath your feet. Without the wind, we wouldn't be able to speak. Water flows all around this place as well, another sign of life. And the sun burns overhead, fire if there was any."

Tan had to smile. Leave it to Amia to recognize the key when it was in front of him.

Marin might want to destroy everything, but doing so was impossible, especially while the Mother existed.

Tan continued pressing his shapings. With each step, he modified the ground, letting the bindings hold so that he could return some of the missing life. Elementals bubbled up as he did, coming through his connection and filling him even more. Tan called to them, asking for the elementals to join him, to return to this place, feeling that it was necessary to weaken Marin.

They walked, taking their time, remaining hand in hand. From above, Tan hadn't noticed whether there were any buildings and now that he was here, he suspected there would not be. Construction meant creation, and Marin was about destruction.

Where would he find her, though? She would have to be somewhere on the island, but it was a massive place, large enough that it would take him hours to walk around.

Maybe he didn't need to walk around it.

Hadn't he seen the key to the island when he'd been in the pool of spirit?

There was another source of power here, one that was similar to the Mother, only the opposite. Darkness lived here, bubbled up here, and was contained here. All he had to do to know where to find Marin was focus on where he detected the darkness.

It came to him like a wound. The darkness was a void on his senses, a pain that he wanted nothing more than to remove, to alleviate. He could feel the source of it and started toward it, dragging Amia with him. She came willingly, her face a flat mask, no emotions evident. He didn't need them to know how she suffered here. The simple fact of this place's existence bothered her.

Tan squeezed her hand.

"I am fine," she whispered.

"We can't be fine while we're here," he said.

"That's not it. It's Alanna. I don't know how she can hold out against the pain I feel here."

Tan smiled and patted her hand. "She is stronger than either of us in spirit. And I don't think she is alone. Her bonded would have come with her, connected to her."

Amia let out a breath and nodded. "You're right. She *is* stronger than us. That's why they want her. Why they think they'll be able to use her."

"I don't think there's anything Marin can do that will use Alanna, but I am concerned about what she intends for her. There has to be a reason, especially if *she* knows she can't use Alanna."

In the distance, Tan noted a gentle rise where a slow peak of black rock began to slope upward. With each step, it became harder to send a shaping through his boots, and harder to set the binding, as if the rock began to oppose him. As they neared, he understood why that was: they reached the source of the darkness itself.

Voidan was here.

When he was no longer able to take a step and set the binding, he shaped himself into the air. Glancing back, he noted a trail of bindings, the rim of protection growing smaller and smaller with each step, until those closest to him were barely larger than his footprint.

As they neared the top of the darkness, pressure built against him and he pushed back, drawing on spirit.

Shadows swirled around him.

They spilled upward from the ground, moving slowly but increasing in both speed and with how much thickness they possessed. There was power to them and he resisted, but there was only so much resistance he could manage. They pushed him back, upward, and away from the island.

If they succeeded in pushing him away, he would lose the chance to find his daughter.

That thought drove him.

Tan pressed, drawing on spirit, drawing on the element bonds, and drawing on the elementals still around him.

It wasn't enough.

He was pushed back, away from the island, and away from Alanna. What he knew wasn't enough to reach her.

26

SHAPERS OF SPIRIT

A s they hovered, Tan discovered a battle taking place. He hadn't heard anything and had seen no sign of it from below. It involved those who had come with him, and they fought disciples—but not *only* disciples.

Figures of blackness—those that could not be real—had taken shape and opposed the shapers. Had he missed other pools of the Mother? That had been the only place he'd seen them.

Those who had come with Tan pushed back, and they managed to fight with strength, but most were mere shapers, whereas these seemed to be creatures created out of the darkness itself. They were more tangible than the dark shapers he had faced near the pool of spirit, and in that way, they were both lessened—and something worse.

They need spirit, Tan said to Amia.

There are not that many who shape spirit, she reminded him.

There hadn't been, but was it something he could unlock? Could he change the shapers—change the warrior at least—so that they would be able to reach for spirit and so that they could oppose the darkness?

Even if he could, there wouldn't be time.

What he needed were spirit shapers, those who had knowledge and training… the kind that Tan had refused to work with.

Not the shapers of the Aeta. There were spirit sensers and there were the mothers among the Aeta, leading their people, who might be able to help, but there were others Tan had rejected.

And in that way, had he rejected someone able to help?

It was possible that he had.

Aeta. You are needed. Archivists. Serve the Mother.

Tan sent it as a shout through the spirit bond and called to the elementals remaining in the kingdoms for assistance. They could help, and they could bring the shapers to him, if they were willing to come. He didn't know if it was too late. Had he upset them too much by rejecting them? They had offered to help, had offered their knowledge, and he had continued to refuse. Had his arrogance created this?

Give them a chance, Amia suggested.

But she did more than that. He could tell that she sent something through the bond as well, a request, one that came from the First Mother, a call to those who could use spirit and would understand what she needed. It was possible that they would respond better to Amia than to him, and he would understand.

Tan unsheathed his sword and drew upon spirit. It flowed through him, through the sword, making the blade glow brightly. With a breath, he unleashed the shaping of spirit, sending it streaking toward the nearest shadow form. Where spirit struck, the shadows evaporated.

The shadows disappeared and he turned his attention to the next shadow form. This one joined with another, and the two of them took on the shape of a draasin, though a dark draasin, one that looked to be completely of blackness, like a draasin of night.

The creature opened its mouth and streamers of black came from it, writhing toward him. Tan withdrew and shaped spirit, barely managing to push it away. Where his shaping struck, the shadow folded but then returned. It was unfazed by his shaping.

Like this, Amia suggested.

She reached through the connection between them and took control.

Tan allowed her to handle the shaping, letting her direct what they did. Her shaping created a funnel of spirit, one that circled around the draasin. As it did, Amia began placing the binding.

The creature pressed out, using strength he suspected came from the source of Voidan, and almost overwhelmed her shaping. Tan added each of the other elements to it and began adding them to the binding before thinking otherwise.

Hold it a moment, he suggested to Amia.

She managed to maintain the shaping and he pressed, using the power of each of the element bonds to constrict the shadows, drawing it into a tight ball. It was much like what he'd done when he faced the strange black shadows near Xsa, when he and Elanne had faced Voidan there. As he did, the draasin deformed, taking on a smaller and smaller space until he placed the full effect of the seal, binding it tightly.

Shadows constricted down into near nothingness.

With a *pop*, the darkness disappeared.

Fatigue washed over him before fading, power pressing into him from the elementals, as if they knew he needed them to lend their strength so that they could succeed. They needed to succeed. Even the elementals understood—particularly the elementals.

There were other forms, and as Tan turned his attention to them, he realized spirit was shaped near him.

Cora, shaping spirit, fought one. Roine, suddenly able to use spirit, fought another. There were two students, both whom he had trained in Par, who battled the shadowy forms using spirit.

Tan and Amia added their strength. They began to push back.

Wind whipped around him and Tan turned to see the translucent form of ara sweeping nearly a dozen people toward him.

They came.

Of course they came, Tan. They recognize the same threat as you. They will suffer the same as the rest of us if Voidan is freed.

The archivists nodded to him but said nothing. They began their shaping, not working alone but working together, connected by spirit and sweeping it toward the shadows. As they did, it pushed back the nearest of the forms and Tan added his binding atop it, forcing it to constrict like the others had.

One by one they fought, each time constricting the darkness, and each time another appeared. They would continue to appear, he suspected, until they did something to force a binding.

Can you help them? Place the bindings with them as they go?

What do you intend to do? Amia asked.

I need to see if we can keep them from escaping. If nothing else, we need to slow them.

She nodded and he shaped himself off, dropping toward the ground. He was joined by three draasin—Asgar, Wasina, and the oldest of the hatchlings he'd helped. They circled around him, breathing fire. At first he thought it more as a threat to keep others away, but he realized that their fire pressed back the encroaching blackness, giving him a chance to do what else he might need to do.

Tan began pulling on his shapings, drawing from the bonds, and formed a massive draw of power. He pressed it around the entire island, slowly making a circuit of the island as he went, using his shaping to seal in the darkness, creating something like a binding in the air. He'd seen something like this in one of the memories the Mother had shown him. It had worked, if only for a while. All he needed right now was to slow the darkness, not destroy it. If they could slow these creations, then his shapers could continue to fight.

As Tan neared the far side of the island, very nearly completing a circuit, pressure built from inside it.

A trio of disciples appeared.

Tan detected that he couldn't stop the shaping he had started. Doing so would disrupt it and force him to start again, if he even could.

Draasin, he asked.

The three draasin turned toward the disciples. Power built from them and flames erupted.

The disciples were able to wrap the flames in a shaping of darkness.

The draasin attacked again, this time together. They formed three points of a triangle. Tan thought that the shapers would fight the draasin one on one, but they didn't. Much like the spirit shapers, they fought together, drawing massive amounts of energy as they did.

Try this, Tan suggested, sending an image to the draasin.

Asgar roared.

Power built through the fire bond as Tan continued his shaping. It was nearly complete. Only a little more and he would be successful in sealing the island, at least temporarily.

When another surge of fire appeared, he glanced back.

Flames burst from each of the draasin, joining together over the disciples. When joined, it took on a shape of a funnel of flame, one that arched toward the dark disciples.

Something compelled Tan to help, like adding his shaping of fire to that within Incendin. He sent a shaping of fire to join, but then had to turn his attention back to his work.

Asgar roared, a victory.

He was nearly done.

A disciple appeared in front of him.

Not a disciple, he realized. Marin.

She was suddenly flanked by another trio of disciples.

Tan quickly finished what he was shaping, tying it in such a way that it would hold, and turned to Marin. Fatigue nearly overwhelmed him.

How much had he been shaping? How much energy had he expended? More than he ever had before. Without the elementals lending strength, he would have died.

He turned to Marin and pulled on spirit, drawing it through the sword. When he pointed the shaping at her, directing the bright, powerful shaping, she waved it away, dissipating his shaping as if it were nothing.

"You have learned so little, Maelen, while I have studied, and I have learned. I *know* what I am to do. Can you say the same?"

She sent thick bands of Voidan at him, and he had to mix the element bonds and spirit to deflect it. The power she controlled was even more than the last time he had faced her. "I know that you must be stopped."

"Must I? Is that what your connection to spirit has shown you? Because *my* connection has shown me a different truth."

"What do you mean your connection?"

Marin streaked toward him, moving in the shadows. "You so foolishly believe that you are the only one who is connected to spirit. What makes you think that you know the will of the Mother?"

As she said it, he noted that she wove a shaping of spirit into her shaping of Voidan.

He had thought her drawing on the pool of spirit, and it seemed that she had, but not in the way that he knew. She pulled on spirit, shaping it, and mixed her connection to the darkness that she also controlled.

Why would the Mother allow her to use it in that way?

It was wrong, but worse than that, it revealed a different truth to him.

He had though that Alanna would be able to resist the shaping of the darkness, but would she be able to resist a spirit shaping? She was powerfully connected to spirit—but so was Marin.

"I see that you recognize a greater truth now, don't you?"

She twisted darkness toward him, and this time, Tan noted very clearly the way spirit weaved through it. "The others who attempted to control Tenebeth failed because they lacked the proper control."

"You can't control the darkness, Marin," Tan said, pulling on spirit. Was that her within the spirit bond as well?

"That's where you're wrong, Maelen. You *can* control it, you just have to be a strong enough shaper in order to do so. And I am *quite* a strong shaper, as your daughter can attest."

Anger surged in him and Tan took a steadying breath. That was what she wanted. She *wanted* him to become angry and to lash out at her. Doing that would only prove that she had greater control than him.

But she didn't have access to the element bonds.

"Don't I, Maelen? You gave access to *everyone* connected to you. Did you think that didn't extend to me? And because of that, you gave me the key I needed to destroy you."

She smiled, and he suddenly understood the strength that he'd seen from her and why it had suddenly changed, increased so dramatically.

Marin could reach the bonds. And it was his fault.

27

SHAPER OF BONDS

As the realization struck him, Tan reached into the bonds, trying to determine whether she was really connected as she claimed. If so, was there any way he could sever the connection? While he reached through the bonds, she moved around him, more powerful than he remembered her being. Had she been a warrior shaper before?

He knew that she had a connection to spirit, but connecting to each of the elements wouldn't develop late like that... would it? What he had done with the bond couldn't have changed that... could it?

She was there, in the bonds.

But, so were all the other shapers he had brought into the bond.

She grinned at him, seemingly knowing that he'd learned she was there, and that there wouldn't be anything that he could do to keep her from it.

It was possible that he couldn't. The element bonds were not his. Everyone was connected to them, as were all the elementals. That was what gave power, and probably gave life.

Yet, he didn't think she could use the elementals the way that he could. That had to give him an advantage. She could reach the bonds, and so could he, but he could also reach each of the elementals who also resided within those bonds.

Power pressed upon him.

It was the power of each of the elements, and Tan could *feel* it drawn through the bonds. He resisted, pushing back against her shaping, but she added a shaping from Voidan to it and started pushing back on him.

"You see, I learned early on how to overcome shapers. Once I discovered the way that Tenebeth could be used, it was very easy to add it to these shapings. It takes barely anything more than a touch, and with that, I can…" Tan was blasted backward and barely managed to control himself, slowing and then turning back to her. "Yes. You see now."

Marin blasted him backward again, and this time, Tan wasn't fast enough. The shaping sent him spiraling away, spinning freely.

Tan noted that he had been thrown toward the island. Spinning as he was—or maybe because Marin had infiltrated the bonds—he couldn't slow himself. He couldn't even shape. Had she somehow shielded him?

It shouldn't be possible for her to shield him. Not since the previous First Mother had he been shielded, and even that he had managed to break free from once he discovered how to reach spirit.

Help me, he sent to the elementals.

The rocky ground came up quickly.

Tan braced to hit. If he crashed into the rock, he didn't think he would survive, not without buffering himself, somehow slowing the descent.

As it loomed toward him, he felt someone grab him by the wrist.

He looked up. Honl floated in front of him, his black cloak flapping in the wind.

"Honl?"

"Maelen. You should really maintain your connection to the elements better."

Tan tried smiling, but concern thrummed through him. He didn't know what he was going to do. How would he stop Marin? She had grown powerful... possibly more powerful than he could stop. If she could use the element bonds *and* she had the power of Voidan, what would he be able to do to stop her?

"You have always underestimated yourself," Honl said, seemingly knowing his thoughts.

"I think arrogance of my abilities has been a bigger issue, don't you?"

Honl laughed, and in spite of the fact that they were so close to the island, and the source of Tenebeth, the sound carried. "I have never considered you arrogant, Maelen. Confident. Sometimes misinformed. Always well-meaning. Never arrogant."

"She reaches the bonds, Honl. Because of me. Had I not—"

"Had you not brought these shapers into the bonds, they would not have managed to help you as they have. Can you not see that, Maelen?"

He looked around, noting the way the shapers attacked. Many were coordinated, fighting in ways they would not have been able were they not empowered to communicate wordlessly and through the bonds. There were dozens of disciples facing off against twice as many shapers. The creations of shadow were confined by the archivists and by Amia, slowly but surely being trapped by the binding. Much longer and they would be stopped.

That left only Marin.

Were had she gone?

He found her attacking his shapers.

Where she attacked, shapers fell, unable to withstand her force. In that way, it reminded him of when they had faced the Utu Tonah and how he had so easily overpowered all of the shapers that Tan could throw at him.

If he didn't intervene, she would destroy everyone who came to help him.

And then she would truly attack.

"Fight with me, Honl?" Tan asked.

The wind elemental nodded. "Always, Maelen."

He had come a long way from the tentative wind elemental Tan had first bonded. Tan could remember the fear Honl once had when confronted with the Utu Tonah. Then he'd been indecisive, unwilling to fully assist, afraid that he'd be torn from Tan and forcibly bonded to the Utu Tonah. This Honl, the one who had joined with spirit, had none of that fear. He was inquisitive, intelligent, and faithful. He had become Tan's friend.

Would he bring this friend to his death as well?

Honl touched his arm and smiled. "We all make choices for ourselves, Tan. Even the elementals make choices. They accept the consequences, as must you."

Tan knew that Honl was right, but it didn't make it any

257

easier to like it. Losing even one friend was difficult. He'd struggled losing Asboel and still hadn't fully gotten past that. He should have power enough that he wouldn't need to lose any friends. With his ability to use the elements and the elementals, he should be a strong enough shaper that he should be able to prevent their loss.

Only, he wasn't the Mother. He could control himself, not his friends.

They reached the first of the Voidan creations. Tan shaped spirit, lancing it through his sword, and created a binding that helped the archivists. Working together, the shaping constricted, pulling them deeper and deeper into the shaping until they were nothing more than specks of dust.

He pivoted, turning to the next attacker, this one a pair of disciples. They attempted to use the darkness on him, but the archivists assisted and together they blocked them. Using spirit, he destroyed their connection to Voidan, leaving them purged of its touch.

One after another he went, facing disciples and shadow creations, accumulating more and more shapers fighting alongside him. They became a torrent of shapers, one that could not be overwhelmed, fighting their way toward Marin.

Tan saw her as little more than a smear of shadows.

As he neared, he glanced over at the friends who had joined him. All now fought alongside him, but shaping on one side of him were Roine and his mother, with Cora and Elanne on the other. Amia had taken his hand.

When he'd been in the pool of spirit, he'd felt the connections and had considered part of it his family. He realized now that he had been partly right. *This* was his family. All of these shapers, all of them willing to fight with him, to come with him and face this horror, they were his family. And he would fight for them, just as they would fight for him.

A sudden urge made Tan send a shaping of spirit washing over them, drawing through the spirit bond, binding them all together.

There had been awareness of them through the bonds, but it surged even greater.

Tan smiled.

We will end this together.

He turned to face Marin.

Darkness exploded from her, a mixture of shaping that combined Voidan with the elements. When it struck them, Tan felt as they were forced back, but almost as one, they resisted.

She used another attack, but he could feel her power building through the element bonds.

Tan diverted what she was able to draw.

He didn't work alone.

Other shapers did the same, pulling on the power of each of the elements. Doing that allowed him to counter her shaping, at least that which was drawn from the elements.

There remained her connection to Voidan.

Marin had become a powerful shaper of Voidan, and she was close to the source of its power. Thick bands of dark energy raced toward them.

Using spirit, drawing on the shaping with the help of Amia and the archivists, he attempted to resist.

Her shaping was too powerful.

It pushed against their shaping of spirit and started oozing through.

A victorious grin appeared on Marin's face. "As I said, Maelen, *you* are not strong enough to defeat me."

Tan maintained his shaping, those with him maintained the shaping, and still they were forced backward. The longer she managed to hold them, the more likely it was that she would push them toward the island and into the pool of Voidan. Marin seemed to be growing stronger as they went, the closer they came to the source of her power making her more powerful.

Her smile widened. She knew the shapers weren't enough. Tan knew it too.

But he wasn't only a shaper. That had never been his primary power. Even when he had managed to reach the element bonds, that hadn't been his strongest connection.

Help me.

The call went out to the elementals, through each of the bonds, through spirit, and rolled away from them.

Marin's eyes widened slightly. She would have heard the call as well. Her skin began to blacken as she shaped, pulling more and more power, turning her body into some manifestation of Voidan.

Tan watched with horrified fascination even as they were pressed back. What she did and what she became reminded him of the lisincend and how they had become twisted by fire. Was Voidan twisting her the same way, or had she already been twisted simply by attempting to reach it?

Help me.

Tan sent the message again. Marin's transformation was complete.

The shapers fought with renewed strength, but it still wasn't enough. Draasin circled her, blowing fire at her, but it wasn't enough. With a single flick of her wrist, she drew enough darkness to counter the draasin.

Help me.

Other elementals began to appear.

There had been those fighting with him from the beginning, those that were bonded to the shapers, and those that willingly offered themselves to the fight, such as ara as it helped hold the archivists in the air. The coming of the elementals this time was like a rolling tide, like an avalanche of power. It started slowly, a rumble he detected through the element bonds, and built as they slowly made their way toward the battle.

Hundreds of different types of elementals came. Many Tan had no names for, but he knew them, just as he knew those he'd bonded. They were each powerful in their own way, and fought with the power of the bonds.

The dark shaping sending them backward eased.

Tan allowed himself a moment of hope. Would they be able to halt her progress? Would they be able to stop her?

Marin's brow furrowed and she redoubled her efforts.

No longer did she shape.

There was no sense of it anymore from within the bonds.

What Marin did now simply manipulated the darkness. She *was* Voidan.

They were pressed back again.

Elementals that attempted to get close failed. Tan had to maintain his connection to spirit simply to counter what she threw at them. There was no time for him to try anything more, though he knew a binding was necessary.

How would they stop her?

The island loomed behind him. Tan could feel the emptiness

of it, could practically taste its awfulness. Alanna was still there, trapped, and if they didn't find a way to stop Marin, they wouldn't be able to reach her.

As much as anything, that drove him.

Help me.

This time, he sent the call to the element bonds.

He had shapers, he had elementals, and he had a connection to the bonds, but could the bonds themselves help in some way?

They needed a solution, if it were possible.

The call surged through the bonds, given life by the joining of spirit that he had added.

The bonds responded, but not in the way that he expected.

Honl appeared, drawing strength from the bond. Tan suddenly understood what had changed about him. Through the shaping, and through what Tan had done, Honl had become a manifestation of the wind bond.

Kota appeared, powered by earth, joining Honl opposite Marin. Tan's bonds were the manifestation of each elemental.

Marin pressed out with her powerful shaping of Voidan.

Nymid came as a soft green shimmering film and coalesced between Honl and Kota. Water surged through it, drawn from Tan and his connection to the bonds.

Marin exploded with power.

The bonds managed to hold it, to confine it.

What of fire?

Tan had no bonded, nothing since Asboel.

Yet fire came as a swirling of heat, flickering out of the draasin, out of shapers—including Tan—and manifested as a draasin of flame. There was something almost familiar about the shape. The creature was massive, filled with the power of the fire bond, and added to the seal placed around Marin.

Marin attacked with renewed fury. The manifested element bonds bulged.

They would not be enough.

Not without something else.

Tan pulled upon spirit. Amia joined him, as did the archivists.

Their shaping came from the spirit bond. When ready, he sent the shaping not at Marin, but at each of the element bonds.

As one, they shook and increased massively.

The bonds began moving, writhing in something of a pattern. That pattern began to take shape within his mind. Tan recognized it, but so did Marin.

She fought, attempting to explode outward with the power of Voidan, but the element bonds confined her.

Shapers added to the power, letting the bonds draw from them.

The binding began to take shape.

The blackness within Marin's skin didn't shrink, but *she* did. It was as if she were one of the creatures of Voidan that she had made. Slowly, she constricted, thrashing more and more wildly as she did until it was clear the element bonds were more powerful than her.

Marin locked eyes on Tan and flashed a malevolent smile. "You've already lost, Maelen, you just don't know it. You will never free her."

With another surge, the binding took hold and Marin disappeared.

FIRE REBORN

Tan didn't dare release his connection to the shaping. He was exhausted, and if he did release it, he worried that he wouldn't be able to reach it again. Instead, he held onto it and slowly, the connection to the elementals rejuvenated him, but they were fatigued as well. There was power within them, but it had taken something out of them to form the manifestation of the bond.

"We need to find her," he said, turning to Amia.

She nodded but said nothing.

Shapers near him were celebrating, but Tan didn't dare, not yet, and not until his daughter was safe. Marin had claimed her like some sort of prize, and he had no idea where she would have brought her.

"Come, Maelen, I will show you."

Honl took his hand, and together with Amia, they drifted toward the island.

"Tan?" Roine asked

He shook his head.

"Where are you going, Tannen?" his mother called after him.

"This isn't over," he said.

"But it is. You stopped her."

He shook his head. "I didn't stop anything. That was all the elements, the bond. All of you," he said, sweeping his hand behind him. "Not me. But this... this will have to be me."

As he turned back to the island, the exhaustion overwhelmed him.

His shaping failed.

Tan began dropping, and Amia dropped with him.

Honl jerked on his hand, catching Amia, but Tan's hand came free.

In the distance, he could see the mound of darkness, that which he suspected indicated the source of Voidan. In the midst of it, there was a glimmer of light, barely more than anything, but enough... enough that he *could* see it.

Alanna.

She was so close... so close, and now he would fall.

Help her, he sent as he fell.

Let the elementals, and those he cared about, take over his task.

Tan closed his eyes, wanting nothing more than to sleep.

The falling stopped. Heat surged around him, a familiar sense, one that he had known.

Thank you Asgar.

A snort of amusement came through his connection. *Maelen.*

His eyes snapped open.

The draasin of flame held him up, supporting him. His other

bonded elementals had remained by him, but he hadn't expected the manifestation of fire to remain.

Tan understood why it had been so familiar.

Asboel?

Maelen.

Power surged through him, and there came a flash of light.

A bond.

Tan gasped.

There had been a void within him since losing Asboel, one that even joining to Light hadn't been able to fill. How was it possible that he had returned?

How is anything possible, Maelen?

The Mother?

Asboel snorted, and flames that seemed an extension of him streaked from his nose. *Normally, the Mother, but this is you.*

How?

You called to the bonds, and you called me out of the bond.

I'm sorry.

I would have been reborn eventually; what does the timing matter? And this form suits me.

This is how you will remain?

I am Fire, Maelen. Just as you created Water, and Wind, and Earth.

What of Spirit?

Asboel chuckled within his mind. *You have already created Spirit, Maelen.*

He looked for Light but didn't see her. He sensed her and knew that she was near, but she was not. *Light?*

Asboel chuckled again. *In a sense, Maelen.*

They reached the mound of blackness. Asboel flew around it. Tan realized that Roine, Zephra, Ciara, Cora, and Fur all had joined them. Honl brought Amia and she looked at Asboel with a strange glimmer in her eyes.

But they were not the only ones to have come.

All the shapers who had answered his call came, pressing inward toward the mound of darkness. They, along with the elementals, formed bindings as they went, driving back Voidan. Life returned to the island, possibly for the first time in a very long time.

The presence of the darkness, of Voidan, filled him, calling to him.

It was there, in front of him, filling a pool with its power. And above it hung his daughter.

Light wasn't Spirit. She was an elemental able to reach spirit, but she was not the manifestation of it.

Alanna was.

The elemental bonded to her had named her the Voice of the Mother, and Tan hadn't understood before, but now he thought that he did. She was his daughter, his creation, much like the other elementals were his creation, those that sprang from the power of the element bonds and fused with spirit. A form of life, of creation, because of him.

Can you fly me to her?

I cannot get any closer, Maelen.

Can you help?

You have never needed my help, but you have always had it.

Power flowed into him.

Tan sat upright and drew upon fire, and managed to reconnect to the other elements: wind next, then earth, and water last. Touching upon them, he drew from the bonds, noting that something had changed within the bond, though he didn't know what. Now was not the time to determine that answer.

As he shaped toward the darkness, toward the pool of Voidan and to Alanna, he reached a barrier and was pushed back.

He couldn't reach her.

"Tan?"

He looked over at Amia. Honl held her aloft and she watched him, her eyes narrowed in concern. Tan reached for her, taking her hand and holding it. Could they get past the barrier together?

When he tried, they were pushed back once more.

There was a sense within him, that seduction of Voidan, almost as if a taunt. It called to him, and he resisted.

Alanna looked over at him. The bright intelligence that he saw so often in her eyes blazed brightly as she stared at him. They were her mother's eyes, the eyes of the two people in the world that he would do anything for.

Voidan taunted him again, this time with more clarity.

Tan understood. He could seal off Voidan, and he could hold the darkness back, but doing so meant that he would trap his daughter within.

Had Marin truly won?

Would he fail, in spite of everything?

Horror dawned on Amia's face as she seemed to understand.

"No," she said, shaking her head.

Zephra joined them. "What is it?"

Tan swallowed, but his throat was dry. He looked around at the shapers surrounding him, friends and family, all of them working with him to do what they could to suppress Voidan.

The darkness around the island changed, drawing inward, life blooming where the bindings had been left, elementals returning.

But all of it served only to trap his daughter more.

Dark laughter filled his mind.

"There's a barrier around her, much like there was around Norilan."

"Can you pass through?"

Tan shook his head. "There is no passing through. It's not a barrier shapers made, not like that one was."

His mother's eyes widened and her gaze shifted past him, looking to Alanna, who hung suspended, no differently than the artifact had once been suspended.

This was the taunt Marin had made, the final defiance. He now understood.

Amia shaped spirit, beating it against the barrier. Other shapers joined, but none were able to do anything other than bat at it uselessly. There would be no getting past this barrier.

What they needed was someone able to reach the dark, to be able to control Voidan.

And they had destroyed them all.

The sense of dark laughter within his mind echoed once more.

29

CYCLE OF LIGHT AND DARK

Tan approached the barrier, hopelessness settling into him. They might be able to seal off Voidan and prevent it from escaping, but they would not be able to reach Alanna. Tan could only imagine the horror she felt, the panic she must be experiencing, knowing that there was nothing they could do.

Only… he didn't see panic on her face. There was peace.

Seal the darkness, Maelen.

The thought came softly drifting into his mind, and he didn't know if it came from her or if it came from Spirit. It could be either. Or both.

Something could get through.

No. I will find a way.

There is no way. Seal away Voidan.

Tan shook his head. Next to him, Amia sobbed, her shaping growing weaker. There were limits to shaped energy, and she had reached hers. Tan had nearly reached his as well as he continued to beat upon the barrier. He was drained. The fight with Marin had taken everything from him, leaving him with only what had been lent by the elementals.

It will only fail again. As it has every time before.

Maelen…

The connection faded.

Tan unsheathed and struck at the barrier with his sword, but it did no better than had he attacked with a shaping.

"Tan, we can't let her stay like this."

The other shapers had completed their binding, and he could feel it constricting. Soon it would overtake the pool, closing it off and trapping Alanna inside. There seemed to be nothing he could do that would stop it, nothing that would bring his daughter back.

And he was empty, powerless now, all his shaped energy exhausted.

The dark laughter echoed in his mind.

He had failed.

All his power, and he had failed the one person he wanted most to save.

You have not failed, Asboel said. *Voidan will be confined. A balance will be restored. That is not failure.*

It is to me.

The darkness laughed again.

Take me instead, Tan said.

He didn't know whether Voidan could answer, or whether it would matter. Would the darkness even want him rather than the Voice of the Mother?

If it were to be confined regardless, maybe it didn't matter.

271

I am the one to trap you this time. I led them here, gave them the power of the bonds to hold you. Take me, and not her.

The darkness seemed to laugh again. *You would be a fool to even make that offer.*

The voice boomed within him, devastating and powerful

Was that what Alanna experienced?

Take me. Torture me. We will be trapped together.

You would know endless torment, Maelen.

Take me.

The darkness laughed again, and there was a surge of power, like a burst that pressed on him, one that reminded him of what he'd felt when Marin controlled Voidan. It struck him, filling him, and he felt *drawn* into the pool.

"Tan!"

He glanced at Amia, wanting to hold her one last time. *For Alanna.*

Shifting his focus to the shapers that had come with him, he sent an image of the binding they would need to secure Voidan. If what he planned worked, if he was successful, then he would seal it off. And if he failed, they would need to do it. Either way, the darkness could not return.

Maelen.

Hundreds of voices, thousands, murmured the name.

Tan wished he had time to respond, but what would he say? What was there to say?

Only sadness.

If he succeeded, he would bring hope.

Him for Alanna. That was a reasonable trade. Even his mother would have to understand.

Tannen. Her voice whispered into his mind like a memory.

With it, he felt his father as well, and then it faded, so brief it might not have been

Then he started through the barrier.

As he passed through, Light appeared and jumped at him.

For a moment, he thought she would try to stop him, but when she reached him, she disappeared, as if passing through him.

Once through the barrier, he thought that maybe Light passed beyond, but she had not. There was nothing but the pool of darkness.

Release her.

The darkness laughed. *I would rather have you both, Maelen. You can suffer along with her, only yours will be worse.*

Tan was pulled, and tumbled into the pool of darkness.

It was like sinking into the night, a black so perfect, so filling, that there was nothing else for him, nothing that he could do. Pain and cold struck him, overwhelming him. Everything seemed sucked from him, an emptiness so absolute that he was left a hollowed shell.

He remained like that for an unknowable amount of time.

There was pain, and darkness, and there was nothing else.

Moment passed that could have been hours or days or even years.

Tan knew nothingness and suffering.

During that time, he felt only the satisfied laughter of Voidan.

There was nothing Tan could do to resist, nothing that he could do to escape. He was trapped, and would remain trapped, for as long as Voidan held him.

Distantly, his mind called on him to attempt to shape, but

there was no power left within him. All that he was had been sucked away, drained by this empty power. No shaping, no sense of the element bonds, and no elementals. Nothing.

Attempts to shape came and went until he decided he never possessed them.

He lost the sense of himself, knowing only that he had come here by choice, though he no longer remembered why.

There was pain. After a while, even that became normal.

There was laughter, a steady dark sound, though he couldn't remember why there should be laughter. Why should there be anything?

There was nothing. *He* was nothing.

Time stretched.

All he had was pain. Cold and empty pain.

In the darkness, he felt a stirring, but how much time had passed since he noted the stirring?

He couldn't tell. Maybe moments. Hours.

Then again, what was time?

It came again, this time with certainty.

It came from deep within him, a different sensation, one of warmth where there had only been cold before. Was there color at the edge of his vision? There couldn't be... could there?

Maelen.

The voice came from deep and far away, but inside of him.

Was that him? Was he Maelen?

Maelen.

It was closer, more urgent.

Now he was certain the darkness faded, replaced by a tenuous light.

The laughter that he'd heard had disappeared.

Had it ever been there?

Maelen no longer knew.

Warmth surged within him, within his chest.

Light came with it, building steadily.

The two combined, warmth and light, and as they did, he *knew*.

He was not alone. When he'd come past the barrier, another had joined him, the last bond, but in some ways, the most important. She had not attempted to go *past* him, but *into* him.

Light? How is this possible?

You are not alone, Maelen. We are here. Your bonds are here.

Tan felt them then. That was the warmth and the light he could see. It came not only from Light, but from Kota and Honl and Nymid and even Asboel. They were with him, brought by some connection to Light.

Then, of course they would be.

Tan had shifted the element bonds. He remembered that now, drawing spirit into them. Light had called to the elementals for him, bringing them with him.

How can I escape this?

There is no escape from the darkness, Maelen.

There had to be something he could do.

Attempting to shape left him weakened and unable to complete the action. Tan tried reaching the bonds, but they eluded him. Even the connection to the elementals was not one of power, but one of comfort and communication.

You're trapped with me.

We chose this, Maelen, much as you chose to sacrifice for the Mother.

I sacrificed for Alanna.

Is that not the same? Light asked.

Tan didn't know how it could be, but that didn't matter.

There had to be some way to get free. Just because the elementals didn't know of it didn't mean it didn't exist.

How to defeat the darkness?

It had attempted to overwhelm him, to show him the nothingness, but he had survived it because of his connections. Did that mean anything?

What of his other connections?

He focused on them, and slowly, so slowly, they resolved within his mind.

Tan? It was the one person he wanted most to reach.

I am here, he told Amia.

What of Alanna?

Voidan seeks to hold her. He focused on Alanna and felt her nearby, the connection to her stronger than what Voidan could overcome. *I will find a way to reach you*, he told her.

He could sense her attempting to reach him, but the connection failed. As much as she might want to reach him, and might want to speak to him, she couldn't get past the barrier that still blocked her.

Without the ability to shape, and without the ability to place the binding, what could he do?

There was only one thing that *could* be done.

Seal us, he sent to Amia.

Tan—

This has to be confined. If it takes me getting trapped, at least she will not be alone.

There has to be something.

There isn't. I can't shape, and there's no way to destroy the darkness.

Even as he said it, he realized the comment felt wrong.

Destroying the darkness wasn't the answer. The Mother didn't *want* him destroying it. Even if he could, he wasn't certain that was what he *should* do.

How, then? There had to be something, some way to stop Voidan and find a way to prevent it from attacking again.

If he couldn't come up with it, he had time.

Eventually he *would* come up with a way to stop Voidan. If not now, in time.

If he didn't, then the seal would fail in time. That was the way of the world. It cycled, the seals fading over time, only to allow someone else to be able to release Voidan and bring the darkness out into the world.

What if there was a way to stop the cycle? Wasn't that what he had to find?

I will stop you, he sent to Voidan.

There was no laughter this time, not as there had been before. *You will not destroy me. Others have tried and they have failed.*

I don't intend to destroy you. Only stop you.

There is no stopping.

Tan felt a surge of darkness and it mixed with the warmth from Light.

Maybe Voidan was right… but so was the Mother.

Which meant there was only one thing that had *not* been tried.

All the other attempts had involved sealing in the darkness.

Tan had seen them, had memories of those attempts gifted to him by the Mother. None had succeeded.

What if it wasn't about destroying, and it wasn't even about sealing it off?

There was risk, and if he was wrong, everyone he cared about would suffer.

But if he was right… this might be able to end. The cycles might stop. He might finally find a way to bring peace and order to things. That was worth something.

Tan pulled on what he sensed of the darkness.

He wasn't able to shape, not here, not where there was nothingness. And he didn't want to use the darkness for his own purposes. That might be where others who might have thought the same had failed. Tan didn't want the power, but he'd been given it over the years. All he wanted was peace.

Balance.

Light and dark.

There was a surge within him.

From that, he realized the Mother wanted the same.

The darkness flowed, going through Tan.

He was connected to the bonds, to the Mother, to everything.

Having darkness pooled like this was dangerous and meant that everyone would suffer were it released in a concentrated form like this, but what if it were diluted?

Tan pulled on the darkness, drawing it into himself.

As he did, he felt the power of the Mother flow into him as well.

In his mind, the pool of the Mother in Norilan drained, drawn away by this.

Light and Dark.

They mixed, but they mixed within him.

Tan pulled on them, accepting them, and then pushed the two back out and along the bonds.

It was not a shaping.

He didn't know what it was, though it felt more akin to what he had done when drawing spirit into the other element bonds.

This was the part he feared.

If the darkness overwhelmed the bonds, they would fall.

Only… as he pulled with both spirit and night, they were in balance.

The Mother countered the darkness.

Night and day.

The balance, as it was meant to be.

In a flash, he knew that there had once been the same balance, but it had been disrupted. In that moment, he sensed how someone had tampered with the power, someone who might have even more power than Tan, and had shifted the darkness, drawing it away.

Tan pushed, letting the flows of power come together, joining. He pushed again, harder, and those flows washed over the world, diluted. There would be no source of darkness for someone to draw upon again. It would be a part of everything, much like the Mother was a part of everything. She was light. Darkness was death. Balance.

They were together again, joined as they were meant to be.

Colors surged around him.

Weight pressed into his waiting arms. Alanna.

He looked down, relief flooding him. He had done it. He had saved her.

Something had changed within him, but right now, it didn't matter.

"Father," she said.

And Tan smiled.

EPILOGUE

Mountains spread out beneath him, and in the distance he could see the edge of the forest, where the line of trees joined the sea, ending in a clear blue line. Tan leaned back, enjoying the sensation of the sun on his skin almost as much as he enjoyed the feeling of Amia in front of him, Alanna tucked between, as they soared over the ground atop Asboel.

There was something very much *right* about riding atop Asboel once more. Several other draasin flew nearby—Sashari, Asgar, Wasina, and even a few of the now dozen or so draasin hatchlings in existence—leaving a trail of shadows across the ground. They traveled in something like a flock, with Asboel at the head, something Tan thought fitting.

Alanna giggled as they banked, turning out toward the sea. She was a natural atop the draasin, her blond hair streaming around her shoulders, the smile plastered on her face. Fearless, in many ways, and changed since the attack. She still had a connection to spirit, only it was not quite as potent.

She could fly with me once more, Wasina said.

It is up to her.

Alanna giggled her reply, and Tan used a shaping of wind to send his daughter to the draasin, settling her on the draasin's back. The shaping strained him but it was a good strain, one that felt right.

Amia glanced back at him and her gaze flicked toward Wasina and Alanna. "She flies well."

"Alanna? She's been flying since before she was born."

Amia laughed and tucked a loose strand of hair behind her ears. "Not Alanna. Wasina. She is such a natural."

"She's a better flyer than her parents," Tan said.

Asboel twisted his neck to look at him with eyes that glowed a deep red. Not quite so flaming as they had been when he had manifested from the bond, but still burning in ways they had not before. *Careful, Maelen, or you will see how I dump unwelcome guests.*

You wouldn't dump me, would you?

Asboel seemed to grunt. *Perhaps once I would not. Now…*

As Tan laughed, they passed a series of nearly formed figures, that of the wind elementals. Ara was no longer quite a translucent, now with a hint of color, barely anything but enough that they couldn't hide as they once had, more like Honl in that, though Honl was something much more than an elemental, and very nearly human now. Since he'd been in the pool of Voidan, and since he'd dispersed it, joining it with spirit and each of the other elements, no elementals could really hide.

Tan sensed fear from the elementals, and they worried about

what would happen to them now that anyone could see them. It was not only wind, but nymid and golud and saa and… all of the elementals had taken on a more physical presence. Mixed with that fear was something that had taken him quite a while to understand: there was a mixture of hope.

He still didn't fully comprehend the reason, but there was time. There would be time.

The elementals hadn't been the only thing to change.

There had been another, and unexpected, change. Shaping began cropping up in others where it had not been before. Tan still didn't understand how, or what that might mean moving forward, but there was something equally right about dispersing the power.

"Do you miss it?" Amia asked.

Tan reached for his shaping strength, for the bonds to the elements, the memory of the power that he'd once possessed still strong, but he no longer possessed the same connection. He could shape, but he was never a particularly strong shaper. Tan could speak to the elementals, but he couldn't borrow strength from them as he once had. And the bonds were closed to him. Tan had power, but no more than anyone else.

"I think I should miss it," he started, "but I don't think I *need* it anymore. Does that make sense?"

Amia smiled at him, and he felt her shaping of spirit building. She sent it washing over him. With it, he felt peace, though he didn't need her shaping for him to feel that. His family was still together. The lands had been united. Shaping was no longer rare, and would only increase. And the elementals were freed.

There was balance.

"Should we return to Ethea? Your mother wanted you to visit again."

Tan smiled as he reached around Amia, holding her close against him. "We were needed in Par first. They had questions about the restoration of the Records. Besides, she didn't want *me* to visit," Tan said, looking back at his daughter. "She thinks to continue her education."

"Can you blame her?"

Tan shook his head. "She will make a fine queen in time."

"You know, ruling suits you as well."

"Par?"

Amia nodded. "There would be others as well, I think. Doma would welcome you, as would Chenir. The Great Mother knows that even Incendin would welcome your rule."

"That is not for me. In Par, I only rule until another is ready," he said. His hand slipped toward her stomach, already able to detect the first tugging of spirit from the boy growing within her belly. Like his sister, this child would be connected tightly to spirit, and in ways that Tan didn't yet understand.

The world was changing—*had* changed. Soon it would be his children's to rule.

He felt a relaxing surge of spirit, a warmth that settled over him, and he smiled. Tan didn't know whether it came from Amia or Alanna.

Maybe neither. Maybe it was the Mother telling him that he could finally relax.

Tan leaned into Asboel, resting his hands on either side of his scaled body, noting the sense of the elementals all around him, and smiled.

Thanks for sticking with Tan's story through everything he's gone through. This is really the end for him, but sign up for my newsletter to hear when I return to the world (there *might* be another series set in the distant future dealing with the aftermath of how Tan ended the cycle).

Keep reading for a sneak peak of Soldier Son, book 1 of The Teralin sword series, which will be 4 books when complete. If you've loved The Cloud Warrior Saga, I think you'll really like this series. I think the first book in the series is one of the best I've written!

D.K. Holmberg

SOLDIER SON SNEAK PEAK

Chapter 1

Endric glowered at his father, but the man had already started off, his wide back deflecting the gaze. Endric's hand itched and instinctively found the cold hilt of the sword hanging at his side. There was a momentary urge to unsheathe the blade and attack, but he suppressed it as he took another deep breath. Still, his shoulders didn't relax.

Instead, he stared until his father disappeared, only turning away when he heard the deep roll of far-off thunder. Dark clouds gashed the sky overhead, inky and black, and flashes of lightning flickered distantly. The coming weather did nothing for his mood. Rain was a constant annoyance in the city, but then, they were high enough that they were practically *in* the clouds, so it shouldn't be a surprise.

Why had his father forced this conversation here, in the

middle of the street, shops on either side of him? People had given them a wide berth, not wanting to distract the general as he chastised a soldier, let alone his son, leaving the street strangely empty. The second terrace of the city loomed overhead, the sheer rock wall rising toward the barracks level, a reminder of the role the Denraen soldiers played in the city. Above everything rose the Magi palace on the third terrace. He couldn't see it today; the thick clouds obscured it.

A quiet scuffing from behind him—too close to be accidental—startled him, and Endric spun, his sword half out of its scabbard before recognition halted his motion. He resheathed more harshly than necessary, snapping the blade back into place. It should not surprise him that Andril still tried to soothe him, yet it did.

"What?" Endric asked.

Andril snorted as he ran his hand across his chin, scratching idly at a small scar—his first. "That's all you can say?"

Endric met his older brother's eyes—defiance flashing through his—holding his gaze steady as long as possible before turning away. Andril had known he would turn away first.

"What?" he asked again, his tone softer. His shoulders sagged, releasing the tension he had been holding since their father first found him in the street.

"You should listen to him. There is much you don't yet know."

"You heard."

Andril nodded. "I did."

Endric scowled at his brother, and a moment of uncertainty passed through him. "He doesn't understand."

Andril snorted. "He's the general. It's not for him to under-stand. He asks because you are Denraen. And his son."

"You know I can't be what he wants."

Andril cocked an eyebrow and his mouth twitched in a small smile. "How do you know you aren't already?" He paused, and the words hung heavy in the air. "Besides, he'll find a way to mold you into the Denraen he needs. He *is* the general."

"Are you to help?" Even to him, the question sounded like he sulked.

Andril shrugged. "I'm Denraen as well." He blinked slowly and sighed. "And your brother. I will not lose sight of that."

"That's why you watched." Andril had known of the diffi-culty Endric had with their father and had not intervened. There was little Andril would have been able to do anyway.

His brother nodded and stared down the dark street.

"Does he know?"

Andril shrugged his wide shoulders. "Probably," he answered. "If not him, then his Raen. Either way, he knows." He slid forward with the dangerous grace of a mountain wolf, and Endric's hand twitched again. The corners of his brother's mouth tugged again, not quite a smile as his eyes flicked to the motion.

Endric inhaled deeply. Andril was not the problem. It would serve no purpose to challenge him. Not that he could win if he did. "What do you want of me?"

Andril again glanced down the narrow street that had swal-lowed their father. "Father is not your problem." He fixed his gaze on Endric.

Endric grunted, unable to meet his brother's eyes any longer. "Not to you. You will succeed him."

Andril shrugged. "Someday." On another man, such a comment would come off as arrogance. From Andril, it was simply a statement of fact.

"Then I will no longer have a problem. Then you can release me from that obligation. I'm no officer, Andril. You know that as well as I. Let me be the soldier I want to be. Let me *fight*."

"The issue will not go away so easily."

Endric frowned. He should know better than to argue with Andril. "Does he truly need for me to follow you in this? Is it not enough that I am simply a soldier?"

"You are much more than a simple Denraen," Andril said as a small smile threatened to crack his face. "You fight what you should embrace. One day you will learn."

Endric grunted and shook his head. "Or one day you will realize the same as Father."

Andril's face almost became sympathetic. Almost. "He doesn't blame you for Mother leaving. Neither do I."

Endric had to look away. Andril knew him too well. "You can't say it wasn't my fault she left."

An uncomfortable silence settled over them. Endric knew there was nothing he could say. Their mother had left shortly after his birth, leaving their father to raise them. Endric had no memories of her, nothing like the years he knew Andril still savored. Neither Andril nor his father ever spoke of her departure.

Finally, Endric broke the silence. "You still haven't answered why you watched if you weren't going to help."

Andril hesitated, his blue eyes piercing and so much like their father's. "I had thought to discuss something with you."

He considered Endric for a moment, then shook his head. "Another time, I guess."

Endric felt his frustration grow. "Now you just taunt me."

His brother spread his arms and smiled, barely a parting of lips. There had been a time that he smiled easily, but no longer. Now he commanded men and directed them in battle. Endric once knew him as happy, but much of the joy that had been a part of Andril was no longer there. That alone would have been reason enough to despise his father.

"There will come a time when you will become more than a simple soldier," Andril said.

"Pray to the gods that day is far off."

"And yet I pray for the opposite."

Endric's eyes wandered, looking past Andril's head to the replica of the Tower of the Gods, which loomed over the first terrace. On this level, there were shops and taverns and temples, including the replica. "I stopped praying long ago," he said softly before turning and meeting his brother's eyes.

A flitter of irritation crossed Andril's face. "Perhaps you are right."

Endric frowned. "About what?"

"I had thought…" He shook his head slowly, not trying to hide his disappointment. "There is much you don't under-stand." He glanced back at the sword hanging at Endric's waist —his hand still hovering near the hilt—and frowned. "Are not ready to understand," he muttered.

A moment passed and Endric waited, knowing his brother well enough not to press. Andril said nothing. Thunder rolled again, closer, a flash of lightning casting his brother's face in a mask of frustration.

"I had hoped…"

Andril never finished. He shook his head before turning and moving silently down the street, disappearing into the shadows.

Endric watched for a moment. It was not like Andril to show hesitation. The man was infuriatingly confident, and deservedly so, excelling in everything he did.

And Endric pushed him.

A wave of shame flushed through him. Their entire life, Andril had been nothing but short of the ideal brother, mentoring him in a way their father never had. He should not take the frustrations he had with their father out on Andril.

For a moment, he considered chasing after him. Another peal of distant thunder echoed and he took a deep breath, pushing the conversation out of his mind. The anger filling him after meeting with their father had disappeared during their talk, leaving him more troubled than annoyed. He didn't know what he would even say if he caught his brother.

Stepping quietly along the stones of the street—not quite with the silence Andril managed—he moved quickly past the row of drab stone buildings until he reached the one he sought. A muted cacophony of sounds seeped through the stone and heavy wooden door, flooding out onto the street.

The Scented Lover was typical for this part of the city and catered mostly to the Denraen soldiers. Heavy smoke filled the tavern. The sharply pungent aroma of rumbala mixed with the thick scent of the hickory log burning in the fire along the far wall. Flames jumped and cast flickering shadows, leaving the room obscured in swaths of darkness. Tables crowded the floor, solid and worn with grime and spilt drink. Some few rested in the pools of darkness that were coveted in places like the Scented Lover.

Endric pushed his way through the patrons, ignoring the brief glares he received. Most men frowned only briefly, turning away when they recognized him. He might not have Andril's skill and certainly not his rank, but he still had earned a reputation, and it inspired more than a little fear, though as he thought about it, Endric wasn't sure that was a good thing.

Reaching the back of the room where the darkness stretched the deepest and the flickering light of the fire barely penetrated, Endric paused and looked down at the small group sitting around a table. No one looked up, though he saw from the stiffness of their posture that they were aware of him.

"Well?"

"You'll have to sit on me for my seat," the man nearest said. He was stout and his head was shaven, leaving the heavy scars across his head shining even in the low light of the tavern.

Endric grunted and placed a hand on the man's shoulder, sliding him over and sitting alongside him. "One day I will sit on you, Pendin."

Pendin laughed and looked up. "Another scar then." Scars were respected among the Denraen, worn like badges of honor. A playful glimmer crossed his face for a moment while he eyed Endric, disappearing as their gazes met. "Something's wrong."

Endric shook his head, but the others knew him too well. They had been friends since their earliest days in the barracks. Those first months of training bonded men—and women, he decided, glancing over at Senda—in a way few outsiders would understand. "It's nothing." He looked away as he waved for a drink, hiding his eyes.

"Looks like nothing," Senda noted.

The waitress brought a mug over for him, leaning over to reveal a flash of cleavage. Endric ignored it as he took a long drink. The waitress scowled, stalking away with a sway to her hips that turned a few heads. She looked back, the scowl replaced by a satisfied smirk.

"Looks like someone else will need to order my drinks tonight," Endric said.

"Maybe you should at least speak to her since rolling her last week," Pendin said and laughed.

Senda frowned at him and sniffed. Olin, a man whose long face matched his height, smiled tightly but said nothing. He rarely did.

Endric shrugged. "There is that."

"Why the mood?" Pendin asked.

He sighed. "The usual. The weather. This city. My father."

"Those never change."

Endric closed his eyes. *They are friends*, he reminded himself. *And good ones at that.* "I argued with my father and took my frustration out on Andril."

"And yet you still live." Senda still frowned at him, and Endric knew that she would be irritated by his treatment of the barmaid longer than necessary. She flipped her tight braid over her shoulder as she looked away from him.

Pendin chuckled, smiling briefly at Senda. "How is that unusual?"

"Something about him was different tonight."

"Perhaps it's because he's been sent from the city," Olin said, barely looking up from his drink.

Senda shot Olin an unreadable expression.

Endric finished his drink and looked up at Senda for confirmation. Her face was blank, and even though she worked with the spymaster Listain, she would say nothing. She looked away from his gaze, and he knew better than to press.

He turned back to Olin, wondering how he knew about it and wondering why Andril had not said anything.

Olin stared back and shrugged. "Rumors. Skirmishes in the far south. Supposedly some kind of cult of warrior priests. Denraen are deployed to investigate."

And Father sends Andril.

His brother had only recently assumed his command and had yet to lead his men in anything more than simple training drills. Was this Father's way of testing Andril's leadership? It wouldn't be out of character for the general to do so. Something about that felt wrong though, and Endric couldn't place why.

"You could ask to go with him," Pendin said, tracking Endric's line of thinking. He pushed his mug of ale over to Endric and winked.

"Not after tonight." Was that why Andril had found him? To see if he was ready for assignment to his regiment?

Endric closed his eyes and visualized his brother, remembering the hesitation he'd shown before leaving. What had his brother intended to ask him? Knowing that he was being sent from the city cast their conversation in a different light. Disappointing his father was for sport; disappointing Andril was agony.

He downed another mug of ale. "I need to find Andril," he said, deciding it couldn't wait.

"Give it time, Endric," Pendin said.

Endric glanced at Senda.

She sighed but answered. "I'm not sure when he's to leave."

"I can't wait," he decided. "I need to know what he wanted." He stood, knocking his chair down as he did. The man behind him hollered and Endric turned, an apology on his lips, but he never got to say it.

The man swung.

The attack was quick. Nearly too quick. Endric ducked and stepped back. "Listen, friend—"

"You damn Denraen are all the same!" the man spat.

Endric took in the man's soiled clothes and thick arms and noted the dirt ground under his nails. A miner.

The mountain city owned one of the few known active mines for teralin, and the mines twisted throughout the mountain. The metal was precious to the Magi, supposedly because it was necessary to speak to the gods. Most who worked the mines did so because they had no other choice.

"Easy, man. It was an accident." He was annoyed but knew better than to attack one of the local miners. The Denraen had a hard enough time with them as it was; it was surprising that these miners would patronize a tavern mostly filled with soldiers. Besides, he had enough trouble from fights he had started. Better to avoid this one.

The man looked down at Endric's sword and sneered. "An accident like the way you pushed me over getting into the tavern?"

He frowned. Perhaps he *had* pushed a little more than was necessary.

Chairs scraped roughly over the wooden floor, and Endric didn't need to turn to know his friends stood to support him. "No need. I'm going," he said and looked over at Pendin.

And was hit.

Endric didn't know how the man was able to hit him so quickly. If not for Pendin's widened eyes giving away the attack, he would have taken it harder. As it was, he managed to pull away and absorb some of the blow. Still, he felt as if hit by stone.

He reacted as a man trained by Denraen would: he attacked.

Endric lunged forward, closing in on the man. Another quick blow caught him on the shoulder, but he had leapt soon enough to miss the worst of it. He jabbed quickly, catching the man in the stomach, and twisted, throwing his arms out to catch him in the throat and knock him down, hoping to end the fight. The man somehow eluded him.

Movement behind him put him on edge and the attacker took advantage, swinging hard toward Endric's face. He twisted and dropped, grabbing the man's arm as he spun. He pulled it down and over his shoulder. Instead of the expected crack of bones breaking, he was left with a handful of sleeve as the man tore his arm away, revealing a heavily tattooed arm. Endric frowned at the markings, tried to make sense of the dark patterns swirling up his arm, but couldn't.

The man smiled. Stained teeth gleamed dully.

He darted suddenly forward, bringing his arm up and out toward his throat.

Endric turned and ducked, punching up and into the man's flank as he passed. A quick kick knocked the man forward to sprawl on his face on the rough floor.

Endric pounced. He landed on the man's back and grabbed the still-sleeved arm and twisted it back. The man pushed up with his free arm, but Pendin was there, forcing him back down. Olin and Senda stood around them, Olin with his sword unsheathed and staff in hand. Their stance dared others in the bar to interfere.

Most turned away and returned to quiet conversation, sliding out of reach of the Denraen. Two men remained. One was short and thin and covered in dark rags somehow holding together. He stared for a long moment at Endric, pushing ratty hair out of his black eyes before he turned. The small man disappeared without a word and was quickly swallowed by the thick throng of patrons.

The other man waited. He was meatier, heavy in the face, and his thick forearms looked perpetually stained with dark smudges glimmering strangely in the muted light. While he was not as raggedly dressed as the other man had been, his dark clothes were nearly as well worn. He stood staring slack faced at them and scratched his arm absently.

Endric pulled up on his attacker's arm and twisted him to face the other. "Is he with you?" he asked. The words were little more than a grunt and thick with the anger he felt.

His father would hear about what had happened. His brother. Another fight. This time, he had done nothing other than protect himself, but it wouldn't matter. The warning after the last one had been clear. Now they wouldn't be pleased. Further disappointment.

Endric shook his head, not waiting for the man to answer, and thrust his attacker forward. The thick man caught him clumsily, then lifted him. The attacker shook him off and twisted, turning quickly to face Endric. A dark smile simmered on his lips and his mouth parted again slightly.

"Go," Endric said, his voice ragged.

The man paused and Endric noted his shoulders tensing as

he slowly eyed the sword and staff held ready. A dangerous glint passed across his face, and for a moment, Endric was sure he would try his luck.

Olin slid forward, just a step, but it was enough.

The man nodded slightly. "Another time," he whispered.

"Go," Endric repeated.

The man turned, pulling his solid friend with him, and they pushed through the crowd. Endric watched until the heavy door opened and then slammed closed, a gust of wind whipping in as it did and sending the dark shadows in the tavern spasming with new life.

"What was that?"

Endric turned to look at Pendin, who stared at the doorway. His eyes were slightly widened and he shook his head slightly from side to side. Senda's face was troubled, her brow furrowed, and she stared at the place where the men had stood. Olin held his sword limply, the point resting carelessly on the floor. The soldier in Endric wanted to admonish him for resting his sword in such a way, but he wouldn't do that to his friend.

"I don't know. Miners, it would seem. Not sure what I did to upset him."

"Tipped your chair back, as far as I can tell," Pendin said.

"You walked into the bar," Senda said, the troubled expression now gone.

Endric watched her for a moment, wondering what she knew, knowing she would say nothing. Her work with the spymaster taught her to keep her lips sealed, so he let the thought go. He needed to find his brother before he left. Perhaps now was a good time to be out of the city.

"I'm leaving," he said.

"We'll go too," Pendin said.

The crowd parted for them as they made their way to the door. The other patrons in the tavern had ignored the disturbance. Nothing was broken, and they had been hidden in the darkness of the back corner. And fights were not that uncommon in the tavern. Especially this tavern. Still, a faint hush met them as they passed on their way out.

The others went out before him, but Endric paused. A strange drumming started behind him, and he turned to see what caused it. He barely saw the heavy board as it whistled toward him, cracking him on his forehead, and he dropped. Something wet dripped into his eyes—tears or blood—and he blinked to clear the sudden flashing lights. He heard the door open again, a muffled whoosh of air.

A dark shape hovered over him briefly and laughed, and then he heard Pendin. His voice was distant, as if coming through the walls, and he heard "Endric—" as he passed into darkness.

Chapter 2

Endric awoke to a throbbing head. He blinked slowly, fighting through the dried crust clinging to his lids. A sliver of light overhead barely pierced the darkness. He was on his back, resting on something rocky and cold, and staring at the slight illumination, hoping his eyes would adjust to the darkness. They didn't.

Loose rubble beneath him stabbed into his flesh like dozens of small knives. He focused on his body to ensure that everything still worked, carefully moving his toes and fingers. When he found that he could, he slowly sat up, ignoring the pounding pressure in his head. A momentary wave of nausea threatened to knock him back, but he fought through it.

He couldn't remember what had happened. They were leaving the tavern, and then something had hit him. Or someone. He tried to remember the face of the person who had stood over him laughing, but couldn't. Could it have been the miner? His head hurt worse trying to think, so he stopped.

Though he couldn't remember what had happened, he could guess what had come next. The all-too-familiar cell he now found himself in was answer enough. It didn't explain why, though.

Endric turned to the thin beam of light marking the upper edge of the door. When he could stand, he pounded forcefully upon the door, ignoring the pain in his head that mirrored the movements of his fist.

When the door opened suddenly, Endric nearly fell backward in his surprise. He hadn't expected anyone to answer, hoping mostly to take his frustration out on the door of his cell. A familiar figure stood framed in the doorway, his face shadowed by the lantern hanging on the far wall.

"Listain."

The man nodded slightly. Endric couldn't see the expression on his face but imagined a slight sneer. His father's Raen had nothing but disdain for him, likely sharing the general's assessment. Listain stood a head shorter than he did and was reed thin, but he still filled much of the doorway.

"Where am I?"

Listain snorted. "That should be obvious. Even to you."

He paused, and Endric imagined him peering into the darkness with narrowed eyes. If Listain was here, that meant the barracks jail. Probably better than the city jail, but not by much. Unfortunately, he had known both.

"Perhaps especially for you."

Endric started forward, unwilling to listen to Listain's comments and intending to push past him, but an iron hand gripped his shoulder. Listain squeezed harder than necessary, and Endric stopped and pushed him off.

"That's what got you into the cell in the first place," the spymaster said in warning.

"I didn't start it."

Listain snorted again. "Witnesses say you did."

"Then they weren't watching."

Endric tensed again, thinking about trying again to push past Listain, but reason got the better of him. Like it or not, Listain was the Raen and far outranked him. Only fear—or respect—of the general had prevented the Raen from punishing him more severely in the past. With his father's current attitude toward him, Endric was uncertain he would be protected.

He took a deep breath and stepped back. "What do you want?"

"Restraint," Listain said, a hint of surprise entering his voice. "It's a start." He took another small step, sliding just past the doorway. His posture was relaxed, but that was deceptive. The man was nearly as dangerous as his father was rumored to be and at least as dangerous as Endric knew Andril was. He resisted the urge to step back.

"The general thinks you should stay another night in this cell."

Endric bit off the first thing that came to mind. "Then why are you here?"

"Your brother thinks you should be allowed to speak on your behalf." He paused for several heartbeats. "Fortunately for you, the general puts much stock in what your brother thinks." The emphasis to his words was clear.

Andril knew he was jailed. That thought bothered him the most. He could deal with his father's disappointment. And Listain was right—it wasn't the first time he had been arrested. But something about this felt different. Especially after how he had left Andril earlier.

"When does he depart?" he asked, not sure if Listain would bother to answer. The thin Raen cocked his head and his lips tightened. "Sir," Endric added.

Listain stared a moment longer before answering. "Two days." He paused another moment, as if considering his next words. "It would be better if you went with him."

The fact that he was right didn't make his words any easier to hear. The chance to join Andril's regiment had probably passed. That he had followed up their argument with a tavern brawl made it even more likely. Endric's shoulders tensed and his hand instinctively slipped to his waist, feeling for his missing sword.

"Better for who—my father? The Denraen?"

"Yes."

The word seemed to echo in the small cell.

Endric shook his head, closing his eyes and sighing. It would be, he knew. Perhaps then his friends wouldn't carry his stigma with them as well. None had ever said anything, but he knew. Pendin—such a skilled and promising soldier—would no longer be held back by his best friend. Olin might find his assignments less unpleasant. Only Senda seemed unencumbered by him, rising to work alongside the spymaster, her analytical mind carrying her beyond the handicap of her friendship with Endric. Occasionally, he wondered if she spied on him to Listain.

"I would go," he said.

Listain cocked his head and furrowed his expansive brow. Endric imagined the Raen smiling at the prospect of him leaving the city, but in the subdued light he couldn't be sure.

Listain grunted and motioned to the doorway. Endric stepped past him and into the dimly lit hall. A few of the other cells were closed, and he worried that his friends had been jailed as well. They had gone out before him and none had been more than incidentally involved. For a moment, he considered asking Listain but thought better of it.

Guards stationed near the end of the hall blocked another door. Behind the door were steps leading to another guardroom. Beyond that, the offices of the highest-ranking Denraen.

His father. Listain. And his brother.

His steps faltered. He couldn't help it.

He felt Listain's eyes on him. The man had a way of seeing and observing fear among the Denraen. Most feared his network of spies, which seemed to miss nothing. Endric knew he was weighed and measured—as he was every time the Raen looked at him—and dismissed as no more a threat than the ash beetles that came out each spring. An annoyance. Little more.

His brother stood waiting at the top of the steps but didn't meet his eyes.

"Listain," Andril said, acknowledging his Raen.

Listain nodded. "You may take him. The general is expecting you."

Andril thumped his fist to his chest in salute. He paused a moment, expecting Endric to do the same. He didn't. Andril ignored the slight and led him off.

They had only gone a few steps before Andril slowed. "You started a fight with a miner." The words were laced with heavy layers of disappointment.

"I didn't start it," he said quietly, knowing the comment wouldn't matter. His history of fighting was damning enough. Worse was that this was not his first run-in with the miners.

Andril turned and faced him, his face the fury of a Denraen officer. Little of his brother remained. "His uncle is Mageborn."

Endric blinked slowly. He had not expected that, though many were born to the Magi without the Mage gift. It was only logical the Magi would have miners in the family as well. "I didn't know."

Andril sighed and turned away, starting forward again. "Would it have mattered?"

Endric couldn't say anything that would sway his brother, so he changed tack. "You didn't tell me you were leaving."

"You are not of my regiment."

"I am your brother."

Andril tilted his head but didn't look back. "I tried," he said after taking a few more steps.

"I would join your regiment if you would have me." For some reason, those words were hard to say.

"I tried," Andril repeated, then shook his head. Then sighed again. Endric saw it as a slow heave of his broad back. "You are not ready. Or I am not ready. I'm not certain which."

"Ready for what?" he asked.

They had reached their father's office. The door was closed and Andril rapped twice upon it before answering. "For the discipline necessary to be Denraen," he finally said.

The door opened and Endric didn't have a chance to counter, though he was uncertain what he would have said anyway. There was no arguing the fact that he was not the ideal soldier. He was skilled with the sword—few were his equal—but that was nearly all he offered the Denraen. Perhaps Andril was right.

Still, it didn't change the fact that he would support his brother. He would rather follow him and act the Denraen Andril needed than remain stationed in the city. Only Andril would know that he simply pretended. And now he didn't want him.

The door opened fully and their father faced him. He was tall —nearly a full fist taller than Endric—and as broad of shoulders as Listain was slender. His bearded face was scarred and worn, and his gray eyes stared at Endric for long moments. He imagined a fleeting look of disappointment crossed them.

"Come." The word was a command, not an invitation.

Andril pulled him through the doorway and closed it after them with a solid thud. Endric suddenly felt more confined than he had within the cell. Months had passed since he had last been in the office—then on somewhat better terms—but little had changed.

The huge map still hung on the far wall, with small dots marking something Endric never understood. Beneath it and facing the doorway was a massive desk. Years had worn away most of the stain, but rather than looking old, it simply appeared more rugged. More fitting of its owner. Papers stacked neatly atop the surface hinted at the amount of work the general sorted through. Rows of bookcases lined the wall to his left. No open space remained on the shelves. The books upon them were all neatly arranged. A huge table rested along the wall to his right, where the senior council of the Denraen met.

Endric looked away. Once, his father had dreamt that both his sons would sit around his table with the council. That dream had died long ago. Only Andril sat among them now.

Few things in the office caught his attention any longer. He had seen it since he was a child and, other than the location of the dots on the map, little changed.

Rather, it was the huge broadsword hanging on the far wall that always commanded his attention. The sword Trill was nearly as renowned as its owner. And just as feared.

Endric wrested his eyes away to focus on his father. The man simply stared at him with eyes of stone. The rest of his face showed nearly as much emotion.

"Were you any other man, you would have been expelled from the Denraen by now," he said finally.

The words were soft, but his father's rasp sliced through him. Endric had not expected the conversation to begin like this. Though they had argued only the day before, it had been about his willingness to lead rather than his desire to remain Denraen. He knew nothing other than the Denraen.

All of a sudden, his heart started hammering in his chest. His throat swelled and he feared needing to speak.

Their father turned away to sit at his desk. His broad forearms rested on the surface and he stared at something on a corner of the desk for a moment before looking up again, his face now wearing the weight of his office. "I am undecided as to your fate. Another fight. And with a miner." His father blinked slowly and shook his head. "You of all soldiers should know the struggles we have had with the miners, and now this!"

"General," Andril interjected. "He is a skilled soldier. The Denraen need men of his skill. I believe he can still be rehabilitated."

His brother didn't turn as he spoke. There was a distance to his tone, as if he were speaking of a warhorse rather than a man. His flesh and blood.

The general turned his hard expression upon Andril. "You would take this task upon yourself?"

Endric allowed himself to hope that Andril had had a change in heart. That he would be willing to let him join his regiment as it deployed.

"I think our relationship would make his discipline ineffective," Andril said, dashing Endric's hope.

Their father blinked again and nodded, sighing deeply. "It should not have to be like this," he said, sounding like a concerned father for once. He crossed his thick arms in front of his chest. Then he straightened his back, furrowing his brow as piercing eyes narrowed, once again the image of the stern general. "Andril. You are dismissed."

Andril nodded and thumped his chest in salute. He turned and left without looking at Endric.

"Endric."

Endric turned his attention back to his father. He had been watching Andril leave, hoping his brother would turn, that he would meet his eyes, but he didn't. "Sir."

The general snorted. "Andril speaks truly. Discipline is needed, though I am uncertain what course to take. Because you are my son, it needs to be someone who can act on my authority and not fear repercussions. I had hoped Andril would be willing to see to your discipline, as he saw to much of your training. Perhaps you have burned even that bridge." He glanced down at his desk, shuffling a few papers. "Listain would relish the discipline too much, and that will serve no purpose. That leaves Urik."

Endric said nothing. At least his father acknowledged that it was Andril who had trained him. And that Listain would enjoy disciplining him. Urik was strict—a typical Denraen—but a good man.

"There is more to being Denraen than being a skilled fighter," the general said. "If you choose to ignore the opportunity I have given you, ignore the chance to lead, then you will learn what is expected of my soldiers."

"I know what is expected of the Denraen," he said.

"No. You do not." His father stood and fixed his eyes on Endric. "You have been protected. That stops now." He grabbed a slip of parchment and scribbled something before folding it and fixing his stamp upon it. "This is your last chance, Endric. Do not treat it lightly." He handed the parchment across the desk. "Give this to Urik. You are dismissed."

Endric took the paper and left. His eyes lingered on the council table, sliding off when he reached the door. He felt his father's eyes on his back. Though he had heard no movement, he suspected the general had sat back down, staring at him from behind his desk.

Endric didn't look back as he turned down the hall.

Chapter 3

He found Urik in his office. It was smaller than his father's and had room for little more than his desk, but Urik had been en'raen long enough that the office was cluttered with stacks of books and papers. Nothing like the clean organization his father maintained.

Endric stood silently before the desk while Urik read the parchment. Endric had resisted the urge to open it and see what his father had written. Whether it was out of fear or respect, he didn't know. Perhaps he truly didn't care. He crossed his arms over his chest so that he didn't reach for his missing sword.

Urik quickly finished reading it and set it down atop his desk. "You know what is said here?" he asked. His eyes caught the crossed arms and narrowed slightly.

Endric shook his head once. He imagined what the general had requested. Discipline had been mentioned often enough that he knew Urik was expected to dole out some sort of punishment.

Urik smiled. It was a slight turn of his lip. It did nothing to make him more remarkable, and it was this plainness that made him a dangerous opponent. Most didn't expect the keen mind and quick sword behind such average features. Yet his father had seen the whole man.

"You are assigned to me."

Endric frowned. "One of your regiments?"

Urik turned his flat brown eyes upon him. "Me."

"I'm not sure what that means."

Urik chuckled, though it came out as a grunt. "Me neither. Seems you have offended Andril. So Dendril assigns you to me. To 'learn the ideals and understand the role of the Denraen.'"

Urik looked up from the parchment and shook his head. "Be easier if you took the commission he offered."

Easier, but not what he wanted. It was simpler to just serve. There was something satisfying in being a mindless soldier. He didn't tell Urik that. Instead, he said, "It's no longer offered, I think."

Urik laughed again. "You don't know your father then. To him, any man can be an officer. He just needs to earn the right."

Endric didn't think there was anything he could do that would regain his father's good graces, let alone warrant earning a commission. Too many years had been spent intentionally antagonizing him. Still, he never let it show. Always the general, never the father.

They were interrupted by a harsh knock on Urik's door. Urik looked over Endric's shoulder and frowned. "Enter."

The door opened to reveal Listain standing on the other side. His face became drawn and tightened even more when he saw Endric. He was clean-shaven, revealing a few old scars along his chin. Most of the officers shaved, but Listain frequently grew out a beard, hiding his scars, though he kept his hair shorn close in the style of the Denraen officers. Only the general wore a beard routinely.

"The general convenes the council," Listain said, flicking his gaze to Urik.

"When?"

"Now. New report from the south."

"I've warned of the south, but you have convinced him that it's not a risk."

Listain shot Urik a hard look. As Raen, he outranked Urik.

Urik nodded carefully. Listain glanced at Endric before

turning and closing the door. "Seems we will start later. Best that your father assigned you to me rather than the Raen."

Endric looked back at the closed door and nodded. Listain would have tormented him and relished doing so. Even his father had acknowledged that.

"I know the two of you haven't always seen eye to eye," Urik continued.

Endric turned to Urik and snorted briefly before he remembered his place. He was assigned to Urik to learn how to be Denraen. It wouldn't do to offend him already. "He is the Raen."

Urik laughed. Emotion never reached his eyes. "Exercising caution already?" He tilted his head, seeming to weigh Endric before smiling slightly. "The two of you are both misunderstood. It is only natural that such misunderstandings lead to conflict." He hesitated, glancing at the door as he considered his next words. "Listain serves the Denraen well. The intelligence he gathers is nearly irreplaceable. You would do well to remember that."

The implication was clear. Listain was irreplaceable. Endric was not.

Urik chuckled softly, breaking the brief tension. "There are some things his spy network does not help him see. Such as the rumors that spread about him." Urik shrugged. "Or maybe he sees and doesn't care." He met Endric's eyes and held them. "Who is to know?"

Endric shifted uncomfortably, uncertain what to say.

"Perhaps he knows his days are numbered. That may be why he suggested Andril head south," Urik said, the comment strangely casual. "Andril will succeed your father someday, and then—"

Another knock interrupted them, leaving Endric wondering what he'd been about to say.

Urik glanced at the door and then grabbed a handful of papers that he stuffed into a small satchel near his desk. "Council awaits." He glanced up at Endric. "I think for your first assignment, we should focus on the ideals of the Denraen." He smiled, his teeth flashing briefly. Turning to his desk again, he leaned and scribbled something upon a scrap of paper, then held it out for Endric. "Take this to Tildan. You have patrol the next three nights."

Endric bit back a comment at his assignment, feeling a surge of irritation flash through him. Patrol was meant for the earliest of recruits… and perhaps that was the point.

Urik watched his face for a moment, then pushed past him as he moved toward the door, holding it open while he waited for Endric to follow. "After that, we will discuss what is next."

Urik hurried down the hall toward Dendril's office and the council. Andril would be there, sitting alongside their father. Endric had never felt that their father wanted the same for him. Not that it mattered to him anyway. He was happier being a simple soldier.

A thought troubled him as he made his way to find his sword and then Tildan. He had not thought of how Andril's eventual succession would affect others. Andril's promotion to en'raen had come with Tordal's retirement. The man had served the Denraen for thirty years and had left scarred but on his own terms. All knew Dendril intended Andril to be general. None in the Denraen debated the logic of the decision; Andril was nearly as respected as Dendril, if not as unapproachable.

But Andril's eventual promotion would impact others. Each

general put their own stamp on the Denraen leadership, and Dendril had been no different. Something Urik had said bothered him. The spymaster was calculating and a skilled planner, traits his father respected and used. But could those same traits complicate things for his brother? Could Listain already fear Andril's promotion?

He started down the hall toward the cells to retrieve his sword, wondering if there was more to Listain's attitude toward him than he had thought and suddenly realizing he might need to be more careful.

Read the rest of Soldier Son now!

ABOUT THE AUTHOR

DK Holmberg currently lives in rural Minnesota where the winter cold and the summer mosquitoes keep him inside and writing. He has two active children who inspire him to keep telling new stories.

Word-of-mouth is crucial for any author to succeed and how books are discovered. If you enjoyed the book, please consider leaving a review at Amazon, even if it's only a line or two; it would make all the difference and would be very much appreciated.

Subscribe to my newsletter for a few free books as well as to be the first to hear about new releases and the occasional giveaway.

For more information:
www.dkholmberg.com

The Endless War

Journey of Fire and Night

Darkness Rising

Endless Night

Summoner's Bond

Seal of Light

The Lost Prophecy

The Threat of Madness

The Warrior Mage

Tower of the Gods

Twist of the Fibers

The Teralin Sword

Soldier Son

Soldier Sword

The Shadow Accords

Shadow Blessed

Shadow Cursed

Shadow Born

Shadow Lost

The Dark Ability

The Dark Ability

The Heartstone Blade

The Tower of Venass

Blood of the Watcher

The Shadowsteel Forge

The Guild Secret

Rise of the Elder

The Sighted Assassin

The Painted Girl (novella)

The Binders Game

The Forgotten

Assassin's End

The Lost Garden

Keeper of the Forest

The Desolate Bond

Keeper of Light

The Painter Mage

Shifted Agony

Arcane Mark

Painter For Hire

Stolen Compass

Stone Dragon

Made in the USA
Monee, IL
13 September 2022